North Sea Shells

By C J Richardson

Copyright © Statement

Fiction Statement

This novel is a work of fiction that is loosely based on an actual event in a real town. The main characters and incidents portrayed in it are completely fictional and are the work of the author's imagination and do not represent actual persons, living or dead.. Any resemblance is purely coincidental.

To my three beautiful daughters
Andrea, Vicky and Christine
with much love

Acknowledgments

I would like to acknowledge the following publications that were invaluable in my research for this novel.

Marsay Mark. Bombardment (The day the east coast bled). Great Northern Publishing 1999

Wood Robert. West Hartlepool The rise and development of a Victorian new town). Northumberland Press. Third edition 1996 .

I would also like to say a huge thank you to my dear friend **Imogen Clark** and my husband **John** who have helped and encouraged me tirelessly along the way.

Finally a huge thank you to ePrintedBooks.com for making this book possible.

North Sea Shells
Chapter 1

December 16th, 1914

The North Sea fog hung about the houses like a wet cloak. Three-year-old William was sitting on a cracket in front of the open oven door, letting the heat pinch his skin, turning it pink. Martha passed him a mug of warm milk and a thick slice of freshly baked bread, slick with dripping. She couldn't help but marvel at how he had grown so tall after being so tiny at birth. The little box bed in the alcove at the side of the range, where George's Granda usually slept, was empty. He often walked over to the dockyard with his grandson. He liked to feel as though he was still part of the crowd that set off for work each morning. She hoped George had made it there on time today; he couldn't afford to be late again this week. Money was tight enough without the shipyard docking his wages...and he'd forgotten his bait for the second time. Rubbing the dull ache in her back, she looked at the tin box and sighed.

The explosion shook the foundations of the little terraced house. The wooden table jumped like a jack-in-a-box, flinging breakfast plates across the room. The cracket flipped backwards and William's head smacked against the cold stone floor. Martha screamed and grabbed her son as a second blast brought part of the ceiling down around them. She scrambled through the broken front door, cradling him, pulling his face to her chest.

More shells whined and whistled, the blasts echoing, lighting the sky every few seconds, tearing into the soupy grey like a thousand fireworks. People were running for their lives, shouting and yelling, pushing and shoving, unsure of which way to go, unsure of what was happening, turning tail each time a blast ricocheted and exploded, showering bricks and mortar ahead of them. Tiles flew through the air, shattering and raining down on the crowds. Martha set off towards Dene Street. She needed to check on her Ma and Da, needed to know they were alright.

'Please, God...let them be safe,' she cried, William holding on tight as she tried to run. She pushed on, passing a young man on Sheriff Street. He wasn't running. He stood alone amidst the chaos, clutching his baby, singing softly, rocking him. The baby's skull was cracked wide open. Blood pooled over the knitted blanket and the man's shirt.

Fighting her way through the debris outside the Star Inn, she became aware of the pungent smell of beer, the pavement wet, and the contents of half-smashed barrels still trickling into the gutter. The brewers dray was lying on its side, the driver and his young mate lying face down, their bodies twisted between the torn and bloody carcasses of the team of horses. One horse, unable to break free, was still alive, breathing heavily, its nostrils flaring, its tongue lolling, its eyes bright with fear. Martha barely noticed them as she struggled on, flagging under the weight of her son.

As she reached the corner of the street where her parents lived, she felt someone grab her arm.

'Don't go down there, Martha. It's flattened. Annie and Cyril, they're... your Ma and Da didn't...' Old Billy Mason pulled her to a stop. He was covered in rubble dust and barely recognisable.

'No... Let go of me.' She fought against his grip, reading his face. 'I have to...I have to.' Dropping to her knees, she rocked William back and forth and screamed like a hare caught in a trap.

She opened her eyes and looked up into George's face. He was on his knees, leaning over her, his face crumpled, the gash on his forehead oozing blood. His normally well-groomed moustache hung limply, dishevelled, drooping like an extra frown on his dirty face. He held her small hand to his mouth and kissed it. The warmth of his lips was reassuring in a world she couldn't quite comprehend for a few seconds. Propping herself up on to her elbows, she looked around, finally recognizing the lake and the wooden benches that lined the path around it. She couldn't remember how she had ended up in Ward Jackson Park. William was sitting on the wet grass beside her, holding on to her damp skirt, his teeth chattering. George ran his hands through the halo of cinnamon curls surrounding her face.

'I looked all ower for you. Home...Your Ma's house...'

'Are they...?' she couldn't finish the question, her wide blue eyes spilling over.

'I'm sorry, Pet. They've gone... Granda, too.' He wiped her tears away with his sleeve turning the dust into a dark trail across her pale cheeks. 'I'll get the bloody bastards,' he groaned.

George helped Martha to her feet before wrapping his jacket around William and picking him up.

Ghosts of people wandered about aimlessly, children clinging to parents, fear and dirt streaking their faces. The shelling had stopped. In the space of an hour, the world had changed forever. A young lad walked past, driving a pair of bullocks like it was any other market day.

'What are you playin' at? Doesn't tha know there's been an invasion?' a man called out.

'I have to get 'em to market. Farmer Miller'll have my guts for garters if I don't.'

'Ha'way, lad. They'll be landin' any minute. There'll be no market the day,' the man said, half laughing.

'An invasion?' someone else shouted. 'I thowt it were a battle out at sea. I saw the guns flashing.'

'They'll still have to gan ower the yard. Can't leave 'em wanderin' about, can I?'

The boy continued through to the north end of the park, disappearing into the thinning mist.

George and Martha made their way back to Dene Street, a fine drizzle soaking them to the skin; stepping over splinters of wood and shards of glass that kept getting caught up in the hem of her skirt; passing terraced houses where paper chains stretched in the rising wind through broken windows and torn nets. Christmas cards were sliding, stopping and starting across the wet cobbles. She needed to take Ma and Da home. They would be cold lying in all that rubble.

From the front, Billy Mason's house seemed to be unscathed; the street wall standing upright; the front door waiting for someone to knock. Martha looked through the gap where the adjoining wall used to be and saw Billy sifting through the remains of his home, oblivious of the danger, trying to find anything worth salvaging. She and George stood on the pavement, William clinging to George's legs.

Martha stared at the space in front of her. It didn't bear any resemblance to the place she had called home for the first seventeen years of her life. She couldn't tell where the hearth had been; the hearth where her Ma had made bread every morning of her married life; the hearth where she set the tin bath for Da when he got home from the colliery, black with coal dust and aching in every limb. Now, the roof and bedrooms had disappeared leaving only the dull sky and a pile of bricks. Somewhere under all this was Ma and Da's iron bed that always squeaked in the night; the patchwork eiderdown that Gran had given her when she married Da; the chamber pot with hand-painted roses on the side. "It's so you won't notice the smell as much," she would say, laughing out loud. On the far side of the debris, she could barely make out what was left of the backyard netty they used to share with Billy and Ethel next door.

'Where's Nana gone?' asked William.

'I'm not sure, son,' replied George.

'They've gan to the dead house at the back o' market yard,' Billy said, placing a smashed wedding photograph carefully on his *to keep* pile.

George put his arm around Martha and led her away. 'C'mon, Pet, we'll go and find them. Granda's probably down there as well by now. There's nowt we can do here.'

The Co-op milk cart overtook them on Hart Road. Fred Bradshaw was leading the horse, man and beast holding their heads down in respect. They could see the unmistakeable outlines of two bodies, shrouded in filthy sheets that were bloodstained and torn. A young girl dashed over to the cart and ripped the sheet away, looking for her missing parents. She retched in the middle of the road as Fred re-covered the mutilated corpses. He set off again. Martha and George followed behind; their pace unconsciously in time with the clip-clop of hooves striking the cobbles until the sound faded and the cart was out of sight.

They made their way across Church Square, entering Lynn Street from the north end. They passed people walking in the middle of the street, avoiding the pavements strewn with glass from the shop fronts. A trolley bus stood in the middle of the road, empty of passengers, the windows down one side shattered, the mangled wheel of the new BSA Ladies

Roadster jammed under the front end. At ten guineas, it was something Martha could only dream of owning. She wondered if the owner had survived. Clinging to George, her feet slowed as they neared their destination.

The trio entered the market yard, where it was evident it hadn't entirely escaped the morning's shelling. Collapsed and broken stalls, vegetables, cheeses, and household goods, baskets of eggs, sacks of potatoes all lay scattered across the cobbled stones. The travelling players had arrived last month to see the winter out here. Their bright caravans parked at the far end were always a welcome sight. The nightly shows would bring the townsfolk from all over Hartlepool and beyond. The familiar sight made Martha remember her parents in happier times. Cyril and Annie would come over often. Her Da would keep company with Robert Colby, the market superintendent, watching the show outside, leaving her and Ma inside with Robert's wife, Sarah.

She saw Robert waving off Fred and the empty cart before looking across the yard at them. The town hall clock was striking as he checked his pocket watch. Twelve o'clock. She quickened her step, grateful to see a friendly face.

'Hello, Mr Colby...Robert, we've come for the key. Ma and Da...I'm told they're... in the mortuary.'

'Martha? I didn't recognise you, lass. I didn't realise...Annie and Cyril? Ha'way, Hinny, off inside and see Sarah. She'll look after you.'

The round face, usually creased with laughter lines, turned pale and grey, his large body starting to shake. Martha could hear his breath catching as she watched him struggling to get control. Putting his hand to the wall for support, he inhaled deeply before leading the way, shouting for Sarah as he went inside.

The front parlour bulged with market traders, players and people in mourning, individual voices indecipherable in the cacophony that gnawed at her head. The air was thick and swollen with the smell of sweat and other bodily odours that made Martha gag. She covered her mouth and nose with her hand.

Robert found her somewhere to sit, his eyes glossy, his brow creased. She knew how fond of her Da and Ma he was. She knew how much her Da had thought of him. Robert Colby's sons were teenagers now, so much bigger than when she used to tell the two of them stories upstairs while her Ma and Sarah sat by the fire and chatted. She smiled as she saw them, sitting in a corner playing card games, glad they were here and safe amongst the crowd. Martha took the hot sweet brew from Sarah without even flinching when her hands cupped the mug. William was sitting beside her at the kitchen table, tucking into a bowl of broth. Poor lad, he must have been starving, she thought, remembering he had barely started to eat when he was thrown to the floor this morning. The memory cut through her and she stroked his back gently.

People vied for space, eager to hear news of the latest ordeal as George told them how a shell had landed in the shipyard that morning.

'I'd barely got to the stores when I heard the first bangs. Harry Bell came running out of the blacksmith's shop just afore a shell hit the offices. I've never seen owt like it. You could see allut railway wagons afire, blown sky high they were.'

The room hushed, everyone's eyes now fixed on him, his chest and voice rising with every word.

'Me and Harry climbed up the ship stocks to get a good look around. I could see the gasworks were on fire when me Gaffer shouted for us to get down. "Bloody fools. Yer could be blown up," he was saying.' George's voice quietened. 'I wasn't feared about the shelling though. No time to worry. I had to look all ower town afore I found 'em in the Park.' He nodded toward Martha and William. 'I thowt she were dead at first, and William was hanging on to her skirts... not even crying. Poor bairn were in shock. He hasn't said much at all...except to ask where his Nan were. There were nowt left of their house.

Just a pile of bricks.' He put his head into his hands. 'Granda...Granda didn't make it either. He'd walked to work with me this morning. He didn't get far on his way home. I found him lyin' in the road across the tramlines; half his chest blown away.'

Martha felt the overwhelming grief rising inside her again as she saw the pain in George's eyes. People made all the right noises, patting his back and offering condolences before turning away, wallowing in their own miseries.

The next couple of hours became a blur as people came and went with more tales of loss and destruction, more cups of tea and sympathy, more bowls of broth. Martha was grateful when Sarah prised her ample frame through the crowd and ushered her and William to the steep staircase that ran up the side of the kitchen.

'You and William get some rest. You both look fair worn out,' she had said putting her fleshy palm to Martha's cheek.

'I need to see Ma...'

'You need to rest first. Plenty of time for that. Your Ma's not going anywhere.'

Martha was too tired to argue. She went upstairs to one of the small bedrooms and laid her son down on one of the single beds that belonged to Sarah and Robert's boys. Stroking his hair, she started singing the lullaby her Da always sang to her.

'Sweet and low, sweet and low
Wind of western sea,
Low, low, breathe and blow,
Wind of the western sea!
Over the rolling water go,
Come from the dying moon, and blow,
Blow him again to me,
While my little one, while my pretty one, sleeps.'

She waited until he drifted off into a deep sleep before lying down on the other bed. Staring up at the ceiling, she bit down on her fist, trying hard not to sob out loud, but the dam had been broken and she gave herself up to it, not knowing how to stop the torrent that followed. Sleep came eventually and she only half-remembered George squeezing into the tiny space beside her and pulling her to his chest during the long night. He had whispered softly in her ear. She had wished it was Da telling her that everything would be alright.

The sun had already burnt through any mist the following morning when Martha stirred. What was the hammering sound? All the shouting? She sat bolt upright. The Germans. They're back. She jumped out of bed and looked through the window at the market yard below. Windows were being replaced in a house across the way. Traders were busy putting up stalls, replacing broken parts, laying out their wares. Chickens squawked, wings flapping frantically, as they were caught and returned to wicker baskets after their night of freedom. She could see the players, in full costume, standing on a makeshift platform and rehearsing loudly for the upcoming play.

'I would my father looked but with my eyes.'

'Rather your eyes with his judgement must look.'

'I do entreat your grace to pardon me—' The would-be Hermia stopped mid sentence, throwing her arms up in dismay, slamming her foot down on the wooden boards. 'Really. How are we supposed to rehearse with that racket going on...I can't think.'

Martha remembered how she would peep through this window with Robert's young sons, looking down on the players in their costumes, performing by the light of torches. A Midsummer Night's Dream was always the favourite. The boys would laugh out loud to see Bottom. Her Da and Robert would be sitting with the crowds by one of several open fires that blazed away in large metal braziers, everyone drinking, laughing and chatting amiably, their faces glowing in the flames as they goaded the actors. The thought of it being performed without her Da there made her eyes gloss over again.

'Morning, lass. How did you sleep?' Sarah was standing behind her holding a tray, her cheeks burning red with the exertion of heaving herself up the steep stairs with a mug of tea and a wedge of bread. There was a glass of milk for William, who was still sleeping, oblivious to the clamour. Putting the tray down, she pulled out the tea towel tucked into the waistband of her skirt and wiped the perspiration from her forehead.

'Where's George?'

'He's out with Robert.' Sarah joined Martha at the window. 'Your Da used to love watching them.' She nodded in the direction of the platform, her eyes filling up as she swallowed the pebble in her throat. 'Do you remember when you and your Ma used to come for a natter while Robert and your Da were out there? I'd put you up here with the boys—'

'I need to see them. When can I see them?'

'Soon, lass, soon. You'll need to brace yer sel.'

'What's going to happen to us, Sarah? Where will we go?'

Sarah wrapped her large arm around Martha's tiny shoulders. Martha snuggled into the woman, who represented the nearest thing to having a mother right now, as if she were a child again. She smelled of fresh bread and comfort. Sarah pulled her close, speaking softly.

'You'll stay here for a few days until your home's put right. Robert and George have gone to sort out the joiners. It'd take months if we waited for the landlord to put it reet. The boys'll share our room. Now, you try and eat some breakfast.' She looked down at the grubby sheets on the bed before adding, 'I'll fetch a jug of water and some soap. And mebbe summat to wear. You could do with a bit of a tidy.'

Chapter 2

'It's not too bad now, Pet.'

George led Martha through the new front door. She could also see that the windows had been replaced and the ceiling looked as good as new, but there was little left in the way of furniture. They both went out into the back yard and started the job of clearing up the pile of broken furniture and household items that George and Robert had put there while the house was repaired. They sifted through, working out what could be made good and what needed to be replaced. The kettle and pans were a bit bent but useable. They carried anything salvageable back into the house. Sarah had given her some blankets and an old mattress for their bed frame, which unbelievably had survived. William's bed would take a bit of work, but it would suffice for now. Sarah had also given Martha another one of her own skirts and one or two of her boys' old shirts for William. They would have something to wear and something to sleep on. The shirts were far too big for William, but she could alter them. She knew how to sew, knit and cook well, thanks to her Ma. Granda's box-bed was still there, but neither of them could face sleeping in it. The rest would take time.

The one thing intact and as good as new was William's cracket, but the child refused to sit on it. Martha didn't push him. It would take time to get over such a traumatic event. She could barely cope. What must it be like for a small child like William?

'There's still no gas for the lights, they can't turn it on again until they've fixed up the gasometers and the pipes to the houses.' George was trying to fix the kitchen table. 'It could be a few days yet, but I've managed to get a bit o'coal for the range and some candles.'

'Is there any water?'

'Aye, Pet. I carried some up from the stand pipe this morning.' He stopped what he was doing and heaved the large bucket over from the corner of the room. 'They say it'll all be running proper by tomorrow.'

Martha filled the kettle and set it on the plate above the fire box before kneeling in front of the range, shuffling around to make herself more comfortable. The ache in her back gnawing at her again.

'Who's coming down from Govan for your Granda's funeral?' she asked, making twists of newspaper. Her heart started to pound. She'd seen the letter sticking out of his pocket when he came to fetch her from the market house this morning.

'Ma's not well; rheumatism's got worse so Da won't leave her... There's only Albert managed to get time off work...He'll be here in the morning.'

'Will he stop long?' Her hands were shaking and her throat felt dry.

'No longer than needs be...It'll be ower afore you know it.'

Continuing to lay kindling on top of the screwed up newspaper, she turned her face up to him. 'I hope so,' she replied.

'It'll be fine. Dunna worry, Pet.' George squeezed her shoulder and looked at William, who was sitting on the floor playing with a small wooden horse that his Great Granda had whittled for him last year. Blonde curls tumbled across the boy's elfin face, hiding his bright blue eyes. He was a perfect miniature replica of his mother; fine boned, a scattering of freckles dotted across his cheeks.

Martha placed a few lumps of coal on top of the kindling and lit the paper. Smoke curled and flames licked the kindling. How on earth was she going to get through this funeral, she wondered. How could she lay Ma and Da under the earth? She still couldn't believe she would never see them again. How could she deal with all this? And what about Albert? How would she deal with Albert?

The three pine coffins were laid out like piano keys on the freshly-mopped floor of the empty front parlour. Her parents and George's Granda side by side. Lids tightly fastened down, hiding their shattered bodies. Martha kept herself busy making tea for anyone who wanted it. She was glad of all the neighbours traipsing in and out, depriving her of thinking time.

'It would a' bin quick, lass. They wouldn't a felt it,' said one neighbour as others nodded in agreement.

She glanced over to see George rubbing his arm after shaking dozens of hands. William was standing by the range, staring at the fire. She watched her husband wink at the boy as he passed through the crowd to greet the latest guests. Poor lad had spoken few words since the bombardment. He was still holding his little wooden horse, Neddy, and looking through the sea of legs in an effort to see if his mother was still there. She caught his eye and smiled to reassure him.

Robert and Sarah Colby arrived and George made his way over. They had organised everything, paying for flowers and funeral costs.

George held his hand out to Robert. 'Thanks for all you've done for us. I'll pay you back as soon as I can.'

'Ha'way, lad. Annie and Cyril were our friends. Dunna be worrying about that. There's no hurry,' said Robert smiling.

' I know but the insurance'll pay out soon. I'll mek sure you get every penny back.'

'I know you will, lad.' Robert patted George's shoulder as he moved away, mingling with the crowd again.

Martha bit down on her bottom lip, twisting the wedding band around on her left hand. Albert still hadn't arrived.

She didn't hear Robert come up behind her. 'Time to go, Hinny,' he whispered, touching her arm gently and pointing through the window. 'They're here.'

The coffins were carried out and placed on the open cart. The townsmen took off their caps and bowed their heads and the women wiped away their tears as the small procession set off from Tankerville Street and marched slowly through the town towards North Cemetery.

George and Martha walked behind the cart, William between them. Martha clutched a handkerchief, swallowing hard, stemming the tears.

Two black horses with gleaming brasses were harnessed to the cart, walking sedately as they were driven by Fred, sitting with his back to the coffins, his legs dangling to the floor. The funeral director strode out in front of them, his tall black hat carried in one white-gloved hand, a ceremonial staff in the other.

'Ashes to ashes. Dust to dust,' Reverend Thomas said in a deep nasal voice as he threw a handful of earth into the hole that contained all three coffins. His large nose was red from continuous wiping and his cheeks were blazing with fever. 'And bay the Lord have bercy on their souls. Aben'

'Amen,' came the chorus of voices in response.

Martha tossed a second handful of earth, George and William following suit.

'Let us bray,' continued the Reverend, bowing his head

and closing his eyes.

George tilted his head to look at Martha, squeezed her hand and offered a smile.

'Alreet, Pet?'

'I...can't bear it...I miss them so...' she gulped between words, choking with grief.

The mourners started to disperse, leaving the three of them to say their goodbyes. Robert Colby was the last to leave.

'You know where we are if you need us, Hinny. Your ma would have wanted us to look out for our god-daughter. You remember that.' He turned and set off after Sarah.

'I know he means well, but it's my responsibility to look after you and William. Not Robert Colby's.'

'He's only doing what he thinks best, George. Don't be angry with him.'

'I'm not, but...anyone would think I'm not capable—'

'Capable of what?' the unexpected voice asked.

Martha whipped around so fast she almost lost her balance.

'Albert.' Her face flushed as her insides coiled up into a ball.

'Where've you been? The funeral's done,' George hissed.

Albert glared at George, his square jaw set as he limped towards him, his left hand leaning heavily on a stick.

'Trying to get a lift. The train lines are still not working from Darlington, or hadn't you noticed the town's been shelled? Fine bloody welcome this is.'

Martha watched as they came together, batting each other's shoulders, smiles tight and forced. Albert nearly knocking his slighter brother over with his free hand. He was still a giant of a man, even with the limp, his broad shoulders developed through years of heavy work in the shipyards. William squirmed behind his mother, hiding his face in her skirt, his bony fingers pinching the back of her legs through the thin material.

Albert turned to her, his mahogany eyes flashing, his

smile wide. She began to feel dizzy and breathless, wiping her mouth as a wave of nausea swept over her.

'Hello, Martha.' He lifted her chin and looked down at her. 'You haven't changed a bit. Still as beautiful as you always were I see.'

Chapter 3

The journey home was strained and silent. Martha walked a few steps behind George and Albert, clutching William's hand. He squealed as her grip got tighter. She was having trouble keeping pace with the long strides of the men. Her heart was racing, the pain in her back getting worse. The streets were beginning to be cleared, but it was still an effort to work their way around bits of masonry and broken glass. George quickened his stride in an effort to keep up with Albert, whose stick seemed to propel him along rather than slow him up. She wondered if Albert's leg still pained him. George and Albert's fifteen year old sister wrote regularly to tell them of their life in Scotland since they'd moved there four years ago. She'd learned from the letters about Albert falling off the stocks whilst working on one of the new warships in Govan. Life up there didn't sound easy, and his sister Edith had said that living in the tenements was a squalid, cramped affair. Each family only having two rooms, regardless of the number of children. They were lucky having only four in their flat. Her, Albert and their Ma and Da. The 'temporary' accommodation had become permanent, as they never managed to save enough to move into something better, what with the rents going up all the time.

William started to cry and pulled on Martha's hand.

'George. Can you carry William...George.'

George looked back at the pair.

'What's the matter, Pet?'

'It's William. The poor bairn's fair whacked and he's too heavy for me to pick up. Can you carry him?'

'C'mon, lad. Let's be having you.' He picked the boy up and swung him high in the air.

Albert watched William's face light up at being up on his Da's shoulders. Albert smiled at the boy and Martha felt the flutter of panic in her chest.

'Ha'way there, young William,' Albert said, looking up at him. 'That's better. You're the image of your Ma when you smile. I'm reet glad to meet you. I'm your Uncle Albert.' William smiled back at the big man. Martha knew he would have felt a lot braver while he was so high up with his Da holding on to him.

'I canna see much of you in him, George. Lucky for him.' He laughed loudly, elbowing George's arm. George stiffened and the group fell silent again, not speaking until they reached home.

'Grand little house; it's a lot better than when we all lived here. Looks like you've got the men folk better trained than Ma ever could.' Albert stood with his back to the freshly blacked range looking around at the room. William's cracket, still unclaimed, filled one corner of the hearth, a flat iron on the opposite side. A colourful, proggy rug, another gift from Sarah, covered the stone floor under his feet. The little window that looked out on to the backyard was trimmed with a lace net, threaded on to wire that was stretched and tacked into place across the top of the frame.

Martha mashed the tea by the stone sink in front of the

window before setting the pot down on the wooden table. George placed his hand over Martha's, staying her.

'Sit down, Pet, you look fair worn out. Are you ailing?' He frowned, narrowing his eyes as he examined her face closely. 'You look white as a sheet.'

'I...I'm tired, that's all. There's no need to worry about me.'

'I'm not surprised you're tired,' said Albert. 'It's a lot to cope with, losing your Ma and Da like that. Our Da's reet upset he couldn't come for Granda's funeral, George. We couldn't believe it when we heard the news. I'm sorry I were late, but the railways have taken a right battering. Bloody Huns. I canna wait to sign up. Make 'em pay for what they've done.' His voice sounded deeper than Martha remembered.

'We'll both go up the town hall in the morning. Most of the lads from Gray's Works are going,' George said, before taking a mouthful of hot tea.

Albert clasped Martha's hand for a second as she passed him a drink. He looked her full in the face. She pulled away, spilling a little of the hot liquid onto his hand in the process. He didn't seem to notice, staring deep into her eyes. William looked up, concerned, as a short gasp escaped his mother's lips, then turned back, satisfied she looked alright, and continued to play on the floor with Neddy.

Martha sat down at the table and cupped her drink. Closing her eyes, she felt the panic bubbling up in her chest. She couldn't think straight. Why had he done that? He couldn't be saying that he still thought about her, could he? She was married. It was unthinkable...She loved George now. She stole a glance as Albert squatted down and asked William if he could play.

'I bet my Granda made that for you. He made me one when I was a nipper.'

What would happen if he went to war? Would this be the last time she ever saw him?... George. She meant George, she told herself sharply.

Martha ladled out the boiled potatoes, flavoured with an onion and a little beef stock. The gas had been re-connected and the lights, along with the fire blazing in the grate, made the kitchen warm and cosy against the black and cold winter's night outside. A loaf cut into wedges and a jug of water formed the centrepiece as they sat down and tucked into their supper and main meal of the day. When they had finished eating, George opened the letter from the insurers. It had been waiting for them when they got back from the funeral.

'Thank you, Martha. I was ready for this.' Albert licked his lips before wiping them with the back of his hand. 'I haven't eaten much since leaving home. Ma packed some bread and cheese for the journey, but it was well past its best. I can't remember how long it is since I ate summat that smelled of meat.'

'It's the same for all of us. You're not the only one struggling. We have to make the best of what we've got.' George sounded angry. 'I need to get back to work tomorrow. There's no money for compassionate leave.'

'You should apply for something on the ships. You can't be earning much issuing stock. You need to do a bit of man's work.' Martha flinched. That was a cruel thing to say. Albert knew George had stopped working on the ships after Rupert had the accident. He couldn't face it when his dearest friend had fallen from the scaffolding during a period of bad weather in the spring of 1910. They had been inseparable all through school and had started work at the shipyard together as soon as they left. George had tried to grab his shirt as Rupert slipped and stumbled backwards, but it had torn in his hand and he'd had to watch as he plunged to his death. He had been killed instantly and George had insisted on carrying him all the way home to his parents. She knew he still blamed himself after all these years.

'It is man's work, and you know full well why I work in stores. Just cos I dunna get dirty like you caulkers anymore.' His face began to flush and his eyes narrowed. He waved the letter in the air. 'Anyway, the money's not only for living. It turns out that Martha's Da let the insurance lapse an' all so we owe Robert Colby a lot of money.' Martha's mouth dropped open.

'Oh, George... no! What are we going to do?' Could things get any worse? Hadn't they suffered enough? 'I'm so sorry. I'll try and find some work to help pay him back. We'll have to cut back...'

'You can forget that, Martha. I won't have you doing that. Married women dunna go out to work.'

'You'll not get far on your wages. Stop being so stubborn. Surely you'll let her take in a bit of washing or summat. You can't afford to be so proud. Dunna be so stupid, man.'

'I'll provide for my family.' George slammed his knife down, rattling the plates. 'I'm about sick and tired of other people trying to tell me what to do. You walk in here after four years and start layin' the law down as if you never left. This is my house; you dunna tell me what to do anymore.' He stormed out, banging the new front door behind him.

Martha stood up quietly and started to clear the crockery.

'I...I'm sorry. I don't know what's got into him...'

'Same as usual,' replied Albert. 'He's hot headed. Allus has been. Canna take advice from anyone.'

'He's a good man. Tries his best for me and William.' Martha's voice was rising. At least he stayed here with me, she thought. Not like you.

'I'm sure he does. You were sharp enough to marry him when I left.' He turned his back to her. 'You said you'd wait...'

'I...I didn't know how long...George was kind...'

'I bet he was...slimy little...' Albert stopped himself, remembering a child was present. 'Allus jealous. Allus trying to get his foot in the door where you were concerned. Managed it eventually, didn't he?'

'That's enough...what's done is done...come, William, it's time for bed...say goodnight to Uncle Albert.' She picked him up and left Albert, red-faced and clenching his fists.

'Goodnight, lad,' he muttered.

William clung to his mother, his face buried in her shoulder as she took him up to his bed, trying to ignore the pain that grabbed her stomach.

She heard Albert go out as she sat with William, waiting for him to go to sleep. He was still having nightmares. Not only about the day of the bombardment, but the sheer panic that took over the town two days after. The Mayor had driven around the streets telling all the residents that the Germans were about to attack again. People were leaving in droves, packing everything they could into prams, wheelbarrows. Loading up flat carts with furniture. It turned out to be a false alarm, but everyone had at least one evacuation suitcase or bag permanently packed from that day. Some kept on going anyway and never came back.

Martha sang softly to her son, calming him.

'Sweet and low, sweet and low
Wind of western sea,
Low, low, breathe and blow...

His eyes drifted shut, opening again each time she moved. Martha smiled, reassuring him that she wasn't going anywhere. The pain in her stomach was getting worse. She knew the cause, but had put off telling anyone too soon. No good building George's hopes up for nothing. It took quite a while for William to succumb, but she wouldn't take the oil lamp away until she was sure he was hard and fast asleep.

Creeping downstairs she was gripped by a blinding cramp. She staggered over to the kitchen table, feeling the blood trickle down her legs before slumping to the floor on all fours.

'Ma...I need you..Ma'

*

She heard George and Albert enter the house quietly. She thought she was going to pass out again as they crept into the tiny kitchen holding their boots in their hands. George held his finger up to his lips and kept saying 'Sssh' as Albert burst into song. Martha reached up from her position on the floor.

'My God, Martha. What's happening?' George flew over and dropped down on his knees beside her. He lifted her head on to his lap. 'Martha...Martha...What's up, Pet? What happened?' The smell of beer, like smelling salts under her nose, sharpened her senses and brought her round.

Albert bent down on the other side, swaying unsteadily, unsure of what to do.

'It's okay, George...get me upstairs. I'll be fine,' she murmured.

The pain knifed through her insides as the pair struggled to carry her up the narrow staircase and lay her on the bed.

'Run and get Sarah Colby, Albert. She'll know what to do.' George sat down beside Martha, stroking her hair.

Albert ran back downstairs and out of the door in a flash, a burst of adrenalin beginning to sober him up.

'It's the baby...I've lost it, George...I'm so...sorry,' she cried as another pain swallowed her up.

'Why didn't you tell me?' George searched her eyes. 'I didn't know.'

'I wanted to be sure. Oh...Oh...' She curled up into a ball. 'I'm sorry...so sorry... '

The pain dragged her down, again and again. Her skirts were soaked in blood.

'You'd better keep her in bed a day or two, George, and she'll be fine. I'm sorry, Martha. Probably the shock of what's gone on that's done it. I'll come back tomorrow and see how you're doing.' Sarah kissed Martha on the cheek and headed downstairs.

'Can I get you anything, Pet?' George's eyes searched her face, the worry making his voice crack.

'I'm fine. Is William alright? Poor bairn must think the world's coming to an end. Bring him in to me, will you, George?'

'Course I will. He's been desperate to see you.'

George disappeared, and Martha curled up under the clean sheets that Sarah had brought, her insides ached and she wanted to sleep. William flew to her side.

'He's feared stiff. Thought you were dying.' George patted the boy's head. 'See. I told you she was alreet. Nothing to worry about, son.'

William climbed up on the bed and snuggled under the covers with his Ma.

'I'll sleep on the floor the night. You and William get some rest.'

'Where's Albert going to sleep?' she asked.

'He'll get his head down in William's room.' he answered, but her eyes were already closed. George looked down at the pair.

'I'll make those Germans pay for this,' she heard him say. 'You see if I don't.'

He lay down on the floor next to the bed. He was staring at the ceiling when she opened her eyes sometime later and looked down at him.

Chapter 4

'It seems like it's becoming a habit. Me bringing you breakfast in bed.' Sarah's round face beamed at Martha as she tried to lighten the mood. 'How are you feeling this morning? Sore I'll bet.'

'I'll live.' Martha pulled herself into a sitting position. William's been looking after me. Haven't you?' She hugged the little boy, who was sitting on top of the blanket.

'Yes, Ma.' His tiny face was still wearing the same startled look that he had the last time Sarah saw him.

'I should hope so, young man. Your Ma needs you now.' She ruffled his hair and grinned at him.

William managed a brief smile.

'He's coming round a bit now, but he's still not saying too much. Except when his Da picks him up and spins him round. He laughs and laughs then. Don't you?' She tickled William until he giggled.

'I'm sorry about the bairn, Martha. It's a sad business on top of everything else.'

'I know. I think George has taken it hard.'

'You're only young. Still only a bairn yersel. Plenty of time for another. Let's concentrate on getting you better for now. I've made a bite for your supper tonight. Sheep's head stew. There's enough for all of you. '

'Thank you, Sarah. You're so kind.'

'Ha'way, with you. Your ma would have done the same for my boys had it been the other way round.'

Martha was glad Sarah was here. It reminded her of how she used to feel when her ma took control and sorted everything out. George tried his best, and she loved him dearly, but it wasn't quite the same as having a mother to help. "He tries too hard, Lass. Always wanting to impress," her ma used to say. She was right; George always felt the need to show he was capable in front of everyone instead of accepting help when people offered. He couldn't even accept her working, even though they owed all that money to Robert and Sarah.

Sarah sat on the edge of the bed chatting away, trying to pass the time while they waited for George and Albert to come back from the recruitment office up at the town hall. The army had made it their temporary quarters since the start of the war in August.

'How long before they have to leave?' Martha asked. 'If they're accepted, I mean. Is it straight away?'

'Pretty soon I think. Mrs Bradley's two boys were gone within a week when they signed up. She hasn't heard a word yet and it's been two months since. Training I think. They'll get some leave before they get shipped out I s'pose. I'm glad my two lads are still too young.'

'I don't know what I'll do when they're gone...When George is gone. It'll be lonely without him.' Martha carried on speaking, to herself as much as Sarah, a picture of George and Albert in uniform filling her head, Albert standing a good head taller than her husband.

'I couldn't bear it if my lads had to go. I hope the war is over before they reach eighteen,' Sarah continued.

'What did you say? Sorry I was miles away.'

'No...It was nothing. Just saying the boys are too young... thank the lord.'

Here I am worrying about myself again, she thought. 'Is Robert going to join up?' Martha asked quietly.

'No...He tried...Hearing's not good enough and his heart's not at its best. Besides, they'll only tek men up to the age of thirty eight. He was upset, but I was glad. I know I shouldn't be, but I can't help it. '

'I'm glad for you.' She hoped they would refuse George, too. Perhaps he wouldn't be strong enough, she thought.

' Robert said there must have been every man in the town queuing up to join when he went yesterday. It took him three hours to get inside the building and another two afore he was seen. Its been like that every day since the shelling. Not surprising when all the papers are baying for blood. They reckon that well over a hundred folk have been killed and about 200 wounded between here and Scarborough and Whitby.'

'It's so terrible. All those families grieving.'

'The papers have named Theo Jones as the first soldier to be killed on British soil. They don't know if he was really. There were four of them went down up at the battery when the shelling first started.'

The slam of the front door, followed by raised voices, heralded the return of the two men. They were shouting at each other and their voices carried upstairs.

'They don't know what they're talking about. Bloody fools. I can still carry a rifle and shoot the enemy, can't I? And I can march as good as the next man. Better in some cases.'

'No good going on about it, Albert. It won't make them change their minds, will it?'

'What do you know? Skinny runt like you and they can't wait to get you on board. Off their bloody heads they are.'

'Face it, Albert. I'm not the pathetic little runt you always make me out to be.' The triumph in George's voice was unmistakeable.

Martha heard the thunder of his boots on the stairs before he burst into the bedroom; eyes flashing with excitement, cheeks flushed with anticipation of what lay ahead of him.

'I'm in. I have to report for training the day after Christmas,' he said, his mouth grinning wider than she'd ever seen it before. 'They won't take Albert...cos of his leg... I'll make you so proud of me, Martha—' He stopped short, the look of disappointment clear on her face.

'What's so good about that? I wish they'd refused you, too,' she snapped. 'Some good you'll be when they blow your head off. You can be all high and mighty then, can't you? Why do you always need to prove you're better than your brother? '

'And why do you allus have to put me down,' he yelled before turning tail and storming back downstairs.

'Aah, Lass. What did you have to go and do that for?' asked Sarah. 'He needs to know you're proud of him.'

'Proud? Proud when I get a letter saying he's dead? Proud when they send me a medal? Proud doesn't keep him safe, does it? He's as good as signed his own death warrant.' Martha buried her head in the pillow and sobbed.

'C'mon, William.' Sarah held out her hand. 'Let's go and make your Da a nice cup o' tea. I've brought some cakes, too. Fresh baked this morning.'

William climbed down and took her hand, his little eyes shiny with tears yet again.

'It's time you pulled yourself together, Martha. This little 'un needs a Ma,' she added as they left the room.

Martha could hear the conversation below as she got dressed and pulled at her curls, trying to pin them up. She splashed her face in the wash basin that Sarah had brought up for her. The bloodied skirt lying on the wooden floor reminded her of the empty space inside her, still raw and sore.

'She's worried about you, George, that's all. She's feared you'll get killed.'

'That's as maybe, but she ought to support my decision,' he growled, biting into the slab of fruit cake that Sarah offered.

'She might if you didn't allus make a pig's ear of everything,' snarled Albert.

'And she might get better a bit sooner if you two weren't at each other's throats all the time,' Sarah added. 'Don't you think she's suffered enough?'

The brothers turned to look at her.

'You're right. I'll go up and talk to her.' George stood up and turned to find Martha coming down the last step.

'No need. I'm down now. I'm sorry I went on at you, George. I am proud of you. I hate the thought of you being out there, that's all.'

'I know, Pet.' He wrapped his arms around her. 'I have to go. Don't you see? To make it right for Granda and your family...and...and the babby.'

'They don't need you to make it right, George. They need you to look after William and me...and maybe...maybe another bairn sometime.' She clung on to him as she spoke.

She saw Albert turn his gaze away as they supported each other.

'It's time I went back to Govan,' he said. 'I'll go first thing in the morning. At least I can do my bit making war ships.'

'Aye, lad.' Sarah looked from the couple and then to Albert. 'Happen it's for the best.'

As Martha looked over George's shoulder, her heart tugged. Albert walked past them without looking up. She heard his stick thud on each step as he went upstairs to pack.

Chapter 5

1910

Albert's breath was hot in her ear as they cuddled in the back row of the Long Room at The Angel Inn. 'I've got something to tell you.'

'I've got something to tell you, too,' gasped Martha, her heart pumping fiercely. She had thought of nothing else all day. Mrs Henry, her supervisor had reprimanded her several times for daydreaming. She'd even got one client's documents lost inside another client's file. "Turnbull and Tilley solicitors have an impeccable reputation for giving their clients the highest quality of service, Miss Palmer, and you very near ruined it in the blink of an eye. Continue in this manner and you will find yourself seeking alternative employment. Do I make myself clear?" Mrs Henry's voice was still ringing in her ears. She ruled that office with a rod of iron and wouldn't tolerate any drop in standards. Ma would be so cross with her if she lost such a good job.

'Me first,' said Albert excitedly.

'Sssh!' whispered a voice from out of the darkness, 'I canna hear what he's sayin'.'

'Sorry, mate.' Albert stopped talking.

There was a tension in the air as they all sat quietly on the rows of wooden chairs, hoping they wouldn't get chosen to be mesmerized and made to do silly things. Dennis Peart was escorted to the front by Mesmero's glamorous assistant, his friends laughing and jeering.

'Me Da's been offered a job up in Glasgow,' Albert whispered. 'Foreman. He starts in a couple of weeks.'

Martha pulled away. 'What are you going to do?' she mumbled, starting to tremble.

'I'm going with him. We're all going. Except our George... says he'll stay with Granda. Stubborn old goat won't budge. Sez he belongs here.'

'When?' she croaked, her voice barely audible.

'Next week. Da's keen to get up there and settle in afore he starts work at Govan. There's a job for me, too.'

'What about us?' her voice cracked. 'Will you be able to visit? '

'I don't know. Hartlepool's hardly a tram ride, is it? ...It's a good opportunity for me ... I'd be a fool to miss it.' He squeezed her arm, pulling her closer; wanting to take advantage of the semi-darkness. 'Don't worry, I'll think of something,' he added before kissing her and trying to undo the top button of her blouse. Martha pulled away weakly.

'Please,' she said. 'Not here.' He sat up straight, muttering under his breath.

They watched Dennis on his hands and knees, barking like a dog. Everyone cheered and shouted. Albert threw his head back, clapping his hands on his thighs and roaring with laughter. Martha cried quietly in the darkness.

He held her hand as they walked home; she gazed up at his handsome, chiselled face beaming under the gas lights. Drizzle danced through the shafts of light leaving a gossamer web of diamonds on their hair.

'I doubt it'll last longer than an hour or two,' he said, tipping his head back and letting the fine spray wash his face.

'No,' Martha said. Her mind was on other things. It wasn't until they reached Dene Street and her doorstep that he pulled her close and kissed her on the lips again. She tasted the cool rain on his skin, the salt on his mouth and the searing heat of his tongue forcing its way into her mouth. Her body responded immediately. Her need to be enveloped by him so powerful she couldn't think about anything else. He stopped as quickly as he started, letting go and looking down at her. The smile on his face showing his satisfaction at being able to illicit such a response. She felt dizzy and out of control as soon as he held her. Totally under his spell.

'Eeh, Martha. I forgot. I've been that excited. What's your news? '

'Oh...I...I'm,' she needed to blurt it out quickly before she lost her courage. 'I'm...It's—.'

'There'll be chance of promotion and good money,' he interrupted. 'I might come back a rich man and whisk you away in a grand carriage. What do you think to that?' He'd already stopped listening. His heart was set on going. What was the point of telling him, she thought. He wouldn't want to know.

'That'll be grand, Albert. Just grand.'

'What were you saying?'

'Nothing...nothing,' she said flatly.

Albert pulled her close again, his chin resting easily on the top of her head, breathing in the sweet scent of her thick, cinnamon curls; stroking her back so that he could memorise the feel and shape of her; the warmth of her cheek pressed to his chest.

'I won't half miss you, Martha Palmer. I'll get word to you as soon as I'm settled. I'll mebbe even come back for you one day, unless some lucky girl up there wins my heart.' A slight chuckle escaped as he shouted back to her and headed home.

She stepped into the house quietly. She didn't want to wake Ma and Da. Didn't want them to hear her crying.

'Is that you, Pet?' her father called from upstairs. He never could sleep before knowing she was home and safe.

She cleared her throat and answered as brightly as she could.

'Yes, Da. Go back to sleep now.'

Martha kept her head down at work over the next couple of days, trying to block out the fact that Albert was going away. He might change his mind. He might realise he loved her too much to leave her. She knew she was fooling herself; she knew deep down that he wouldn't decide to stay. He had been so full of what he would do up there. The opportunities that were waiting for him. She'd missed her chance. She prayed she was wrong, willing her body to give her some sign that everything would be alright. After all, it had only been a matter of days since the date circled in her diary. The diary she kept hidden under her mattress.

She saw Albert once more before the family left. He came round to her house with a bunch of roses a day or two later.

'To remind you of me,' he said pulling her towards him on the doorstep. He kissed her hard on the lips. 'Will you wait for me, Martha? It could be a long time afore you see me again.'

'Would you come back quickly if I needed you, Albert?' she asked, looking directly into his eyes.

'Why are you asking that?' His face wrinkled into a frown.

'I need to know you care for me, Albert. Do you?' She held her breath, waiting for him to give her the answer she desperately needed.

'I wouldn't have time to run up and down from Scotland every time you called me. I've a career to build. Yoos'll have to be patient. I'll come back when I can. What's the matter with you, Pet? Is there summat up? '

'No...you go and make your fortune; You can't miss a chance like that.'

Albert kissed her again and she clung to him as if her life depended on it. He removed her hands and placed them firmly by her sides. 'Steady on, Pet. That should keep you happy for a while. I'll not forget you, Martha.'

Martha touched her fingers to her lips as she watched his back disappearing around the corner. She managed to hang on to the sound of him whistling for a few seconds more.

Chapter 6

December 25th, 1914

Martha and George watched William pull the string bow undone and peel back the brown paper.

'A horse. Another horse to play with Neddy,' he beamed, jumping up to show them. He immediately picked up Neddy and introduced them. 'This is your new friend. He's come to play with you.'

'I'm so glad you managed to find it. It would have been a shame if it had got lost in all the mess.' Martha squeezed George's arm.

George smiled and wiped the shine from his eyes; picturing his Granda carving it with love for his great grandson. 'He would a' been so pleased to watch him open it.'

'I'm sure. I wish Ma and Da could have been here.'

She got up to check the potatoes boiling on the range. A mutton and onion broth, with a sprinkling of barley, bubbled away in another pan. The rich smell made it feel more special. Christmas last year had been so different. Such a lavish affair compared to this. The three of them and Granda had spent Christmas day round at Ma and Da's house. Ma had made the most wonderful spread of goose and potatoes and enough vegetables to feed the street. The whole family had groaned with pleasure after dinner, sitting around the fire and playing games with William, getting him to repeat words for them, everyone roaring with laughter when George got him to say "*Ha'way Pet*." Da nodded off after he had drunk two or three beers. He rarely drank, and it had gone straight to his head. They had arms laden down with food to bring back home. It had lasted for days. George's Granda said it was the best Christmas he'd ever had. "Your Ma can't half put on a good meal," he had enthused for a week afterwards. "Where does she get all that food from? More to the point, how can she afford it?" Martha had laughed. "She's quite friendly with a chap down at the market," she had replied, thinking of Sarah and Robert Colby.

The memory filled her with a nostalgic sadness. Turning back to the broth, she sighed. She had to make the most of today. George would be gone in the morning.

'Open your present, George,' she said forcing a wide smile. 'I hope you like it.'

He tore open the package and pulled out a soft woollen scarf and matching brown gloves. 'How? When did you manage—'

'I didn't. I'm sorry. I'd been making you a new waistcoat. Yours has seen better days... It was at Ma's house. Sarah gave these to me. I prom—'

'We can't keep relying on them, Martha. We owe them enough already.'

'Hold your horses. I promised to knit some for her sons in return. For goodness sake, George.'

'I'm sorry...I—'

'You always are, George. You always are...' She turned back to the cooking. The whole atmosphere was spoiled. 'They're to keep you warm...out there.'

He stepped up behind her; wrapping his arms around her waist; resting his head on her shoulder. 'I don't know how you put up with me,' he said, his hot breath seeping through the fabric of her blouse and warming her skin. 'I promise to try harder. Let's not fall out on my last day at home...please ...please?'

She swivelled around in his arms and held him close. William looked up and smiled before turning back to his beloved horses.

'I'm sorry too, George. I shouldn't have shouted. People are only showing kindness. You have to learn to accept it...accept it's not about your capabilities...it hurts to hear all that bitterness in your voice.'

George kissed her lips softly and she felt a sudden warmth in her groin. Realising their time was short; she held his face in her hands and returned his kiss with fervour.

The day passed in a haze, playing games with William, making him laugh and giggle. It was the first time since that terrible day and they made the most of it, pretending their Christmas dinner was the most sumptuous meal they had ever had; pretending they were King George and Queen Mary and William was a young Prince Edward.

George got on all fours, neighing and snorting like a horse. 'Would the young prince like a ride on his favourite stallion?' he said in the poshest voice he could muster.

William squealed with delight.

'Yes please, Da...err...Neddy.' He scrambled up on to George's back and squeezed his heels into his father's sides. 'Giddy up, Neddy. Giddy up.'

George hobbled around the floor as fast as he could manage, wincing at the hardness of the stone under his knees. Martha squealed with laughter as William kept pulling George's collar back and George snorted and raised his arms up in the air. William screamed with delight and clung on to his father's shirt so hard his knuckles turned white.

'Neddy needs a rest, young prince. Neddy needs a rest.' George let William slide off his back before standing up. 'Would the queen like a ride?' he asked Martha, his eyes flashing wickedly at her. Martha blushed.

'Maybe later, my dear King,' she replied with a curtsy.

'Have a ride now, Ma. You'll like it,' William urged her.

'I'm sure I will,' she replied, her eyes still firmly on George. 'But this queen needs to clear all these dishes now.'

'As you wish, Your Majesty,' said George with a sweeping bow that set them all into fits of laughter all over again.

They flirted with each other endlessly, and when night fell, they climbed the narrow staircase, George carrying William, who was fast asleep, in his arms. Falling into their own bed, they made their last night together one they would always remember.

It was dawn when he crept from their bed. Martha woke later to find a small package on the pillow beside her. She smiled.

Chapter 7

January 25th, 1915

Dearest Martha,

I am settled in and enjoying my training. I'm not right good at this letter writing, but I'll try my best. Jimmy Saltburn is here and Arthur Simms, as well as another half dozen from Grays, so I have pals around me. We have to do drills each morning and we go on route marches most afternoons. My feet are covered in blisters and that sore I can't sleep proper. The food is good and we get three meals a day. They've put Jimmy and me in stores, as we're used to that sort of work. They reckon we'll go overseas in a few months.

I miss you and William all the time and I hope to get a chance to come home and visit before they ship me out. They call it furlough in the army. Funny name for a holiday. Thank you for the vest, it's proper warm. Did you like the lace handkerchief? I thought the woman embroidered your initials real pretty. I know it weren't much, but it was all I could afford. Are you managing on your own? Keep smiling, Pet. I'll be home afore you know it.

Your loving husband,

George.

Ps. Can you send me some writing paper? I had to borrow a piece from Jimmy to send this letter. A few packs of cigarettes would be good if you can manage it.

'Well it sounds as if he's alreet, Lass. At least he's safe for the time being.'

Sarah passed the letter back to Martha and took a sup of tea. 'This is the first time in weeks that I've come round to find a smile on your face. You usually look like a wet weekend every time I see you.'

'I know. It's the thought of him getting...what was it...furlough? It sounds like I'm describing a cat with short legs.' She laughed aloud. 'It is a funny word isn't it?

'It is. See... life isn't so bad. Yoos are alreet, aren't you?'

'I suppose so. William's boots are getting too tight and I don't know where the money'll come from for new. The separation allowance is fine for food and coal and gas and such, but there's never enough for extras. I've no idea when I'll be able to start paying you and Robert back for the funeral costs...'

'Now don't start on about that again. I've told you. Robert says you can pay him back when the war's over and George is back at work. It can't be too much longer, can it? And he won't hear of you helping out at the market he says. Doesn't think married women should go out to work. Old fashioned devil, he is.'

'Sounds exactly like George. I don't know what to do. I hate being on my own all the time. I need company.'

'Yoos are doing fine, lass. You've managed so far without George. You can get by. You just need a bit more confidence, that's all. Dunna worry. If you're really struggling, there's allus me and Robert to help out with food and such. You know that.'

'I need a job. Something to keep me busy until he gets home. I heard something about sending parcels out to the men at the front. I could help with that.'

'Mrs Clarke's running that effort. I can introduce you.'

'You mean her from Clifton Avenue? Isn't she one of them suffragette women? '

'Yes. She's got women knitting for her all ower town. Socks, vests, gloves. I do some as well...Robert doesn't like me being around her, but he knows it's a worthy cause. Yoos could do that, couldn't you?'

'Of course. I've been knitting for George.'

Sarah picked her cup up again and fiddled with the handle before taking a long drink.

'I've got summat to tell yer. You mustn't tell anyone. Least of all my Robert. He'd kill me if he knew.' Her eyes were serious as she looked hard at Martha.

'Knew what?' Martha swallowed, wide eyed and all ears.

'I've joined 'em. The Women's Freedom League.' She paused, waiting for the reaction. 'It's about time we women stood up for our sels. Mrs Wicklow says we're as good as the men and we should have equal rights.' Sarah's voice sounded passionate and the colour in her cheeks rose as she emphasised her words, flinging them out before Martha could interrupt her. 'It's people like my Robert who hold women back, she says. She's right. Robert would keep me in the kitchen all my life if I let him. I'm better than that. I've got a mind of my own. Yoos have got a mind of your own. We have to change things. Change the way men think of us...Trouble is, I daren't tell Robert. Not yet anyway.' Sarah took a deep breath and waited for Martha's reaction.

'Oh, Sarah. What are you thinking? You can't get involved with the likes of them Pankhursts. You'll end up in prison.'

'Not them. The Women's Freedom League. We're pacifists, well most of us are, we don't have anythin' to do with them militant sorts. Well, apart from Mrs Wicklow. She's a proper militant sort. Anyway, they've all called a truce for the duration. They only want volunteers to help with the war effort any way they can. You know, nursing and fund raising for the Belgian Refugees. Yer can help us...with yer knitting, putting Red Cross boxes together and such. Just don't let on to anyone that I'm a member...especially Robert. He thinks they're all out to cause trouble.

Martha saw how serious she was and squeezed Sarah's hand.

'He won't hear it from me...I promise...' She sat quietly for a few minutes, drinking from her mug; digesting everything Sarah had said before eventually coming to a decision. 'Now then, Sarah,' her voice sounding positive. 'When do I get to meet your Mrs Clarke?'

Well...what harm could it do, she thought, trying to hold back the flutter of fear...or was it excitement?

Sarah's face relaxed, and she smiled at Martha before getting up and making her way to the door. 'There's a meeting at her house on Monday night. Can you get someone to look after the bairn? I'll tell Robert I'm coming here if that's alreet with you, Lass,' she said as she opened the front door and stepped out.

'I'll ask Ethel, next door. I'm sure she won't mind looking after William for an hour or two.'

'Good idea, and you can say we're off to the new Canada Picture Palace. Everyone's talkin' about it.'

When Sarah left, Martha set about her housework with a new vigour.

'Well, I never, William Hubbard. Your ma will have such a lot of work to do; you'll have to help her. You'd like that wouldn't you?' she said with a grin as she picked him up and twirled him around. There was a spark of enthusiasm in Martha's voice, her eyes shining for the first time in such a long while. William looked at his mother, his puzzled expression making her laugh.

All the homes on Clifton Avenue looked grand to Martha. She stood beside Sarah, staring up at the large semi-detached house in front of them. Martha swallowed nervously. The stark white colonnades of the front porch complemented the red bricks. A pane of stained glass topped the heavy front door; a country landscape in greens, blues and yellows, glowing in the gas light that shone through it; throwing patches of colour across the front of her worn black coat. She had never been in such a fine house before, except for the time her Ma took ill with the influenza while her Da was at work down the mine. She had been sent to fetch Dr Bartholomew and even then, she didn't exactly go inside his home. She remembered being told to wait on the step by some snotty nosed housekeeper who thought she wasn't fit to step inside the door. The doctor had been a kind man who let her hold his hand while she pulled him along the streets, desperate to get back home where he could make her ma better. He called in a couple of times after that to see how she was doing. Even now, if he saw Martha in the street, he would acknowledge her and ask after Ma and Da.

Mrs Clarke was peering through the large bay window at the front of the house and smiling down at the two women.

'C'mon, Lass. She won't bite,' said Sarah, taking Martha's elbow and ushering her up the step.

A young girl with dark hair, in maid's uniform, pulled the door open and stood to one side. The pale face and haunted look in her eyes seemed unnatural in someone so young. Martha thought she half recognised her but was so taken by the hallway and stairs as they entered, she didn't take the time to think about it for more than a couple of seconds. The columbine print on the wallpaper seemed so real she almost thought she could smell its fragrance. Paintings of highland cattle and wild stags were hung at eye level to ensure any visitor was treated to a view of the wilderness called Scotland. Martha marvelled at the beautiful creatures and wondered if there would ever come a time that she may see such things. The girl, who was about fourteen years old, took their coats and hats before knocking on the drawing-room door.

'Come in. Come in.' The voice had a warm tone and as Martha entered the room, she was greeted by a brilliant smile and outstretched hands. 'Do come and join us, Mrs Hubbard. You are most welcome.'

Martha was shown to a high backed chair, beautifully upholstered and padded for comfort. She and Sarah were offered tea in delicate china teacups. The cup and saucer rattled in her hands as she tried to compose herself.

'Th...Thank you...Mrs Clarke.'

'Not at all. We're pleased that Sarah was able to persuade you to join our cause.' Mrs Clarke swept her hand around the room as if to introduce the dozen or so women that were already there, sipping tea and chatting amiably to each other. Martha felt out of place in a second hand white blouse. She fidgeted, brushing imaginary creases out of her plain black skirt and adjusting the matching hat she had worn to her parents' funeral. She had felt quite smart when she had set out with Sarah, but now...now she was here and surrounded by all these ladies in beautiful, full, taffeta skirts and ruffled silk blouses, wearing hats with brightly coloured plumes and pins...now... she felt as if she should be in the kitchen working alongside the young maid that had let them in.

'I...I would like to help with the parcels. Knit things and the like. My husband's in the army— '

'And I'm sure you're proud of him, as we all are.' Celia glanced at the photograph of her husband in officer's uniform that stood in an ornate silver frame on top of the piano by the window. An electric lamp with a Tiffany shade was strategically placed to shed a warm pool of light on the soldier's face. 'There'll be plenty of knitting for you to do...Now, ladies. Let's get this meeting underway, shall we? Has everyone got a copy of the agenda?'

Martha shuffled uncomfortably in her seat, trying not to rattle the crockery. Sarah seemed oblivious to her and joined in the discussions as they worked their way down the agenda.

'Item One. Where are we with the Belgian Babies Appeal? Are people donating enough boxes of clothes?...'

As the night wore on, Martha found herself drawn into a world where women were discussing politics and the plight of the Belgian people since the invasion. Of the number of refugees who had ended up in London. The Thanks Offering Day appeal was well under way and two of the ladies had been guarding the entrance to the public market rattling their tins at the shoppers. Sarah was leading this appeal and even managed to get some of the stallholders to donate a percentage of their takings. The hospitals needed all the funds they could get after the Bombardment and this was a way for the townsfolk to show their appreciation. This was one cause that Robert supported fully without realising that the women involved were actually suffragettes. They discussed jobs where women might be as capable as men and could be of service while the men were at the front. Working on the trams, trains and in the hospitals that were apparently bursting at the seams with casualties and the general sick. It sounded ridiculous at first and she wanted to laugh. She could just hear what George would have to say about it all. No wonder Sarah didn't want Robert to know she was a suffragette. However, as the night wore on, she found herself agreeing with some points and even asking questions.

'Do you think women could do some of the harder jobs that our husbands normally do?... in the shipyards say?...but only until they get home from the war, I mean? Keep their jobs going for them so no-one else can jump in?'

Everyone looked at her. The silence seemed to last for an age. Had she said something stupid?

'That's exactly what we could do, Martha. Exactly.' Mrs Clarke broke the spell and all the other ladies beamed at her as if she was one of them. All except for a tall thin woman with a downturned mouth and small, beady eyes. She was dressed totally in black and reminded Martha of a cat that had cornered a bird and was getting ready to strike. It made her shudder. The woman looked down her sharp nose at Martha before standing up and approaching her. Martha kept her head down, staring at her teacup. From the edge of her vision, she could just see the woman's long bony fingers and the protruding veins that ran, like roads on a complex map, crossing and intertwining across the back of her hands.

'What Mrs Clarke means is that women are perfectly capable of doing the same work as a man and we don't need to either depend upon them or suffer their patronising attitudes. All this nonsense about taking work away from the men because we accept lower pay has to stop. The real problem is that women's wages should be on a par with what the men get. Good day, ladies. Let me know when the next fund raising event is, Celia,' she ordered before marching from the room. Celia scurried after her, chattering apologetically and wringing her hands together, 'Of course, Gladys. Of course.'

Martha was bewildered by what had happened. Who was this woman?

'Don't worry, she's a bit strong headed is Mrs Wicklow. Widowed and a bit of a tartar, but she does a lot for the cause. She's not feared to say what she thinks either. I told you about her. Yoos'll get used to her.' Sarah touched Martha's shoulder in support.

'We're all a bit scared of her really,' squeaked a small woman dressed in grey and squeezing the drawstring purse in her lap. 'My Harold says we should stand up to her, but it's not easy, is it ladies?' She forced a weak smile, looking for confirmation from her immediate neighbours.

'No...But she's a good sort underneath all that bluster. Don't worry, Martha. She wasn't being personal,' said a young woman who appeared to be a similar age to herself. Martha wasn't so sure it wasn't personal, but she decided not to let it ruin the evening. She was convinced that these women felt the same as she did about doing men's work. After all, it would make sure that George had a job when he came home and she wouldn't mind going back to the way it was. At least she didn't think so. She only hoped she was capable of doing such work.

It was difficult to find sleep that night as she lay in bed. So many thoughts dancing around her head. Was she doing the right thing getting involved in all this women's rights business? Mrs Clarke seemed nice enough and the other women had all been nice to her. Except for Mrs Wicklow. Scary, that one, she thought, remembering those thin hands and bony fingers. She sounded like the women she'd read about in the newspaper. What would her ma have said if she had known that Sarah was involved? Would she have tried to talk her out of it? Probably not. She had always pushed Martha to make the most of herself. Her Da's views had always been plain when it came to the Pankhursts. "Men in women's clothes," he'd say, "I hope my girls dunna get any silly ideas like that. I wouldn't want to be visiting either o' you two in prison." The thought of her parents made her eyes fill and she remembered where she'd seen Daisy, the housemaid, before. It was the young girl who'd pulled the sheet from Fred's cart and vomited in the middle of the road.

Chapter 8

April 15th, 1915

Dear Martha,

The weather is improved now and the route marches seem much easier. We did twenty miles today and my feet didn't hurt at all. They seem to have hardened to it. You should see the muscles on me now. I've never been so strong. I canna wait to show you and William. I still dunna like the drilling though. Sarge says it'll mek us work as a team once we're out there in the field. Be able to follow orders better. I think they just like to see us jump to it when they shout.

We have been training in the use of bayonets for the last couple of weeks. It's a bit of a laugh stabbing sandbags that are hanging from a wood frame and they even have ones that are hiding in ditches to mek it more real, but when I bed down at night, I think about what it might be like when it's a real German I've got to fight. I canna imagine killing someone for real. Mebbe it'll all be ower afore we get sent out there. I hope so.

How is my big boy? Does he miss his Da? I miss him and you so much. It feels like years since I've seen you both. All the lads miss their families. Sarge says it won't be long till we get some furlough and I'll be home as fast as my legs can carry me. He thinks it'll be afore the end of April. I dunna know how much time we'll get, but I hope it's a couple of weeks.

Your loving husband,

George.

Martha read the last paragraph out loud to her son.

'Do you hear that, William? Yer Da will be home soon. We can have a party for him. Won't that be good?'

'Will there be cake? And... And jelly and cream, Ma? Will there?'

'There will that. Cake and jelly and maybe even a bit of fruit,' she answered, mentally working out how much money she would need and what she could do without. William danced up and down, pulling at Martha's skirts. 'Da's coming home. Da's coming home,' he sang loudly.

'Now give me a hand with all these socks and gloves. We need to take them up to Mrs Clarke's and get some more wool.'

They sang together as they tied all the knitting into bundles, including all the pieces Sarah had brought round last night, saying that Robert was getting a bit difficult about her disappearing for hours on end. He said she should drop off her knitting at Mrs Clarke's and come straight home instead of sitting and gossiping with them. He didn't want her getting any silly ideas. Martha would have to do the fetching and carrying for a while and explain the situation to Mrs Clarke. She hoped that Sarah wasn't risking too much. She would hate to see her and Robert fall out. They always seemed such a happy couple. Always laughing, always ready to help anyone, always united in their beliefs and love of all things family. It occurred to her that she would also have the same problem when George came home on leave. Still, that was a couple of weeks away and she could do extra between now and then to make up for time lost while he was at home.

They walked the short distance to Clifton Avenue, William

carrying a small bundle of socks for his mother. Obviously enjoying the responsibility placed upon him, he marched along with his head held high and his woollen bundle hanging over his left shoulder. His right hand was tucked inside Martha's. On William's first visit, Daisy had been asked to take William down to the kitchen and find '*something nice*' for him to eat. She had cut him a slice of fruitcake that Mrs Finch, the cook, had made. It was so big; he had to take some home to finish at suppertime. The second time he went, Daisy and Mrs Finch gave him a slice of apple tart that was glazed on top. He couldn't put it in his mouth fast enough. The sticky sweet fruit was caked around his cheeks when he had finished and Daisy had to wash his hands and face before returning him to his mother. As the weeks passed, the pair became a familiar sight along Clifton Avenue, and Martha knew that William would be hoping that this trip would be as fruitful as all his previous visits. It was difficult for her to provide many treats for her son.

Daisy opened the door almost as soon as Martha knocked.

'I'm afraid the missus is busy this morning, Mrs Hubbard. She's not been feeling very well and Dr Bartholomew is with her now. I'll take the bundles for her.'

Martha and William handed her the knitting.

'I'm sorry to hear that, Daisy. Nothing too serious I hope?'

'A telegram arrived. She fainted and I went for the doctor. I haven't seen her since.' Martha put her hand to her chest; her heart was beating so loudly it echoed in her ears.

'Is there anything I can do?' she asked, reluctant to go. She was becoming quite fond of Celia Clarke, who always treated her as an equal and who seemed to value her opinion.

'I don't think— '

'Is that Mrs Hubbard, Daisy? Please show her in.' Celia's voice was faint but audible through the parlour door.

'Yes, Ma'am,' said Daisy, ushering Martha and William into the hall.

Martha opened the drawing-room door before looking

back at Daisy. 'Could you?'

'Course. C'mon, William, let's see what we can find today,' she said, taking his hand. William didn't need asking twice and pulled Daisy towards the kitchen.

Celia Clarke was lying on a scarlet-red chaise longue by the bay window, her skin as pale as a winter's moon. She dabbed at wet slate eyes with the corner of a lace handkerchief.

Dr Bartholomew looked over to Martha, his face now beginning to line with age, his brow furrowed with worry.

'I'm afraid Mrs Clarke has had some very sad news, Mrs Hubbard... Oh! It's Martha,' he added as recognition hit him. 'It's nice to see you again. I'm sorry it's not under better circumstances. How are George and young William?'

'They're fine, thank you. William has gone through to the kitchen. George is at training camp.'

'I'm pleased to hear they are well...I must be going,' he added, putting his stethoscope back in his leather bag. 'Please try and rest, Mrs Clarke. Take the tablets; they'll help you to sleep. I'll drop by in a couple of days to see how you are progressing.' He nodded at both the women and started to leave the room. 'Don't get Daisy, I can find my own way out...I'm so sorry for your loss, Mrs Clarke.'

They heard the front door close behind him.

Celia turned her face to the window.

'It's Godfrey, Martha. He's gone.' She passed the telegram over.

To Mrs C Clarke, 17 Clifton Ave, W Hartlepool

Regret to inform you that Lt Godfrey Clarke was killed in action on April 17th 1915. He was a gallant officer who gave his life in order to save others and will not be forgotten by his fellow soldiers. Lord Kitchener expresses his sympathy.

Martha knelt down in front of Celia and took her hands, stroking them softly.

'I'm so sorry, Celia,' she whispered.

Chapter 9

They heard the whistle and saw the steam curling high in the sky long before the train pulled into the station at Church Square. William was squealing with excitement. Neither he nor Martha had slept last night. Decorating the house with coloured streamers as if it were Christmas. They baked cakes and made jelly. Martha had baked bread and squandered a little money on butter, cream, ham and even some bacon.

'Is it here yet, Ma? Is it here?' William stood on tiptoes shielding his eyes from the morning sun. A light breeze sent a pink, confetti cloud from the cherry trees sailing across the platform and down onto the tracks. Tiny blossoms caught like jewels in Martha's hat and the shining curls she'd spent an age trying to pin up and bring under control. She had taken her time, brushing it repeatedly until it resembled spun silk. The scent of spring and the warmth of the sun were exhilarating and Martha couldn't stop smiling. The trundle on the tracks got louder and louder and echoed in her ears as the train rounded the bend, whistling loudly, and pulling into the station, the steam gushing and erupting from the funnel like a volcano over the roof of the engine.

The minutes seemed endless as they waited. Passengers stepped down on to the platform where porters rushed forward to take their bags through to the taxis and horse - drawn carriages that were waiting out front. The steam billowed around the whole station and Martha's view of the train became obscured.

'I canna see anything, Ma? Where is he? Where's Da?'

People were pushing past them in a hurry to get out off the platform and into the sunshine.

Then he was there, looking over the shoulder of an elderly gentleman and his wife; looking past the porter who was loading the couple's cases onto a luggage cart. He gazed at them across the platform; his kitbag slung over his right shoulder, his thumb hooked in the strap. He lifted his peaked cap and waved it high in the air, trying to get their attention.

Martha slowly drank in his features. The thick, dark hair smoothed down flat on his head, the gleam in his eyes, the moustache painted neatly over his top lip. He looked taller somehow, more handsome. He was smiling from ear to ear.

'Da. Da.' William threw off Martha's hand and ran as fast as his little legs could carry him. George put down the kitbag and squatted to catch him. He lifted him high and up on to his shoulders.

'My you've grown, lad. I could barely lift you.'

William snatched the army cap from his father's head and put it on his own as George continued to grin at Martha. He marched over to where she was waiting, too stunned by the sight of him to make her legs move. He looked down at her face, lifted her chin and placed a kiss firmly on her mouth.

'Hello, Pet. I'm reet glad to see you.' She felt her stomach somersault and her legs go weak at the sight and feel of him. He had changed so much from the slight man that had left her a few short months ago. She could see the muscles straining through his uniform. His chin seemed broader, his dark eyes twinkled and he had the look of someone who oozed confidence. He breathed in the sweet scent of her hair before he picked the cherry blossom from it and put it in his breast pocket. 'To remind me of today,' he said, still smiling.

To remind you of me, Albert's voice echoed George's as the memory of Albert leaving her all those years ago crept into her head. She pushed it away.

'We've got a surprise for you, Da. C'mon, Ma, let's get home.' William dug the heels of his boots into George's chest, bobbing up and down as if on horseback, pulling on his Da's hair.

'Yes, William,' she replied, pulling herself together and looking up at her son and her very handsome husband. 'Let's get home.'

She offered her arm to George and they walked out to the front of the station. She couldn't have felt more proud of him. Her husband, her man, was home on leave from the army and she was going to make the most of every moment.

'You shouldn't a' gone to all this trouble, Pet. We can't afford it.'

'It's fine. I've been putting a bit away every week. We couldn't have you coming home to nothing.' Martha poured the tea and they sat down to eat the feast she and William had prepared. 'Tell me about training camp. Is it hard? Your letters make it sound easy, but I'm not so sure.'

'I canna say it was easy at first, but yer get used to it quick enough. I feel as fit as a flea. The lads are all grand and most of my pals from Gray's yard are there. We're waiting for orders, so I dunna think it'll be too long afore we go off and show them Huns who's boss.'

'Don't talk that way, George. It frightens me.' Martha dished some jelly on to a plate for William. 'I hope it'll all be over before it comes to that.'

'Dunna worry, Pet. I know how to look after mi sel.'

'Ma says we might go to the fairground after dinner, Da. Can we, Da? Can we?' William shovelled the jelly down, swallowing each piece whole.

'Now that sounds like a grand idea, William, but there's nowt to hurry for. Enjoy the jelly. Yer canna taste it when it doesn't touch the sides afore yer swallow.' He laughed loudly and Martha and William laughed along with him.

The fairground was in the market yard, and they caught the tram as a special treat. William persuaded them to climb the stairs to the open top.

'I want to see everything from high up,' he said.

It wasn't often they went anywhere on the tram. Money wasn't to be squandered and shanks pony was good enough for them Martha always told him. George was shocked to find a female conductress taking the money for their tickets.

'What's all this about? Where's the real conductor?' he asked the girl.

'Fighting for his country like you,' she answered as she made her way to the next customer.

'Surely they don't need a slip of a girl to do the job. She won't be able to handle any troublemakers on a Saturday night. She won't last five minutes,' he said to Martha. 'Don't you be gettin' any ideas, Pet. I wuddna be able to sleep at night for worryin' about it.'

Martha didn't respond. She knew it would be pointless.

William stared in fascination at all the shops along Lynn Street, the crowds of people window shopping, the carriages and horses, even a couple of motor cars.

'I wish we had a motor car, Da,' he shouted above all the noise.

'One day, son. One day.'

People smiled and doffed their caps at the trio when they got off and walked the final stretch. Men patted George on the back.

'You're doing a fine job, lad,' they said, and William looked up in awe of his father.

*

They walked through the crowded aisles of the Public Market and out into the yard. The fair was usually gone by Easter, but this year, due to a slow start to the spring, it had stayed put for an extra couple of weeks. Now the weather had turned they would soon be pulling out. Memories of her childhood came flooding back again as Martha entered the melee and inhaled the wonderful smells, sights and sounds of the fairground. The scenic railway was the centrepiece with a real waterfall and ducks on the water. The queue was long, people chatted animatedly as they waited their turn. Everyone marvelled at a great steam organ playing a recital. Favourite opera pieces played out on request and even something a little more modern. Songs for the troops were very popular and crowds sang along. The large gilded figures on the front of the organ were animated and clashed symbols or blew trumpets, moving their heads and arms in time to the music. The smaller stalls were almost as busy with people desperate to see the fortune tellers or try their hand at darts. Coconut shies were always a favourite along with the Aunt Sallies and shooting galleries. Children dashed from stall to stall, pleading with parents to let them try their luck and the air smelled of toffee apples and the mouth-watering, rich aroma of roast pig turning on a spit.

George kept tight hold of William's hand as they made their way over to the shooting gallery. 'Watch this, son,' he said, leaving go of the boy and picking up a rifle.

'No soldiers,' said the stallholder.

'What? Ha'way, man. Yer canna be serious, can yer?' asked George. 'My son wants me to show him what I can do.'

'Aye. And I dunna want all my stock gone in five minutes. I'm sorry, lad, but it wouldn't be fair, not when you lot are all trained in shootin'. The man took the rifle from George and set it down.

'I s'pose. C'mon, William, let's have a try at the Aunt

Sally.' He marched off leaving Martha amazed at his mature response. Looks like he's finally grown up, she thought, following him with renewed pride. George flung the wooden balls and easily hit the stuffed canvas heads, knocking their grotesque painted faces to the ground. A stick of chewing gum was the prize that he shared with William, Martha telling the boy to be careful not to swallow it or all his insides would be stuck together. William dragged his mother over to the scenic railway that travelled merrily round and round and up and down when they seated themselves. Martha was enjoying the ride as much her son, and George waved to them each time they passed. Still a little dizzy, William persuaded George to take him on the Helter Skelter next. Martha watched as George sat on the mat at the top with William between his legs. She held her breath as they corkscrewed, on a slide, around the outside of the wooden tower at great speed before landing in a heap at the bottom. They staggered to their feet, laughing until there were tears in their eyes.

'Da. Look. The Striker. Do the striker, Da,' yelled William.

George took up the wooden mallet and swung it high before bringing it down on the striker that shot up the column and rang the bell at the top.

Martha pictured a day long ago when Albert had made the Striker ring out. They had just started walking out together and they had gone to the fair along with George and his friend Rupert. Albert had pushed George forward to have a go. He must have known that George was neither big enough nor strong enough. Albert had laughed, calling him a weakling. George had been embarrassed and walked off. Even she had laughed.

She felt a sudden rush of shame as she thought about it and gave George a peck on the cheek. 'My hero,' she said, smiling up at his puzzled expression. His face glowed at her praise as they headed over to the steam gondolas.

While George and William were being tossed up and down in 'The Mauritania', Martha spotted Mrs Wicklow with one or two women. She couldn't quite see what they were doing, but there seemed to be some sort of a commotion and a crowd was gathering. She looked up to see if George and William could see her before prising her way through the throng to get a better view. A small woman was waving her parasol at Mrs Wicklow and shouting vehemently.

'You take that back. How dare you call my husband a coward? He works at the shipyard. He's needed at home to do war work.' She spluttered the words, angry tears rolling down her cheeks.

'Sitting at a desk in an office is hardly helping the war effort is it? I've no time for shirkers. He should be at the front with the rest of our men, not hiding behind his wife's skirts.' Mrs Wicklow stood tall, her chin raised.

'Come along, dear,' whispered the woman's husband, his face burning with embarrassment. He slipped the white feather into his pocket and pulled his wife away. A few people jeered and booed him as he went.

Martha was shocked by the incident. That poor man and his wife. How could she be so cruel? She had heard of this sort of thing happening but had never witnessed it until now. Mrs Wicklow was a dangerous woman, and Martha was sure she wanted nothing more to do with her. She looked over to the women and wondered if Celia was aware of what they were doing. They were supposed to be pacifists, weren't they? She recognised one other lady from the group and decided that it was time for her to stop going to the meetings if Celia condoned this sort of thing. She was about to turn away, when she saw Sarah approach the women. She seemed nervous, looking around all the time as she spoke to Mrs Wicklow. Surely she wasn't involved? She made her way back to George, her mind trying to make sense of what had just happened. She arrived at the ride as they both dismounted, looking positively green from being thrown up and down on the make-believe ship.

Chapter 10

'What on earth did you think you were doing? That woman is wicked. And anyway, Robert could have been anywhere nearby. What if he'd seen you?' Martha was furious with Sarah. She spat on the flat iron before pressing down on a petticoat. The anger had been building up inside her. It had ruined her precious few days with George. All she could think about was what Sarah was risking and what she would say to Celia about Mrs Wicklow's behaviour.

'I was as surprised as you to see what happened. I went over to tell her, but she was so busy spouting about cowards and such, I didn't have a chance to open my mouth. She's a reet wasp. Allus trying to sting someone. I'm with you on that. We'll have a word with Celia Clarke on Monday night.'

'I'm not sure I want to go anymore. It's getting a bit dangerous. You need to be careful, Sarah; Robert won't take kindly to being made a fool. You can't keep lying to him.'

'Ha'way. You can't keep taking a back view when so much needs doing. The League opposed going to war for months before it started, but now it's here...it's different...Our men are fighting for us and we should be helping in any way we can. I want to do my bit for the war effort, and I dunna just mean knitting. I want to work. Munitions...Nursing...Anything that keeps the lads out there going. Lads like your George. He needs all the help he can get.'

'He's not even out there yet...what difference does it make whether we women work or not?'

'Don't you listen to anything at the meetings? It means we can send more soldiers and get this war finished. The sooner the better, I say.'

'I suppose...but I won't do what Mrs Wicklow does...is that clear?'

'Clear as a bell, Lass. Now get that kettle on; I'm fair parched with all that shouting.' She grinned at Martha, who found herself smiling back.

'You get it on. Can't you see I'm busy,' she chuckled as she folded the petticoat, relieved that they had cleared the air.

'Where's William gone? He was here a minute ago?' Sarah asked.

'He's in the backyard using the netty. Thinks he's big enough to do it on his own now. His drawers tell a different story but don't let on. He'd be shamed.' They both looked the other way when he came back in, trying not to smile and pretending not to notice him.

'I'll be fetching the rest of that washing in now. Mind you don't go near the flat iron, William. It's red hot.' Martha went into the backyard and started to unpeg the clothes from the line. She tutted at the colour of William's Sunday shirt. It was beginning to turn grey from so much washing. She needed to raid her little jar of coins again. There was always something that stopped the pennies from reaching the rim.

'Robert asked if you'd like to come for tea on Sunday. He's wondering why I haven't asked you over for a while,' said Sarah, coming to stand at the back door. 'Truth is I've been scared one of us might say something out of turn.'

'I'm sure it'll be fine. I'd love to come. You'd like that wouldn't you, William?' she shouted through to the kitchen so that he would hear her.

'Oh, yes, Ma. I like Uncle Robert,' he shouted, running to the door and ducking through the gap under Sarah's arm. 'Can we go now?'

'It's great to see you, Hinny. Where've you been hiding? 'Robert kissed Martha's cheeks before taking hold of both William's shoulders. 'You've fair grown, lad. What does yer mother feed you on? Beef steaks?' He laughed and his eyes lit up.

'What's a beef steak?' asked William, his face puzzling.

'Have you never had a beefsteak, lad? Well we'll be putting that reet the day. Did you notice that succulent smell coming from Aunt Sarah's oven?' William was already drooling at the rich aroma that filled the market house kitchen. He nodded, looking eagerly in the direction of the range. 'That's a big slab o' beef cooking. That's what it is.'

Martha stared incredulously at Robert. He winked at her.

'Friends in high places...' he said, tapping his nose with his finger. 'Now then young man, I hope you're hungry.'

'Yes, sir,' beamed William, scrambling on to a chair at the scrubbed wooden table.

They all laughed at the sight.

'It's not ready yet, William. Ten minutes. Come and help me lay the plates and cutlery,' said Sarah. She opened drawers and cupboards and let William pull out knives, forks and spoons. She showed him how to lay the table properly. Robert's sons came in from getting the stalls ready for the following morning. Edward stood nearly six feet tall at seventeen and fifteen-year-old Joe wasn't far behind. They both had a look of their father, but the younger boy was heavier set like his mother. The boys smiled to see the visitors and made a fuss of William, but Martha could feel a tension in the air whenever Edward, the eldest boy, spoke to his father.

'It's time I was getting out in the world. Doing my bit,

instead of clearing market stalls and tidying up the yard.'

Robert's fist came down on the table, making the cutlery jump in the air.

'I've told you enough times. That's not going to happen. You're too young. Now let's hear the last of it.'

They all sat down to a feast of vegetables, potatoes, thick slices of beef and gravy. This was followed by a large bowl of patriotic pudding, made with grated potato and oatmeal and topped with fresh cream. No-one's favourite, but it salved Sarah's conscience after serving up beef.

'What do you think, Martha? Your George is out there. Shouldn't we all stand up and be counted?' asked Edward.

'I...I think—'

'What did I say? Dunna bring Martha into it. I make the decisions in this house. Not another word.' Robert's face was almost purple with rage, and Martha saw his hand come up and snatch at his heart. William cowered against his mother. Sarah put her hand on her husband's arm.

'Don't be upsettin' yer Da with such talk, Edward. You know he's not been well.'

Edward backed off and continued eating his pudding. His brother Joe had kept his head down the whole time.

The boys went straight back out when they had finished eating. There was no sign of the fairground now that had gone back on the road earlier in the week. William was so full he fell asleep in a corner of the room.

Robert sat in his favourite chair, and Martha helped Sarah wash and dry the dishes.

'Now then, tell me what you've been up to since I last saw you. Sarah tells me nothing when she comes back from your's. How's George? Does he write?'

Martha could see Sarah's face relax at the mention of George. She knew her friend would be glad that the conversation wasn't about Edward or what she and Martha did together whenever Sarah came over. 'He does, Robert. He's enjoying his army life,' she replied as she pottered around the kitchen, putting things away. 'You should see the size of him. Muscles everywhere. He looks like he's been working on the docks all his life. There's lots of men from Grays in his battalion he says. You remember Jimmy Saltburn?' Robert nodded in response. 'Well they're best pals now. They never liked each other when they worked in the parts shed together, but George says they get on like a house afire. I'm pleased he's happy, but I hope this war ends before he can get sent out to the front line.'

'Aye. It must be hard for you. Our lad, Edward, keeps on about joining up. Over my dead body I told him. Yer too young, I say, but he says they've taken loads o' boys at sixteen or seventeen. They lie about their age and the army doesn't argue. These recruiting officers get paid half a crown for every man they sign up. No wonder they turn a blind eye. It's not right. I have to keep my eye on him otherwise he'd be gone like a shot. Once they've signed up, there's no chance of getting 'em back.'

Sarah stood behind Robert's chair and rubbed his shoulders. 'He won't go. He knows how much it would hurt us.'

'Sarah's right. Edward wouldn't do that to you. He's always been a good lad.' Martha tried to reassure him, even though she wasn't at all convinced of what she was saying. There had been something in Edward's manner that suggested he was very serious.

'I hope you're both right. It'd kill me for sure,' he said closing his eyes. Martha and Sarah tried not to react as he screwed his face up, his hand clutching his left breast.

Chapter 11

May 28th 1915

Dear Martha,

Sorry I haven't written sooner. We left England as soon as I got back to barracks but this is the first chance I've had to write. We were supposed to carry on training away from the front for a few weeks but we've been thrown in at the deep end.

You will have read in the papers by now about the terrible gassing of the Canadians and our lads outside a certain small village last month. Our men joined the York and Durham divisions for a counter-attack the day after but Fritz stayed in control of the village. Our lads tried again the next day and we were successful but had to retreat again as we had a great number of casualties. We have an infirmary on site and the wounded were brought here for treatment. You can tell the ones have been gassed as they march in single file, holding on to each other's shoulders. It seems to have been non-stop fighting since then. Poor Arthur's been badly wounded. He'll be shipped home if he survives. At least it's been a short war for him. Give his wife my best if you see her. Tell her he's keeping his spirits up and looks forward to seeing her soon.

I miss you and William so much and I keep the photo we had done when I was at home, close to my heart. It makes me feel safer when you're pressed close to me. I can just picture you and William on the scenic railway. I imagine you lying next to me at night and I can fair smell your sweet hair.

Jimmy asks if you can go and see if his Ma is alreet. She hasn't sent any word to him for a while and he's worried about her. He said she was wheezing a lot the last time he saw her and he's feared she might be worse. (I think you know what I mean, what with his Da dying not long since).

We can receive parcels out here. It's like lightning, how quick they arrive. Sarge's wife sent a parcel on Monday last week and it was here by Wednesday night. The mail trains are running non-stop to make sure we all get word from home. Sarge says it helps keep morale up. He's right, I don't know what we'd all do without our letters.

Can you send me another razor and a strap? Someone's pinched mine. Cheeky sod whoever it is. I've got nearly half a beard sprouting out of my chin and my moustache looks like a ferret hanging off the top of my lip. I have to use scissors to keep things under control but I'll be on a charge if I can't shave soon. A bit of taffy would go down well if there's enough in the jar but don't be leaving yourself short.

Sorry I won't be there for William's birthday in June but there won't be any furlough in the next few months. I can't believe he's almost four.

Take care of yourself my darling

Your loving husband

George

Martha could feel the tears stinging. There had been quite a few Form B letters delivered to friends and neighbours recently. It didn't seem right that officer's wives got a telegram straight away and ordinary folk sometimes didn't get the letter until days after. Ethel Barnby, who lived next door, got a letter from her husband last week, announcing he'd got a few days leave while he recovered from a minor shrapnel wound. She'd been shopping in order to celebrate his pending homecoming and had come home to a green envelope. Apparently, he had died the same day he'd sent his letter. She spent the afternoon organising a memorial service.

Martha prayed George would be home sometime soon. The longer she was without him, the more she realised how much she loved him. It was a shame he wouldn't be back for William's birthday, but they could put up with that as long as he came home safely in the end.

'C'mon, William. We need to go and visit Mrs Saltburn on Broad Street. Pop your boots on. There's a good lad.' Martha brushed her skirt down and checked her hair in the mirror. There were dark patches under her eyes.

'What does Da say? When does he come home again?'

'Not for a while, William, but he's very well and misses you.' she reassured her son.

She was tired and having difficulty sleeping. She stroked her hand over her stomach and sighed.

At least he wouldn't be around to see her lose this one, she thought. Something wasn't right. It felt like the last time and the time before. She hoped she wouldn't have to carry it too long before the inevitable happened. It always made her realise how lucky she was that William survived. She remembered how touch and go it had been when he was born. Barely weighing a ha'peth of taffy.

She knocked hard for a second time. Still no answer. She tried to peer through the lace curtains, but to no avail. Mrs Saltburn probably wouldn't be sitting in the parlour anyway. Most folk around here would sit in the back kitchen in front of the fire.

'Are you looking for Alice? She never answers her door nowadays. Can I help?'

Martha turned to the middle-aged woman next door. Large arms folded across an equally large bosom. She looked at Martha with suspicion, the jowls on her cheeks hanging low and colliding with the ripples on her neck.

'I'm Mrs Hubbard. George Hubbard's wife. My husband and Jimmy are serving together.'

'Ha'way. You must be Martha... I'm Nellie...Nellie Wagstaff.' She held a dimpled hand out for Martha to shake. 'Alice talks about you and George a lot. Jimmy's reet fond of George. Come in and I'll take yer through the back to hers. I've got a key. She's not been well.'

Martha and William followed the woman through to the shared backyard and into next door,

'Alice,' shouted the woman. 'It's only me, Nellie from next door. You've a visitor. George's wife...Eeh Alice...'

Alice Saltburn was lying on the floor, her face almost as grey as the stone beneath her.

'Oh Alice,' cried Nellie as she dropped to her knees beside her. 'I told yer to let me fetch the doctor. Yer silly woman.'

'I'll run and fetch Doctor Bartholomew. Come with me, William.' Martha pulled her son away hoping he hadn't realised that the woman was dead.

'I'm not sure how to word it. What do you think?' she asked Sarah.

'You can't sugar coat death, can you? Best get it out and tell him straight. Let him break the news to Jimmy. He already knew she was dying. TB dunna tek any prisoners. Poor lad, it's less than a year since he lost his Da from the same thing.

Sarah finished clearing the lunchtime plates from the table. Robert and the boys were back out in the yard. 'Martha...why won't you come back to the meetings?' she asked quietly, afraid that Robert might walk back in any minute.

'Because I don't believe in what that awful woman is doing. I don't want to be part of it. There's enough suffering without women putting men down so low as they feel ashamed of themselves. I heard she goes around putting white feathers into any man's hand that hasn't got a badge to say his job is vital to the war effort. So what if some are against fighting. They're entitled to their own beliefs. It doesn't mean they're cowards.'

'Alreet, lass. Ger off yer high horse. Yer entitled to your views, but so is she. Her husband was killed in the Boer war. A Major or something, he was. Broke her heart losing him. Some of his men ran off during a battle and left him to die. Yer can understand why she teks against men who won't fight.'

'I didn't know... I'm sorry for her, but...' Martha wondered how she might be if that happened to George and found herself sympathising with the woman. 'I suppose... it must be hard for her...I can't agree with what she's doing though.'

'Look... Celia has been asking for you. She misses you. Can't you come for her?'

'Maybe. I'll see.'

The atmosphere was tense...electric...the ladies waited for the response.

'Who are you to tell me how to behave? What right have you... a slip of a girl... to tell me what I can and cannot do. You're the one who shirks her duties. You're the one who hides behind other women's skirts instead of facing the situation before us. You are not fit to call yourself patriotic.' Mrs Wicklow seemed to grow taller with every word. Her beady eyes bulged with fury, her bony finger pricked Martha's chest as she prodded and prodded with each word. Martha stepped back as the woman's spittle sprayed her face and took a deep breath.

'I...I...What you are doing has nothing to do with being patriotic. It's cruel and vindictive.' Martha's eyes pricked as she tried to stand her ground. 'That poor man will be shunned wherever he goes now, and my guess is that some of our soldiers are only out there because of women like you pushing them into it.' Martha was shaking from head to toe.

'Don't you dare put down women like me. We fight for what we believe in. We're not timid little mice like you...Celia, if you don't get rid of this woman, you'll get no more support from me.'

'I...I'm sorry, Mrs Wicklow...Gladys. I'm sure we can sort this out amicably—'

'No need, Celia. I'm leaving.' Martha retreated from the room. 'Are you coming, Sarah?' Sarah lowered her gaze without speaking. It sickened Martha to see them all cow towing to that woman. She had been stupid enough to think that Celia, or at least Sarah would have backed her up. She ran from the room, hurt and humiliated. Sarah was on her own from now on. Nothing was worth turning neighbour against neighbour, friend against friend.

Whether it was the upset or her apparent inability to carry babies successfully, she didn't know, but the miscarriage happened that night. It was as sudden as the last and painful, although not so bad that she needed help this time. She was saddened by the loss of the unrecognisable, tiny life that had hardly started to grow inside her but glad not to be bringing another child into the world right now.

Chapter 12

June 26th 1915

Dear Martha,

Say happy birthday to William for me. I hope he liked the little farm we got him. I wish I could have been there for him.

Jimmy's not the same since his Ma died. He doesn't seem to care about anything. He'll get his head blown off if he's not careful. We're still in the thick of it. The sound of the artillery and mortars is enough to make you deaf and it goes on and on.

I've been trained in stretcher bearing and first aid now as well as trench warfare. They need as many men as possible. We have to go out into no-man's land, between the fighting, to bring in casualties. I've been given a dog. A little spaniel called Bess and she's trained to find the wounded. Brave as any soldier she is, darting about looking for men that are still alive. We follow the sound of their cries and she growls real low when she finds anyone. She knows not to bark. Capt Briggs allus comes with us. He won't see his men go out on their own. He's a grand officer. We're lucky to have him.

Some of the men are scared of going back out when they've been patched up. They'll try anything to get a blighty. One man ran in front of a wagon that was pulling cannon. The horses swerved and barely missed trampling him to death. He's going to be court martialled next week, poor sod.

Thank William for the drawing. Tell him I'll allus keep it with me for luck. Thank you for the cake, it made it here safely. I will share it with Jimmy. See if I can't cheer him up a bit.

Dunna worry about me, Pet. I'm fine and dandy. It'll tek more than Fritz to see me off.

With all my love

George

Martha was lying in bed, reading George's letter by candle light. She daren't open them in front of William anymore for fear of what they might say. She didn't want to frighten him.

William's birthday had been a quiet affair. Martha and William had spent most of the day alone. He had been so pleased with the little wooden farm from her and his da. Neddy and Dobbin, his precious wooden horses, had been put in the beautifully crafted stable along with a donkey that he named Dandy. There were cows, chickens, sheep, pigs and even a farmer and his sheepdog. Sarah had called round to give him some taffy she'd made, but the atmosphere was strained and she didn't stay very long. William didn't seem to notice. He was only interested in gobbling up the sticky sweets. Martha thanked her for remembering and offered tea, but Sarah said she was too busy and left. Martha felt sad to have lost the friend who had helped her through the darkest of times when her Ma and Da had died. She wanted to run after her, but the thought of showing any weakness in her opinion of the League would be a betrayal of her own views. She had to stay strong in her belief that men were doing their best, even when they were too afraid to fight, or firmly believed that war was wrong and refused to fight, becoming conscientious objectors. She did not look on these men as cowards, like Mrs Wicklow and some of the townsfolk; she looked on them as being brave enough to stand up for peace and even go to prison on trumped up charges for it. She had watched in fear as Mr Parkin, from the bakers on Lynn Street, had been pulled down from his soapbox and attacked by the crowd. He was eventually carted off to the police station, the crowd booing and jeering him. One woman, who had received a letter concerning the death of her son the previous week, spat in his face saying he should have been the one hit by a German bullet. The Northern Echo had reported, the following Thursday, that he had been given three months detention for causing a public nuisance and inciting violence. It was common knowledge that men like him were treated badly by other prisoners while the guards turned a blind eye. The shop was boycotted and Martha had heard that his wife and six children had left the town to live with relatives in Durham. The whole world seems to have gone mad, thought Martha. She wondered what it would be like when this dreadful war ended. How many men would come home? How many families would only have a telegram or a Form B to say that their loved ones were dead? No funeral. No grave to mourn over. She prayed for George and William and right now...sleep and oblivion for a few hours.

Around three in the morning she woke with a start to what was now, not a regular, but a familiar sound. Shell fire. They must be practising over at Heugh Battery. Why they did it at night was a mystery to her. She never took it for granted though. One night, it might not be practise. She crept through to William's room and carefully carried him downstairs. They both crawled under the table and stayed there until things quietened down again. She wondered if George was sitting in a trench somewhere thinking about her and William, or if he was crawling through no-man's land with a stretcher. Whatever he was doing, she hoped he knew that she was thinking of him. She sang William's favourite song softly as she rocked him.

'Sweet and low, sweet and low
Wind of western sea,
Low, low, breathe and blow...

*

It was almost five o-clock and broad daylight when she put William back in his bed and Martha decided to get on with some washing rather than climb into her own. She wouldn't be able to sleep now. She was too wide-awake.

'Martha! Martha!' Sarah was hammering on the door.

'What on earth's the matter? You'll have the door down,' Martha shouted as Sarah stumbled into the house.

'Edward's gone. He left a note.' She fell into Martha's arms, sobbing. 'Robert and Joe are out looking for him. What shall I do? What shall I do?'

'Come and sit down. Robert will find him. You'll see.'

She guided her friend into the back kitchen and sat her down at the table.

'How long? When did you find the note?' Martha asked getting mugs down from the shelf.

Sarah leaned across the table, her arms folded. She sank her face down into the ample flesh as she babbled. 'First thing. I'd just got down and found it on the mantel. Leaning up against the clock.' She fumbled and pulled the note from her apron pocket. 'Here,' she said, looking up and handing it over to Martha.

Dear Ma and Da,

Don't be mad at me. I couldn't stand it no longer. Me being here while all my pals are out there fighting. I'm nearly eighteen so I'd be going in a month or two anyway. Don't come after me. I won't change my mind. I'll write as soon as I am able.

Your loving son

Edward.

'I'm so sorry, Sarah. I'm sure Robert will find him before it's too late.' Martha put her arms around Sarah's shoulders, trying to soothe her. Their falling out seemed petty right now. Her friend needed her and that had to be her priority. She sat down and held Sarah's hand, praying for Edward's safe return to his mother. William must not have heard the banging on the door. There had been no sound from upstairs.

When Robert and Joe eventually returned, it wasn't good news. Robert's face was grey as he collapsed into a chair. 'He hasn't been to the local recruiting office,' he wheezed as he tried to tell Sarah what had happened.

'Tek your time, catch yer breath,' Sarah told him. Martha fetched a glass of water.

They waited until he could speak properly.

'They said he could have gone anywhere. Lads who run off usually go as far from home as possible.'

'We'll never see him again.' Sarah started to cry.

'He's a big lad. He'll fool 'em easily. That recruitment officer said they wouldn't push him too hard about his age. They need as many volunteers as they can get.'

'It's not reet,' Sarah was becoming hysterical. 'They can't tek him. They can't.'

'Now then, Sarah. You screamin' and bawling isn't going to change anything. He's gone and there's nowt we can do.'

Joe looked at his Ma, his eyes shining, his hands balled into fists at his side. 'It's all Edward's fault,' he spluttered.

'It's the governments fault. If women had been in charge, there wouldn't be a war in the first place. It's time we stopped all this killing,' Sarah screamed.

'What? What are you talking about woman?' Screwing his face, Robert gripped his chest, his breathing more and more laboured.

'Robert? Are you alright? Shall I get the doctor?' Martha said, trying to calm the situation. Sarah wasn't thinking straight. Robert didn't need to hear about her political views right now.

'I'm fine. I don't need a doctor.'

Sarah started to panic at the sight of her husband's face contorting. She took a deep breath and took hold of Robert's hand. 'Alreet, Robert. Take yer time. Breathe nice and slow,' Sarah got her emotions under control and spoke slowly and calmly. 'Fetch him some sweet tea would you, Martha? Have you got sugar?'

'Come and help me, Joe. I think we all need a drink,' said Martha already preparing the pot. She was sad for Robert and Sarah, but she was also glad that something had brought them back into her life. She would write to George straight away and ask him to keep an eye out for Edward.

Chapter 13

Every day, Martha and William made the journey over to Robert and Sarah's house to see if there had been any news of Edward. It had been over a month now and Robert seemed to have shrunk into himself. There had been no more mention of women's rights from Sarah. Her remorse for screaming at her husband when he was already so distraught at the loss of his son tormented her constantly. She did all she could to coax him along. Cooking all his favourite meals where possible. Filling in for both him and Edward out in the market yard. Collecting rents, dismantling and mantling stalls as required. She looked exhausted, her face permanently red, her normally tight-fitting clothes beginning to hang loosely. Martha tried to help wherever and however she could. William stayed in the house with Robert while she worked outside. Martha did the cooking sometimes, particularly when Sarah was finding it difficult to cope.

'I canna bear it, Martha. I'm so worried about Edward and what's happening to him. Robert's so ill, and Joe canna concentrate on his apprenticeship studies down at the marine works while he's helping me all the time. What am I to do? Is there any news from George?

'I'm sorry but George says he's no more likely to know where Edward is than any other of the thousands of soldiers out there. Not until you know what regiment he's in anyway. You've got to stay positive. You'd have heard from the army if anything had happened to him, and besides, he's probably not even out there yet. It's early days. '

'I know yer reet, Lass. I only wish he'd drop me a line or somethin'. Anything to say he's alreet.'

'When's his birthday?'

'First of September. Why?'

'I think you'll get your letter then. He knows they won't send him home, even if you go to wherever he's training once he's past eighteen.'

'Do you really think so?'

'I'm sure so, Sarah. You wait and see.'

'Mebbe so. Mebbe so,' Sarah conceded. 'Will you stay for supper again? I've made too much as usual. Can't get used to three instead of four.'

'We'd love to, wouldn't we, William?'

'Yes please,' replied William, who was always hungry these days. No matter what she fed him. He must be going through a growing spurt, thought Martha.

'C'mon, Robert. Time to eat,' Sarah said nodding at her husband, signalling that everyone else was already seated at the table.

He looked up briefly. 'I'm not hungry. Start without me.'

'Starvin' yersel is not going to bring Edward back. You've another son who needs you and a wife if yer hadn't noticed.' Sarah held back the tears while she served potatoes and a minced beef stew. Joe touched the back of her hand as she sat down.

'It'll be alreet, Ma. Give it time,' he said trying to be the man of the house. 'We'll manage the business 'til Da's feeling better.'

'You need to do yer training. Yer'll not pass your

apprenticeship if you don't.'

'Me? I can do it standing on my head. Dunna worry about me, Ma. I'll be fine.' He smiled widely at her.

'I know you will, son.'

'Ma, tell 'em about Da's dog. He's got a dog, Uncle Joe. Tell him, Ma,' said William.

'That's a good idea, William,' said Martha, grateful for an opportunity to change the subject. 'It's so clever. It takes messages up the line to other battalions to let them know what's happening and then it brings another message back to George. I don't know how it can know where to go?'

She didn't mention its duties in full. Message taking was probably enough detail apart from the fact that she didn't want William knowing about the other side of things. Robert's family had enough imagination without her adding to what must be filling their heads. Images that already tormented her every waking hour.

The letter had arrived on September third. Edward had sent a photograph of himself in his full regalia, begging his father to be proud of him while he did his duty and fought for King and Country. Robert had cried for an hour solid, after which, he had stood up and proclaimed that he had to be strong for his son and went out to work in the yard. The lack of food and exercise for several weeks had left Robert weak, but he struggled through for most of the day before collapsing in the late afternoon. A couple of stallholders carried him in and Sarah sent Joe for Dr Bartholomew.

Martha and William arrived as the doctor was talking to Sarah.

'His heart is very weak, Sarah. He needs to be in the hospital but he's refusing to go. Says he has to be here in case there is more word from Edward. I can't force him. Try and make him comfortable. That's all you can do.'

Sarah went back upstairs to sit with Robert until he fell

into an uneasy sleep. Martha and the two boys stayed downstairs. Joe kept William busy while Martha made a start on the evening meal. It was an hour later when Sarah joined them. She was pale and her eyes were bloodshot and swollen.

She told Martha about the letter and what had happened to Robert.

'Edward's at Larkhill in Wiltshire. He's in the final weeks of training with the Royal Field Artillery. He says it won't be long before he's sent overseas.' She spoke softly and without emotion. 'He says the talk's all about how the army can't afford to spend much time training the men now.'

Martha remained silent, knowing questions wouldn't help her friend come to terms with what was happening around her.

'He said that trains are coming home every day, packed with wounded soldiers before being loaded with fresh troops and ammunition and being sent back out to the front line.' She took a deep breath and looked straight into Martha's eyes. 'He says he's enjoying his time at Larkhill and can't wait to get down to what he's being trained for.' It was all too much for her and she put her head in her hands.

'And Robert?' asked Martha.

'He shouldn't have been out in the yard. Thought he ought to pull himself together. For Edward's sake. He was too weak, Martha. I should have stopped him.'

'If anythin' happens to Da... I'll...I dunna know what I'll do...The selfish...' Joe didn't finish the sentence. He ran out to the yard, slamming the door behind him.

Martha and William stayed with them for the next few days as they watched Robert labour to get his breath. His appetite was next to nothing and he drank little. He tried to speak once or twice, but Sarah quieted him saying that she would tell him the minute they had another letter from Edward. He held on to his son's photograph right up to the point of death on the third night.

Chapter 14

November 26th 1915

Dear Martha,

I hope all is well with you and William. Nothing much has changed here except we were sent up to a nearby village for a couple of days rest last week. We even got to have a bath. Some of the local women washed our clothes for us as well. It felt nice for a bit but the bloody fleas and the mud soon took over again once we got back. It has rained solid for weeks. The trenches are flooded and my boots and puttees don't even start to keep the wet out. It's nigh on impossible to dry out between forays and half the regiment are starved with the wet and cold. Poor little Bess has to be carried over the top else she slips straight back down into the pool that leaves all our feet and legs numb with cold. Even then she nearly drowns in the mud while we are out trying to find our poor men that have been wounded. Some of the craters are like blooming lakes and one of our lads was lying in one for two nights before someone found him. It was too late of course but we made him comfortable and gave him a tot of rum to soothe him before he went. Still, we all keep our chins up. Nothing else for it except to cry and none of us will do that. The Huns must be suffering the same fate as us so we get some comfort from the thought.

The pounding of the shells doesn't get any less and I think I've lost the hearing in my left ear. At least I know I'm still alive while I can hear out of the other one. Jimmy had a narrow escape last week. Got hit through the thigh by a sniper bullet. It went in one side and straight out the other. The medics patched him up and he was back on duty after three days in the infirmary. He complained about how bad a shot Fritz was and if it had been him doing the shooting the man wouldn't have been well enough to go out and fight again.

Parcels are not getting through as easy now with the roads being thigh deep in mud but please keep sending them, as I will receive them eventually. Except for cakes and home baking. The last cake you sent took a month and it was in a right state when it arrived. A bar of chocolate would go down well.

Give my best wishes to Sarah. Are you still helping her out? I don't mind you doing it. I wanted you to know that it's alright by me. Times change and we have to help each other as much as we can. It's a good job she has Joe there. I still haven't heard anything of young Edward but the Royal Field artillery is here and I may get to know something soon.

No signs of me being home for Christmas. All leave cancelled now.

Your loving and very cold husband
George

'Do you want the job?' asked Sarah. 'I know it's hardly helpin' the war effort but it'll help me a lot. I haven't time to cook and clean at the minute. I'm chasing my own tail most of the time.

'Of course I'll help you. You don't need to pay me to do it. You're my friend, Sarah. That's what friends do,' Martha continued sweeping the floor as Sarah washed up the breakfast plates.

'I know, Lass, but I want it more formal. You've been helping me for weeks and I canna let you keep on doing it for nowt. I need to be out there with Joe. Doing Robert's job properly. The last thing I need is the council trying to replace us. They came over again last month wanting to see if things were still being done properly. It's ridiculous the way they suggest I'm not capable. I've told them that Joe has been helping his Da since he was little and deserved the chance. The fact that men are short on the ground is the only reason they're allowing me to carry on at all. They'll be back to check up again next month. Can you understand now why I joined the cause? I can't pay much, Martha, but you'll get three meals a day thrown in and it'll save you worrying about who could look after William if you did other work...what about it?'

'I...' she saw the desperation on Sarah's face. 'I'll do it. Thank you, Sarah. Whatever you can afford is fine. It'll always come in handy.'

'Good. Now that's settled, I'll leave you to it. We'll be in for a bite to eat at one o-clock. You know where the larder is... and thank you. It'll make all the difference.'

Sarah left Martha to start her new job as housekeeper. She'd been more or less doing the job anyway. The only difference would be that she'd get paid.

Poor Sarah had so much on her plate, Martha thought as she set about her cleaning routine. Keeping up with the job, her home, worrying about Edward and it had broken her heart that Joe had to give up his chance of an apprenticeship to work at the market full-time. She had written to the war office demanding they send Edward home, but she'd heard nothing back. Martha still hadn't told her about the letter she'd had from George this morning. She'd wait until later. Perhaps they hadn't sent Edward over. He was supposed to be nineteen before he was sent overseas. Worst of all was the great hole Robert's passing had left in all their lives. How the world she lived in had changed over the last year. She wondered if she would ever feel some normality again. If any of them would? She turned to see William setting the table. The sight of her son, eager to make sure his dinner was on the way, dragged her back to the here and now, making her smile.

'It's a bit too early for that. There's a lot of work to do

before it's time to eat again.'

'I'm hungry,' said William.

'You're always hungry. Let's have a look in that larder and see if there are any of Aunt Sarah's wonderful biscuits.'

Wilson Bros. was full of Christmas decorations and delicacies, and there was a large notice asking people to get their Christmas Orders in early 'To avoid Disappointment'. Martha pushed her way through the crowds in the grocery department. William's eyes bulged as he passed the shelves and shelves of toys. The food section was stacked with baskets full of bread, fruit and vegetables. Barrels of potatoes and flour with scoops and scales for weighing by the stone were set to one side; a wiry man wearing a white apron waited to serve the growing crowd. The shelves behind the glass topped counters were weighed down with jars of sweets, candies, liquorice and liquorice root at one side and packets of split peas, pulses, lentils, barley on the other; all sorted by colour for those too old to have benefited from the current education system and unable to read. One section of the counter had paper bags filled with broken biscuits, advertised at threepence a bag. Martha bought flour, beef suet, sugar and some dried currants. Carrots completed the order and once cooked and mashed would add moisture to the mix. It wouldn't be as good as the Christmas puddings she had eaten before the war, but it would be a welcome change to some of the concoctions she had made recently. It had always been her ma that had made the Christmas pudding at home, easily large enough to share with Martha and George to spare them the expense. She checked her list to see if she had all the ingredients she had set out for and found that the almonds needed for a sweet sauce was still outstanding.

'Please, Ma,' said William staring up at the jars of sweets.

'Just a ha'peth then.' She pointed to the jar of bon bons and the girl weighed out a few into a paper bag. Martha filled her basket and passed the sweets to William. She turned to leave and found herself face to face with Mrs Wicklow. Martha turned her head away.

'E...Excuse me,' she said as she tried to edge her way around the dreadful woman.

'Wait...Mrs Hubbard. How is Mrs Colby? I heard about her poor husband. '

Martha was surprised by what sounded like genuine concern for Sarah.

'She...she's as well as can be expected. I'm afraid I need to get back. Please excuse me.' Martha managed to find a gap in the crowd and slipped through it, holding fast on to William's hand. Relieved to get away, Martha relaxed again as they wandered down the high street, looking in windows, stopping at Marks and Spencer's penny bazaar and marvelling at the array of goods for one penny or less. They stopped outside Able's toyshop and William pointed out a box of lead soldiers.

'Ma, soldiers like Da. There's some riding horses and look, some horses pulling a cannon.

Martha looked at the price tag. Six shillings was a lot of money. She would check the jar when they got home. Sarah was paying her five shillings a week and all their meals, so she was putting a good sum away every week now.

'You should be very proud of your father, young man. He's doing an excellent job for his country and you.' Martha saw the tall stick-like figure through the shop glass. Mrs Wicklow's nose looked even sharper than she remembered in the reflection.

'Yes, Miss. He is,' replied William, turning around and beaming up at the lady.

'I heard Mrs Colby's son has volunteered. It must be hard for her.'

'It is...very hard.' Martha felt her hackles rise. 'That's the reason Mr Colby had a heart attack. Because his son felt he had no choice but to run off and fight this war.'

'We all have our crosses to bear, Mrs Hubbard. Some of us

hold our heads high while we do it. There are many things in life we don't agree with, but we do our duty and help where we can in order that those who fight for this country don't feel it is all for nothing. Men like your husband and Mrs Colby's son whose own lives depend so greatly on the men that stand beside them. The war is a fact, whether we agree with it or not, and when we see others who neither support nor give the best of themselves and shirk their duty, it is our responsibility to point out the error of their ways. I do hope we understand each other a little better.'

She left Martha staring after her. She wasn't sure what she felt. Anger? A small amount of admiration, for someone who didn't falter in her mission to fight for what she believed? When it came to George and Edward, a slight feeling that they were on the same side pricked her conscience and settled itself down beside her abhorrence of all things war.

Christmas day at Sarah's house felt strange. No George, no Robert and no Edward. Joe kept William entertained playing with the soldiers and horses. Creating pretend battles. William insisting on being his Da so that Joe had to pretend to be a German soldier and lose all the time. Martha and Sarah passed the day making socks and vests for their men after they had cleared the Christmas dishes and wrapped the leftovers...

'I wonder what they're doing right now?' asked Sarah. 'I wish with all my heart that Robert was still here, but he'd be sitting and worrying himself sick over Edward. Reading the newspapers used to make him ill. I'd to tell him to stop buying it, but he couldn't bear not knowing what was going on.'

'And we all know what that did to him,' Joe snapped. Poor Joe, Martha thought, it's so hard for him.

'I remember how he used to sit and tell stories to me and the boys when he and Da came in from watching the players?' Martha reminisced, lightening the conversation. 'You remember, don't you, Joe? We used to pretend to be asleep when he came in the room, but he'd sit down and start telling us all about when he was a boy. He knew we weren't really asleep...I used to love that.' Martha smiled at the memory.

'I know,' said Sarah. 'Then he'd pretend he had to wake you up. Tickling you and the boys. He'd fetch you downstairs and your Da and Ma would take you home. I used to say it was alreet for you to stay, but Cyril couldn't bear the thought of you spending a night away from him. You were always his princess.'

'I can't believe it's a year since they were killed.' Martha eyes filled. She pulled herself upright. 'Mustn't get all maudlin. Da'd tell me off for that. "Allus look for the sunshine in everything, “Martha. It'll be there somewhere" he used to say.'

'Where's the sunshine in all this war then? Tell me that.'

'We're still alive and so are George and Edward. There's the sunshine, Sarah.'

'I don't think he could see much sunshine when you got married so soon after you and George started walkin' out. I remember him sayin' it were strange how one minute you were walkin' out with Alb...' Sarah stopped speaking for a moment. 'Martha...Do you love George?'

Martha dropped a stitch. Trying to pick it up, she avoided looking at Sarah. 'That's a funny question. Course I love him. Why do you ask?'

'Do you hear anything from George's family? His Ma and Da... Albert?'

Martha felt herself turning pink. What did she know?

'They write to George sometimes. He tells me what they're doing. Why are you asking, Sarah?'

'Ah...it's nothin'. Tek no notice of me. I don't know what made me ask.'

Martha settled back in her seat; knitting George's vest, an uncomfortable silence hanging in the air. Sarah stood and picked up the kettle.

'Who's for tea and Christmas pudding then? It looks grand, Martha. You did a good job.'

'Me please,' yelled William jumping up and knocking his soldiers over.

'I was asking anyone who has a normal appetite, not someone who can't get enough into his mouth at any time of day.'

They all laughed and Martha's discomfort disappeared in an instant.

Chapter 15

1910

'Stop moping about, lass. You're making yourself ill. It'll not bring him back. Hurry up now or yoos'll be late for work.' Cyril Palmer guided his daughter, ushering her towards the front door. Her tiny frame, inherited from her mother, looked miniscule against his large hands and strong arms. Twenty-six years in the pits had made him the large man he was today. Martha shrank from his touch. 'Careful, Da. Your hands are still dirty.'

Martha knew he was right, but it didn't make things any easier. She'd cried herself to sleep yet again last night.

'Stop badgering the girl, Cyril. She'll be fine.' Annie Palmer's soft voice drifted through from the kitchen. The sound of water being poured into the tin bath echoed and gurgled through the house.

'Yoos'd think she was a queen still in her night clothes at seven in the morning.' Her Da's small round eyes winked at her from a broad, square face, still covered in coal dust. 'Oh yes, I forgot. She is a queen. You can tell by the way she talks all posh.'

Martha usually laughed but could hardly muster a smile this morning. How many times a day did he refer to her Ma that way?

'She's definitely queen in this house. Anyway, I like the way she speaks.'

'I know. You speak all proper too since you started work at Turnbull and Tilley's solicitors. I'm that proud of you. Now... It's time my little princess stopped feeling sorry for herself and got off to work. 'Your Da needs a bath and some sleep afore his shift tonight.'

He tried to kiss her forehead as he opened the door, but she ducked out of his way.'I'm going, Da. Stop going on at me.'

Stepping out on to Dene Street and a particularly beautiful autumn morning, she set off towards Cleveland Road where she would catch the tram to town and her job at Turnbull and Tilley. The sudden rush of nausea made her gag, reaffirming what she had hoped... prayed was only her imagination. Stopping for a moment to regain her composure, her mind filled with the utter reality of the situation. She was a single woman who was going to have a baby and it would soon be apparent to the whole world. The nausea gripped her again and her hand flew over her mouth.

Ma would be so upset. Ashamed of her. What would Mr Turnbull think? He'd only given her the job because Ma had worked there before she married Da. Mr Turnbull had even arranged elocution lessons for her mother because he wanted his establishment to be regarded as high class at all times. Her family had been surprised when she said she was marrying, Da, her Ma had told her. "Love's more important than anything else, Martha. You remember that. Wealth and status amount to nothing if you don't have love." Her Ma was a real lady in Martha's eyes. Turnbull and Tilley didn't employ married women and asked Martha's mother to leave. They knew that she wouldn't stay after the babies started to arrive. She never complained about having given up her career. She kept herself and their home spotless; dressed immaculately; knew how to exchange views with anyone, regardless of gender or position; maintained high values and genuinely cared for other people. She was always volunteering to help those less fortunate than herself, even though she and Da had little of their own since she gave up work and got married; a lady who expected her daughter to behave like a lady, not like someone who came from the gutter and didn't know any better. She was so glad that her Ma had found someone like her Da to love. Martha knew she would join Da in bed after his bath. Whenever he had been on the night shift he loved Ma to bathe him and then they would go back to bed together for an hour. Her Da was the kindest, sweetest person in the world. It would break his heart when she told him. He had such high hopes for her. She was seventeen...a woman, but to him she was still a little girl. She was the most special person in the world they always told her. The little girl he and Ma, who had so many miscarriages before they had her, had waited so very long for.

Albert had been gone for over a week and hadn't written yet. She would go round to his house on Tankerville Street after work and get his address from George or Granda Hubbard. She would have to write and tell him. He'd surely come home when he knew. Why on earth hadn't she told him before he left? Because she had been afraid he would have left anyway. The thought made another bout of nausea come over her, making her feel slightly faint.

'Come in, Martha, Pet. It's grand to see you.' Albert's Granda opened the door to her. His features were similar to Albert's, and she could see he would have been a handsome man when he was younger, but years on the docks and nights in the pubs around the town had taken their toll and the once broad, six-foot three man was bent and shrivelled. The skin hung loosely on his frame and his hands were lined with deep veins and age spots. His toothless smile always made Martha want to laugh and his kind voice made her feel at home whenever she came to visit.

'Hello, Mr Hubbard. I'm sorry to bother you. I was wondering if you might have Albert's new address.' Martha stepped into the short hall and followed Granda through to the back room. All the terraced houses on this side of town were similar but a little older than where Martha and her family lived. There were two rooms downstairs and two up. There was a simple range with a fire burning. Granda always seemed to be cold whatever the weather, she thought. His box-bed fitted snugly in the alcove at the side of the range. Albert and George had slept in it as bairns when they were small, and their mother and father slept upstairs in one bedroom with Edith. Granda and Grandma slept in the other bedroom until Grandma died in 1901 from consumption. Granda couldn't bear being in the room anymore, so the boys, who were getting quite big by then, moved upstairs and Granda moved down. He still didn't want to sleep upstairs, even though there was plenty of room now.

'Yoos'll have to wait 'til George gets home, Martha. I canna read. Never went to school much. I was working in the shipyards by the time I were eight. George looks after that side of things now.' The old man sat down in the rocker and his body curled over towards the fire, like a flower seeking out the sun.

Granda's pot was on the hearth and it was half-full. Martha could feel the bile rising in her throat from the stench. 'I...I'm fine here,' she said from the doorway back into the hall, trying to hold her breath. She heard the front door slam and moved out of the way to let George through.

'Martha. How grand...For God's sake, Granda. Yer could have emptied it,' George snapped as he picked up the pot. Screwing his face up and holding his nose, he headed for the back door and took it out to the netty. The rush of cool air allowed Martha to take a deep breath. She hoped George would leave the door open, but Granda had other ideas.

'Shut the bloody door, lad. I'll freeze to deeth in this weather.' He hunched his shoulders, pulling a threadbare scarf around them. 'It's alreet for you with all that fat on yer. My bones feel every bit of this wind.'

'Yer canna leave that next to the fire. Yoos'll gas us all out,' he snapped, coming back inside. 'I'm sorry, Martha. It's good to see you. Canna get you a drink of summat? Tea?'

'I'm fine thanks, George. I came to ask if you've got Albert's new address. I...I.' Martha stopped short. The meagre contents of her stomach had decided to make a bolt for it and she ran through to the yard and into the netty before George could shut the door. She heaved and wretched, bringing up only bile. Everything she had eaten for lunch had been brought up in the toilet at work. She had excused herself several times, claiming to have an upset tummy. Mrs Henry, her supervisor in the office seemed to accept the story and hadn't questioned her too much. In fact she had been encouraged to leave early before a very important client was due to arrive.

'Ha'way, Pet. What's up?' George was behind her; holding her shoulders until she had finished.

'Something I've eaten. Nothing to worry about,' she said standing up and wiping her mouth with the back of her hand. 'Could I have a glass of water please, George?'

'Course you can. Come back inside. I'll walk you home. Canna have yer on yer own when you're out of sorts.'

Martha could feel Granda's eyes on her as she sipped the water. George had gone upstairs to fetch a letter that had come from Govan. It had arrived a few days earlier. 'You alreet, Pet? Nowt too serious is it?'

'No, Mr Hubbard. Something I've eaten, that's all.' Martha felt uncomfortable. He knows, she thought. I can tell by the way he keeps looking at me.

'Nothing you need to talk about?' he pushed.

'Stop being so nosy, Granda. Martha's not well. That's all

you need to know.' George apologised to her. 'I'm sorry, Martha. I canna put my hand to it reet now. I'll have a look for it and bring it round to your Da's as soon as I can. It didna say a lot. Just that they're all settled in at work. He's not too happy about the lodgings. The tenements are as bad as those at The Croft apparently. Only two rooms, but they're managing. They hope to move somewhere better when they've earned some wages. Come on, I'll walk back with you. It's getting a bit dark now the nights are drawing in.'

Martha sighed. It meant she couldn't get a letter in the post as soon as she'd hoped. Still she could write it and have it ready.

'Thank you. I'd like that,' she said, desperate to get away from Granda's prying.

Chapter 16

January 6th 1916

Dear Martha,

I was glad to get your letter. It must have been hard for Sarah this Christmas. Robert was a good man. Still no sign of Edward but I'll keep asking.

The Christmas parcel, with sweets and cake was a great success with my pals out here. I didn't have to wait too long for it and it was still in good shape. I think they must have put on extra deliveries for Christmas. More socks and vests are what I needed most so a big thank you for those. We got some plum pudding from the Red Cross too and packets of woodbines and thick slabs of taffy. It was a good day. I won't say it's the best Christmas I've ever had 'cos that wouldn't be true. It could only have been the best if I was at home with you and William but it were grand and we were all laughing and larking about. Even though it was bitter cold, it didn't matter for that one day. The parson came to see us and we had a proper service and sang hymns and Christmas carols and such. Even Jimmy perked up a bit and joined in.

I've got some news from Govan. Our Edith is getting married. Ma's as mad as can be. She's only sixteen but she's ...well you know what I mean...so it's for the best. The lad's a union member so Da's alreet about it. Albert says she's too young but she's made her bed and all that. He's a fine one to talk. Showed his true colours a long time ago, didn't he? Anyway, I thought you should know. You being able to understand what she must be going through. Perhaps you could drop her a line.

We're still having our heads pounded with the shells and mortars and Bess still has lots of men to find every day between bouts of fighting. It's a wonder there's room in the hospitals for them all. It breaks my heart sometimes, the state I find them in. Surely the war must be over soon.

Take care, Pet. Have a happy New Year

Your loving husband

George

Apart from Sarah's strange comments, it was the first time she had heard Albert's name in months, and the fact that it was in relation to the news about Edith made it worse. It would have been better if George hadn't mentioned it at all, but she supposed it stirred unwanted memories for him, too. She put the letter away, determined not to let it spoil the day. She hoped Edith would be happy with her union man. She would write to her tomorrow.

It was May, and Martha was enjoying her work at Sarah's house. It felt good to be earning a wage, no matter how small. She had opened a savings account at the Yorkshire Penny Bank on Church Street and religiously put half her earnings in every week. The way she saw it, she had managed without that extra money so far so it could be used to pay back Robert and Sarah's funeral loan in the future. With the rest, she kept her eye open for pieces of second hand furniture for the small front parlour at home and managed to furnish it for very little over the following months. She kept George informed and asked his opinion on every purchase whenever she could. He seemed pleased with what she was doing and didn't raise any objections. Working as a housekeeper for Sarah appeared to be acceptable in his eyes, particularly as it provided an opportunity to pay off their debt to the Colbys. Sarah and Joe were doing a good job at the market and the council were not looking at replacing them, as the Colby's accepted the same wage Robert had been on and they shared it between them. Sarah left all the heavy work to Joe and she attended to all the paperwork and negotiated the rent for the players and their caravans over winter.

'I've had another letter from Edward.' Sarah's face was glowing with excitement when Martha arrived one morning.

'I'm so pleased for you, Sarah. It must be a load off your mind.'

'He says he's well and coping with the cold and wet. He asks if I can send him a parcel, as he's missing my home cooking. I hope he's getting enough to eat out there. He's still growing.'

'I think they do, but it's much the same every day. George likes it if I send him a bit of taffy and a cake when I've baked. He'll be needing lots of socks and spare puttees mind. George says it's like a bog and they can't get anything dry.'

'Edward says he and his pals are all infested with lice; they can't get rid of them even when they are given special soap, and he said that rats are running round everywhere. The thought meks me feel sick.' Sarah's cheeks wobbled as she shuddered.

'I know. I try not to think of it. It's terrible what they have to deal with.'

Martha took her coat off and rolled her sleeves up. She didn't say she remembered George saying that the rats even built nests in the bodies of the dead soldiers in one of his letters. She'd been sick in the chamber pot the night she read it.

'Do they bite?' asked a shock-faced William.

'I shouldn't think so,' Sarah smiled down at the boy. 'Soldiers are much too tough to eat. The rats'd have to spit them out they'd taste so awful.'

William grinned. 'Good ', he quipped. 'I don't like rats. I think my Da'll shoot them with his rifle. Bam! Bam!' William raced around the kitchen firing at imaginary rats with his imaginary rifle.

'Good, lad. Mek sure there are none of the little blighters in my kitchen.'

'Yes sir!' He saluted Sarah then continued his mission in earnest.

Sarah left them to their tasks and went out into the yard that was buzzing with the usual daily activity of setting up stalls. Martha put the water on to boil for the dolly tub and went upstairs to strip the beds. She glanced down at the yard and remembered the day of the bombardment again. Her Ma and Da had been taken from them and now Robert was gone as well. She wondered if people met up again in heaven. She hoped so.

The knock on the door was so light that Martha didn't hear it the first time. She wondered who might be calling. She didn't get many visitors.

'Celia,' Martha was surprised to see her. In all the time they had known each other, Celia had never been to her house. They hadn't had any contact since that day last year when she had left after her argument with Mrs Wicklow. She was dressed in mourning black as usual. Martha felt a pang of sympathy as she remembered the day of the telegram and how distraught poor Celia had been.

'Martha...I was told this was where you lived. I wondered if I might take a little of your time.'

'Of course. Come in...Please.' Martha made way and showed her through to the now partially furnished parlour. I'm afraid you'll have to take us as you find us,' she added in an apologetic manner.

'Oh...What a delightful little room,' enthused Celia. 'So cosy and neat.'

Martha pointed to one of the two padded chairs that straddled either side of a small round table. She'd been thrilled to get them from a large house clearance last month.

'I'll make some tea. It won't take long.' She left the room. William, who had followed his mother to the door, decided to stay in the parlour with their guest.

When Martha returned with a tray of tea and home-made biscuits, she saw that William was staring at a basket that Celia had set down by the chair. It was covered by a blue and white checked towel, and from the warm scent of apples that filled the room; Martha guessed that it must contain one of Mrs Finch's delicious crumbles that William loved so much.

'William, don't stare. Mrs Clarke will think you very rude.'

'Not at all. It's a gift from me and Daisy...and Mrs Finch of course. We've missed your company.'

Martha poured tea and sat down to wait for Celia to tell her the reason for the visit.

'I'll get right to the point, Martha. You will have probably read or heard about Mrs Pankhurst's 'Right to Serve' protest march in London last summer. She held her hand up as Martha started to rise. 'Please...Please hear me out.'

Martha sat down again, tense and uncomfortable. She didn't want to have anything to do with these militant women down in London.

'Like you, I do not agree with violence when protesting, or chaining oneself to the gates of Buckingham etcetera...but this time...there is an opportunity for women, not only to go out to work, but more importantly to realise their dream and get the chance to vote. Have their voice heard in parliament. Mrs Pankhurst made it a negotiating point in her talks with the government. One of the politicians, Mr Lloyd George, is supporting the campaign and even saying that he would support votes for women if he gets elected as prime minister.'

'I see,' Martha thought of Sarah. Surely she was the most appropriate person for Celia to talk to. 'How does this concern me?' she asked warily.

'I had dinner with Mr Gray last week and he told me that he was giving over part of the of the Marine Engineering Company for the manufacture of shells. I managed to resist saying that it was about time. He should have done it a year ago, but that is beside the point. At least we have managed to get some women onto the trams and on to the railways. The point is that the government are asking more and more companies to help in this area. Our men on the front are not being supplied with arms fast enough to keep pace with the Germans. Mr Lloyd George's main worry is manpower, as he doesn't want to move men from building warships. He has great trouble in staying on schedule with them, as it is while the men up in Glasgow keep going on strike.' The mention of Glasgow made Martha think of Albert again. She wondered if he had been part of the strikes. He had always been quick to support any sort of industrial action. 'A great many more men have enlisted since conscription in January, and now that they've upped the age to forty one, even less are available.'

'What is it you want me to do?' Martha pulled her mind back into focus. She couldn't work out how she could be of help.

'It seems that the results in the south have not been repeated here and we are lacking in women volunteers. Could you talk to your friends, neighbours...persuade all the women, particularly married women, that they wouldn't be doing something totally unthinkable, but in fact helping their husbands and sons who are away fighting. Not only that, I am assured by Mr Gray that the wages will be exceptionally high compared to domestic work. He is also working closely with National Union for women workers, which means that women's rights are looked after, and they also keep a close eye on working conditions. He pretends he has thought about it seriously, but the truth is that we women have won the right to a man's wage. It is finally considered that munitions work is dangerous enough to be classed as equal to that of the highly skilled traditional and dangerous work normally left to the stronger sex. What do you think?'

'I...I'm not sure. I'll speak to Sarah.'

'That was my next request. I thought that Sarah or you...could hand out leaflets supporting the 'Right to Serve' campaign. Not walking the streets of course, there are plenty willing to march, but at the public market as people come and go.'

'I...' Martha's head was swimming. She was asking such a lot of her. She still wasn't sure she believed it was the right thing to do. She would be going against what George believed. Celia stood up and made her way back into the hallway.

'I'm sure you can take this through to the kitchen for your mother, William.' Celia said, handing the basket to the boy who grabbed it eagerly. She waited until he had left the room before standing. 'Martha, you would be doing a great thing for the country; our men overseas need us to do this, George included... and you'll be helping women all over Britain.'

Martha felt like she was being swept along by the passion in Celia's voice, and the emotion that was clearly visible in her face. She followed her to the door and let her out onto the street.

'Please think about it...I won't pressure you anymore, but if you decide that you can help, you know where I am.'

The slightly built woman strode away leaving Martha with a great deal to think about.

'What do I think? Ha'way with you. Of course we'll do it. Look at the opportunity for women to earn a decent living for their family while the men are away.'

'But don't you think the men would be against it? '

'Of course they will...for a while. But they'll see sense. Particularly when they see the results. More arms reaching them faster. It's bound to bring the war to an end sooner rather than later. Anything that'll bring my boy home safe is good enough for me. We can be part of bringing that about and getting votes for women at the same time. Don't you want to be part of it? This is history in the making.' Sarah was practically bouncing around the kitchen.

'Well...When you say it like that,' Martha felt Sarah's enthusiasm taking over her own body. She felt slightly light headed. Was it euphoria? Was she finally going to be helping to bring the war to an end. She had to believe that. She did believe that.

She rapped on the door, briskly. Daisy was surprised but pleased to see Martha and William again. 'Come in, Mrs Hubbard. Come in.'

'Martha's fine by me, Daisy. No need for formality.'

'Mebbe not with you Mrs...Martha but Mrs Clarke'd have summat to say about it,' she whispered.

'Is that Mrs Hubbard, Daisy?' Celia's voice pierced the drawing room door. Daisy grinned.

'Yes, Miss.'

'Then show her in immediately.'

Martha handed a perfectly ecstatic William over to Daisy before entering the drawing room.

Chapter 17

Martha stood at the entrance to the public market on Lynn Street while Sarah manned the back exit that led to the outdoor stalls. William was at Celia's house. She had offered Daisy as a childminder for the day in order that Martha could do this job. William had jumped at the chance to spend time with her. Apart from his mother and Joe, Daisy was his most favourite person in the world.

Martha pressed the leaflets into the hands of passing shoppers. She hoped they would be well received. It had taken a lot of courage for her to step out of her own little world and take some responsibility for helping the war effort. She was filled with trepidation at how she would be looked upon by anyone she knew.

I wonder what the dreadful Mrs Wicklow would make of it, she wondered. She'd possibly faint with surprise or... no that wasn't possible... crack a smile? Martha almost giggled at the thought.

She waved the leaflets in the air to attract attention. They were emblazoned with 'Women's Right to Serve' across the top. The younger single women were keen to hear about the new munitions factory that paid good wages. This was their opportunity to rise above the poverty line that came with more traditional roles such as domestic service or shop work. The factory would be open for business by the middle of June, and anyone interested should put their names down for an interview at the earliest opportunity. The older, married ladies, particularly those of a working class background were a bit more dubious at the idea. Middle class and upper class married ladies seemed to be signing up as quickly as the young singles, and that eventually persuaded the rest.

'If them well-off sorts can get their hands dirty and help out, so can we,' shouted a woman nearby. She was dressed in similar clothes to Martha and looked to be in her early twenties. She had the wildest looking red hair that Martha had ever seen. 'And anythin' that'll help feed my brood at home while my man's away is alreet by me,' she added.

Martha smiled at her and the woman winked back before coming to stand beside her.

'Florrie,' she said holding out her hand. Florrie Mason.'

'Thank you,' said Martha.

'You're George's wife, aren't you,' said Florrie. 'You don't recognise me, do you?'

'Should I? Your name sounds familiar.'

'I live on Dene Street. Across the way from where yer Ma lived. My mother Agnes was friends wi' your Ma. You're lucky to have George, he's a good man.'

Martha could hear the genuine warmth in her voice as she spoke. 'Of course. You left school the year before me. I remember. You had a twin brother. Freddie, wasn't it?'

'That's it. Freddie and Florrie with the frizzy hair. That's what everyone called us.' Florrie's sage green eyes twinkled as she spoke.

'Is Freddie...?'

'He is. Been out there since day one. He was one of the first volunteers. Ma cried her eyes out. Da were that proud...not now though. He's feared all the time. Cries as much as Ma wi' worry. Good job mi little brothers are not old enough they keep sayin'.'

'My friend Sarah's the same. One of her sons ran off to join up,' said Martha. 'Your brother...Is he alright?'

'I think so. Not heard from him in a while. Usually writes most weeks... Must be on the move.' Her eyes clouded as she spoke.

'That's probably it,' said Martha, trying to sound positive. 'What about your husband? Is he out there?'

'Husband? What husband? I only said it so those women who weren't sure would take a leaflet. Nothing wrong with a little white lie now and then if it gets the reet result, is there?'

Martha saw the flash of mischief cross Florrie's face and smiled.

'I'm sure there isn't,' she replied with a knowing smile. She felt as if she was going to get on very well with this woman.

Martha soon realised what an asset Florrie was. She seemed to know an unbelievable amount of people. When she told her that she had worked at Wiley's butcher's stall in the market since she'd left school, Martha understood.

'Hi, Florrie, not working today. What's that yer doing?'

'Hi, Florrie, Betty told me about the new factory. let's have a look.'

And so it went on, all day. Every leaflet gone by four o-clock.

'I'll have to go and see how Sarah's faired and then collect my son William. Thank you so much for your help, Florrie. Would you like to come with me and then back to mine for a cup of tea?'

'That'd be lovely, but Ma'll need some help wi the boys. I'll be applying for a job though. It'll mek a big difference to the family. I'm the only one who works. Da's too old now and his rheumatism stops him getting about. I've lost some extra income I used to get and I need to earn more than Wiley's pay to make ends meet.'

'Well, thanks again. I might see you at the factory when I

get William into school next month.' She hadn't thought about it before, but the idea was suddenly appealing. Spending the day with Florrie had shown her how much she'd enjoyed passing time with someone her own age for a change. She loved Sarah dearly, but it was more like a mother-daughter relationship than close friends. She would run the idea past her. There was no way she could leave Sarah in the lurch if she was still needed, but it would be nice....

'Dunna worry yersel about me, Lass. Joe's doing a grand job and I can manage a bit of housework on mi own. Besides, I canna stand in your way. You've got to grab the chances when they're there.' Martha looked closely at Sarah's face. She seemed genuine?

'Look, Sarah. Don't be saying that if it's not alright. I mean it. I'll tell them I've changed my mind. I should never have applied. Of course you still need me here. I'll be able to help you even more when William starts school.'

Martha pushed the peg down into the dolly tub, rotating it vigorously at the same time, the carbolic soap flakes creating a rich lather to clean the bed sheets and Joe's shirts.'Don't be silly, woman. Put that down and come and sit inside with me. It's blummin' cold out here. I've made you a hot drink to keep the chill off.'

Martha was far from cold. She wiped the sweat from her forehead with the back of her hand and went inside to join Sarah at the table. Even though the weather was particularly miserable for early June, and there had been virtually no sunshine, Martha's exertions were keeping her very warm indeed and the air inside the kitchen seemed stifling with the range on.

'You are not going to miss this opportunity to earn good money and that's the end of it. If I was a bit fitter, I'd be joining you, make no mistake. Joe's proved himself capable of doing the job and it won't be long afore our Edward's sent home now. They've moved him off the front line to some base for under nineteens.'

'Do you think they will actually send him home? He'll be nineteen in a couple of months.'

'I hope so. A couple of months home'll do him good.'

'I hope you're right, Sarah.' Martha had read in the papers of some boys being held at these bases until their nineteenth birthday and then being sent back up the line. It seemed it was only under eighteens that were sent home.

'Who'll be taking William to school when you get the new job?'

'I haven't thought that far ahead. I don't know if I'll get taken on or not yet. I'll cross that bridge when I come to it.'

'I can do it. You can bring him here afore you go then I'll walk over to Murray Street with him. It'll only take five minutes and he can come back here after.'

'It's at least twenty minutes walk for you. I can't put extra on you, Sarah. I already feel guilty enough about leaving you as it is.'

'Ha'way, with you. I've already said I can manage quite well without you now that Joe's up and running with it all. I can allus get another lass to help if needs be.

Martha thought about it for a minute. Florrie's younger brothers and sisters all went to Murray Street primary school. Perhaps William could go with them?

'It's very kind of you, Sarah, but I can't put on you like that. I know someone who might be able to help and, besides, I owe you enough as it is and I want to start paying you back, not adding to the debt.'

Sarah stood up, a flash of anger crossing her face. 'I'll not tell you again, young lady. You don't need to pay me anything back until the war's over and your George comes home. And if I hear one more word about it, I'll not be speaking to you again and that'd hurt both of us a sight more than anything else.'

'Alright. I hear you.' She smiled widely at her surrogate

mother. Her Ma and Da would be looking down and smiling too, knowing how well she was being cared for by this wonderful woman. 'But I'm still going to try and find someone else to take him to school.'

There were two letters waiting for Martha when she arrived home that evening. One penned with the familiar hand of her husband and one in an envelope with the Marine Engineering Works Logo on the front. She decided to open the latter first. Her hands shook with excitement.

It was brief and to the point.

We are pleased to inform you that you have been successful in your application. Please report for your shift on Monday 3rd July at 6:00 am prompt. Training will be given on the job. Stout shoes are recommended. You will be issued with overalls and a cap. Canteen facilities are available at a nominal cost.

'I've got a job, William. Ma's got a job.' She danced around the kitchen with her son, laughing and singing.

'Will I come with you?' asked William.

'No, son. You'll be going to school next Monday. Won't that be wonderful?'

William nodded but his face wasn't agreeing with his head.

'Don't worry. You'll like it. There will be lots of friends to play with.'

'Is that my birthday present? Going to school? I wanted a toy to play with.'

'No...There'll still be a nice surprise for your birthday...as always.'

'That's alright then.' He grinned, dancing around happily with his mother.

Martha waited until bedtime to read the letter from George.

June 15th 1916

Dear Martha,

I hope all is well at home. Things are not so good here. We seem to be getting ready for something much bigger than we've seen so far. The officers are pushing us all very hard. We lost Capt Brigg last week and our new officer is fresh from training so he'll have to prove himself before we can trust him. There was a skirmish a couple of days ago and we lost quite a few. I'm afraid Jimmy was one of the unlucky ones but I heard he was extremely brave and saved a couple of the pals afore he went down. The thought of being here without him hurts me badly. I miss him.

I wish I could come home now. The dead and dying are everywhere you look. Bess is well and still doing her duty, thank God. I'm finding the noise a bit difficult to deal with. I can't seem to get any rest at all but I'm sure it is the same for everyone here. Dunna worry about me. I'm just feeling a bit sorry for myself. I'll be back to normal as soon as I can get a some sleep.

Will write again soon.

Your loving husband

George

Martha sobbed into her pillow. Poor Jimmy. Poor George. He sounded so down, so dispirited. The tone of his letter was different. She could read his sadness in the words, no hint of hope or cheer at all. How could she be glad for herself when he was going through so much?

Chapter 18

Martha felt William's hand gripping hers tightly as they entered the Murray Street school yard and stopped to take in the scene before them. She had emptied her jar and even withdrawn a small sum from the bank to make sure he was dressed properly. The most expensive item had been the new Norfolk jacket and knee length shorts, both of which had pleased her son. All the pockets would be especially useful to put his best marbles in and the used bullet cartridge his Da had given to him when he came home on leave last year. He had put Neddy in his shorts pocket, until Martha had explained that he might lose it in the playground. He put it back with his other animals in the wooden farm, even though he didn't usually go anywhere without his little wooden horse.

William kept tugging at his long woollen socks with his free hand and scraping his new boots on the rough surface of the playground, the studs making a bright spark each time he did it.

'These stockings are itchy, Ma'.

'If you don't think about, it'll stop. Put your mind to how

much you'll enjoy being at school. All the friends you'll have to play with.'

'Yes, Ma,' he replied, still fidgeting.

There were several mothers standing outside the gate, sharing the latest news on loved ones away on the front line, their children already playing with friends. Squeals of laughter were ringing out across the yard, boys shouting, chasing each other with imaginary guns and making rat-a-tat-tat noises. A group of girls formed a small intimate circle, holding hands and skipping around, singing favourite nursery rhymes. Martha remembered from her own days at school that it was only the closest of friends that were invited to join in. She also knew it didn't feel very nice if you were the one left out. One girl raced past, her stick keeping a metal hoop wheeling along the ground, her dress and white cotton pinafore billowing in the wind; ringlets and ribbons flying out behind her. William's eyes followed the girl's every move. He didn't have a hoop.

Florrie was standing with Mrs Appleby, the teacher, by the girl's entrance. She wasn't smiling and Mrs Appleby was speaking to her with a stern look on her face. Florrie shouted across the yard to a young boy who rat-a-tat-tatted his way over, pointing his imaginary rifle this way and that as he came; a shock of red hair announcing his family connection to Florrie.

'Frank! Get ower here now,' she bellowed at the little boy. Bare elbows protruded through large holes in the grey woollen sweater he was wearing as he ran over and stood between the two women. 'What have I told you about fighting? Mrs Appleby'll stop you coming at all if you carry on much longer. Then where will you be? Unemployed and a layabout by the time yer fourteen, that's where.'

'Sorry, Florrie. Sorry, Mrs Appleby,' he muttered, shuffling his feet in worn out boots that looked two sizes too small for him; sniffing hard to retrieve the candle that was sliding down over his upper lip. His stick thin legs were bruised and grubby and his knobbly knees sported several half-healed scabs.

'That's all well and good, Frank, but your sister is quite correct. This is your last warning. The next time it happens, you will be expelled. Do I make myself clear young man?'

'Yes, Miss. Can I go now please, Miss?'

'Off with you. I will be ringing the bell in five minutes, you better make the most of what free time you have left.' Mrs Appleby dismissed him with a wave of her hand before looking up and catching sight of Martha and William. She beckoned them over. 'Mrs Hubbard and this must be William,' she said touching Martha's son on the head. 'Welcome to Murray Street Primary, William. We are very pleased to have you. Come and stand by my side until I ring the bell. I'll introduce you to the other children when we get inside.' She took his hand and held him by her. 'Say goodbye to your mother. She'll be back to pick you up later.'

Martha could see the look of fear on William's face. It would be the first time he had spent a whole day without her, except for his day with Daisy when she'd been handing out leaflets at the market. She bent down to her son and dabbed his cheek with her handkerchief before kissing him. Seeing the damp streak had made her own eyes sting. Her chest felt tight and she could hear the quick drumming of her heart reverberating around her head; as every mother did when leaving their child at school for the first time.

'Now you be a good boy for Mrs Appleby. Listen to everything you're told and you'll soon get the hang of it. I'll be here the minute school finishes to take you home and you can tell me all about it. Isn't that right, Mrs Appleby?' she said standing up again and looking at the middle-aged woman in front of her.

Mrs Appleby smiled tightly at Martha. 'We find it better not to make much of it. Rather, the mother can sometimes make the wrench harder by sympathising. William's a big boy now and will cope admirably with the situation. Say goodbye to your mother, William, and you can help me ring the bell. How about that?'

William's eyes lit up as Mrs Appleby placed his hand on the bell handle and covered it with her own. She raised his hand high and swiftly down again. Up and down. Up and down. The clanger rang out and the older girls and all the infants (boys and girls) rushed forward to line up in front of the door where Mrs Appleby stood and the older boys to queue in front of their own entrance, where Mr Cartwright waited; pocket watch in hand.

Martha walked back to the gate, swallowing hard, and stood by Florrie who was waiting for her.

'He'll be fine. Dunna be worryin' ower him.'

'I know. It just feels strange...leaving him on his own.'

'I've had a word with our Frank. He'll look after him 'til he finds his feet.'

Martha wasn't sure whether she should be glad or worried, bearing in mind what had happened with Frank earlier. It suddenly occurred to Martha that Florrie and her twin Freddie and now Frank all had names beginning with 'F'. How strange she thought.

'How many other siblings have you, Florrie?' she asked

'Well, there's me and Fred, then there's Frances who's fifteen and in service, Violet is twelve, she's the one who's standing a foot higher than anyone else in the girls line and thinks she's all grown up. Right handful she is and then there's Frank, he's six,' she finished, nodding at the little brother who had been in trouble a few minutes earlier. Martha heard Florrie's voice soften as she spoke. Frank was obviously her favourite even though she had reprimanded him not five minutes earlier.

'Violet?'

'I know. Da couldn't believe she were his, so he insisted on giving her a different name to the others. She was so big and long when she were born and all of us were underweight and skinny. Her hair's a different colour as well. Dark as night instead of red like Da's. Ma swears he's being daft, but he's sticking to his guns about it. I feel a bit sorry for her sometimes. Whatever the truth it's not Violet's fault, is it? Although, I can see Da's point as well. You wouldn't be happy if you thought your wife had been with someone else, would you?'

'No...Of course not.' Martha felt a pink rash slide up her neck and colour her cheeks. She found the topic uncomfortable and changed the subject.

'Have you had a letter? From Gray's. Did you get a job?'

'I did. I'm that excited. I start on Monday. Six sharp. How about you?'

'The same. I'm not sure what I'm going to do with William before and after school though. What do your brothers and sisters do?'

'They're with Ma until it's time for school and then Violet takes 'em. Your William can come round to ours and do the same. We can go to work together then. What do you think?'

'I...I'm not sure...Won't it be too much for your mother?'

'No. Anyway, Violet'll keep 'em in order.'

'That sounds fine...I think,' Martha answered. She hoped she wouldn't regret the decision.

'Right, now that's sorted you can walk down to the market with me and we can sort out times. Will you get a knocker-upper? It's a lot easier than hoping you'll wake up on time.'

'That's a good idea. I used to go on at George about getting one, but he said he wouldn't waste money on it. I think it cost us a lot more than the price of a knocker-upper each time he got up late for work and got his wages docked.'

'Yes It's a bit hard to manage sometimes. When you dunna earn that much.'

Martha had never opened up to anyone about her husband before and she wasn't sure why she was doing it now. Probably because she had spoken so fondly of George. She felt comfortable with Florrie. She hadn't had a close friend since she'd left school at fourteen and gone to work at

Turnbull and Tilley Solicitors as an office clerk. None of the girls at Turnbull's were what she could call close friends, but she had enjoyed going out with them sometimes with the small part of her wages that her Ma gave back to her each week. That was when she had met Albert and his friends and his younger brother, George. George, who always seemed to stay in the background. She would never have guessed that she would be married to him one day.

Martha collected a very excited William from school. He talked incessantly about his new friends and what he had been doing in class. 'I can do letters, Ma,' he started. 'A and B and C. I can draw them in a straight line like the teacher showed me.'

'That's my big boy. You can show me when we get home,' she answered.

'We have our own slate and a chalk to write with. I'm not allowed to bring it home. It has to stay in school. I can rub the letters out and start again if it's wrong. Mrs Appleby says I'm doing it good.' William barely paused in an effort to tell his mother everything. 'Frank Mason played with me in the yard, and he showed me his catapult. He didn't let me have a turn, and Mrs Appleby took it off him when it hit the window, and John played marbles with me and let me off when he won my best one. Said it was alreet this time, but he'd keep it if I lost next time. Can he do that, Ma? Is he allowed to keep it? You don't keep it when you play with me. I don't think I'll take them tomorrow, Ma. We talked about the king and how proud he is of all our daddies who are fighting and we said prayers for everybody to keep them safe. And...' He paused and took a deep breath.

Martha chuckled as her son chattered on and on. He obviously liked school and she had worried needlessly. She took the opportunity to interrupt. 'Would you like to go and see Daisy? I need to go and see Mrs Clarke about some more leaflets.'

'Oh, yes please, Ma. I can tell Daisy all about school. Does Mrs Finch bake on Mondays, Ma? Does she?'

Daisy let Martha and William in. Celia was in the drawing room. Martha could hear her talking to someone.

'It's Mrs Wicklow,' whispered Daisy before announcing their arrival.

'Oh.' Martha hoped there wouldn't be any sort of confrontation.

'Come in, Martha. Do come in,' beckoned Celia from within the room.

Daisy took William as usual and Martha could hear him spouting about school again before they got to the end of the hall.

'How are you, my dear? You remember Mrs Wicklow?' she said as if Martha could possibly forget.

'Of course,' Martha replied glancing at Mrs Wicklow before planting her gaze firmly on Celia.

'We've been discussing the latest news, Martha. The government have agreed to revise the voting registers now they have realised that all the men who are fighting are no longer eligible to vote.'

'I don't understand? Why?'

'Because they have lost their residency requirement. They'll have to give the vote back to them by changing the law.'

'Oh.' Martha wasn't sure what else to say. Celia grinned.

'The prime minister has recommended extending the vote to include some women. "They have taken the place of men in the workforce and as such are servants of the state." Isn't it wonderful.'

'Absolutely. You must be delighted.' Martha wondered if Sarah knew. Celia turned her attention to Mrs Wicklow.

'Martha has worked wonders with the leaflets, Gladys. Mr

Gray says he has been inundated with requests for work. Goodness. Where are my manners. I haven't even asked why you're here. Come and sit down, Martha. To what do we owe the honour? '

'I...I've run out of leaflets and I thought I might take some down to the promenade on Saturday. Lots of people take the sea air at the weekend.'

'What a splendid idea. What do you say, Gladys?'

'I say, I'm pleased to see Mrs Hubbard taking such an interest in the cause. Welcome on board.' She nodded at Martha to show her pleasure. Martha even thought she saw a hint of a smile on the narrow lips.

'I have some other news, Ce... Mrs Clarke. I won't be available to distribute the leaflets after this week. That's why I'm offering to do the promenade on Saturday.' She felt as if she were dashing Mrs Wicklow's hopes of another recruit, and it somehow built her confidence and made her feel a little less vulnerable.

'Martha...Please call me Celia. I thought we'd abandoned the formality between us. We are friends' now...not ...acquaintances. Why are you deserting me? I thought— '

'Oh, no. I'm not deserting you, M...Celia. I decided to apply for a position at the factory myself. I start work on Monday.'

'Bravo,' said Mrs Wicklow. 'You are doing your fellow women a great service, and your husband will be proud when he hears.' Martha wasn't so sure about that. 'Celia and I have joined the staff up at the VAD hospital. Normanhurst. Helping in any way that we can.'

'That's excellent news, Martha' Celia joined in. 'Perhaps, between us all, we can shorten this dreadful war and help more of our men come home safely.'

There was a gentle knock at the door and Daisy carried the tea tray through.

'We can help ourselves, Daisy. No need to stay. I think you're needed more in the kitchen by a certain young man than you are in here.'

'Yes, Miss,' said Daisy, smiling at her mistress. 'Young William is telling me and Mrs Finch all about his first day at school.'

'That's wonderful. Does he like it, Martha? What will happen when you go to work next week? Who will look after him?' asked Celia, concern beginning to line her face.

'That's all taken care of. I know of a family on Dene Street with several children at the school. The Masons.' Celia and Mrs Wicklow looked at each. Martha wondered if they knew of them. 'William will stay with Mrs Mason each morning and walk to school with the children. They'll all go back to Mrs Mason after school until I can collect him.'

'The Mason's? I see. What hours will you work?'

'It's a twelve hour shift from six in the morning.'

'As interesting as all this is, I'm afraid I must be off, Celia. I have a pressing appointment.' Mrs Wicklow rose to her full height. 'It was nice to meet you again, Mrs Hubbard. Will you excuse me? I'm sure our paths will cross again.'

She sounded almost courteous and Martha was glad the encounter hadn't been too onerous.

'I'm not sure about your arrangements for William,' said Celia when Gladys Wicklow had gone. 'I think it would be much better if Daisy took charge of William for you while you are at work...'

'But...' Martha started to open her mouth, but Celia continued as she picked up a pile of leaflets from on top of the piano and handed them over.

'Let me finish. Daisy will have very little to do with her time now I'm going to be up at the hospital most days. She's very fond of William, and I'm absolutely sure that William adores her. She can pick him up from your house and bring him back here before she starts work. She can take him to school when it is time, then collect him and bring him back here for his tea. You can call for him after your shift. Now, what do you say?'

'The Masons are a good family,' said Martha defending them.

'I'm not suggesting anything to the contrary. It's...I remember there was talk...'

'What sort of talk?'

'About Florrie...Something about a child being born out of wedlock. A boy I believe.'

Martha could feel her insides curling up.

'I don't listen to gossip. People tend to exaggerate things.'

'Possibly. Anyway, that's by the way. The point is more that it's such a big change for William and he will probably feel safer with people he has known for a long time. Don't you agree?'

Martha could see the logic behind Celia's view.

'Put like that, I won't argue with you. You're very kind, Celia.'

Martha realised she was relieved that William didn't have to spend long hours with Frank. It wasn't that she was looking down her nose at the Masons, whatever the truth of the matter, she could never point the finger, but she couldn't help but think that William would end up in all sorts of trouble, left to little Frank's influences. Florrie would understand. It didn't mean that she and her couldn't still be the best of friends. At least she hoped not.

Chapter 19

July 5th 1916

Dear Martha,

Life in the trenches is becoming unbearable. It's allus wet and these damn rats'll be eating us alive given half a chance. Things are getting much worse. We all went over the top a few days ago. You'll have read about it by now I should think. Top brass ordered a massive artillery bombardment on Fritz for the last few days of June. You've never heard such noise in all your life. I thought my ears would burst from it. The sound wouldn't leave me at first. I could hear it all the time. We attacked at seven thirty in the morning on the first of July. We all marched out in lines. They said it would be alright as Fritz was all but finished. We all thought it would be a pushover but it turned out that there were still thousands of them waiting for us. Half the bloody shells we'd thrown at them hadn't exploded. They mowed men down with their machine guns like they were skittles. There's barely a man left in my battalion and quite a few others so we've all been put together and been attached to the 150th. I've a couple of flesh wounds but I'll live so there's no need to worry about me. I've lost Bess. It was after I was hit by shrapnel. I must have been knocked cold by the blast for a while. I think she must be a goner. Maybe she's gone over to the other side to help

Fritz but I doubt it. No-one's had sight of her.

I've never seen so many dead and wounded. They're everywhere. There's no opportunity to bury the poor buggers properly. There's nothing but mud as far as the eye can see now, not a blade of grass or a building for miles.

I understand why you've gone to work at the factory. It hurts to think of you having to do it but a lot of the lad's wives are doing it and I know you wouldn't stand by when we need everyone's help to make more arms. When did you meet Florrie? I'm not too happy about you being around her. I think you should try and make new friends. The Masons are not well thought of and nothing good will come of it.

I miss you Martha. I must be due some furlough soon but I dunna think I'll be allowed to come home.

Give William a big hug from his Da.

Your loving husband

George

George's letter played over in Martha's head as she stood by her machine, one of many, in long, evenly spaced rows across the huge warehouse. How could he be so narrow minded? Florrie had nothing but good things to say about him. It didn't make any sense; there must be more to it. She put it out of her mind as she concentrated on the job in hand. Her foot pressed down on the bar to tighten the chuck that held the cutting tool against the spinning shell. Sparks flew, long ribbons of metal swarf gathered on the floor by her feet. The driving belt that operated each lathe came down from the line shafting that ran the length of the shell shop to where it was driven by an electric motor. The heady smell of cutting fluid invaded her nostrils, cloying and thick. It remained with her night and day, invading her clothes, the sheets on her bed. No amount of bathing and washing seemed to make it disappear fully.

Between each row of lathes were wooden benches where each shell would be placed after she and the other operators had roughed trimmed them. Other women would then gauge and measure each shell before placing it on to a four wheeled truck that could be pushed along to where the shells would then be turned and milled before copper bands were driven into the grooves. The shell cases were heavy to transfer onto the benches and the work was tiring, but today it gave her a sense of purpose as she measured and gauged the shell herself, "*Half the bloody shells hadn't exploded*" The words were ringing in her ears. Was it their fault all those men had died. She couldn't stand by as if nothing had changed. She would speak to Mr Castleton. They needed to improve checking methods. It needed to be done at every stage to ensure the shells went down to the shell filling factory at Chilwell in perfect condition before the explosive was added. She was the one whose strength her family depended upon now. Especially George. She was so worried about him. He wasn't coping anymore. The handwriting had been clumsy. Not at all the neat style he had developed working in the stores at Gray's and been so proud of; more like a child's hand. The thought of all those rats scurrying over dead bodies made her feel physically sick. She hadn't been able to sleep at all last night and had been out of bed and downstairs well before the knocker-upper tapped on the window.

'Penny for 'em,' yelled Florrie over the constant noise, standing a few feet away, doing the same repetitive work.

'Oh... George's latest letter. He doesn't sound very good.' She pulled the envelope out of her overall pocket and waved it. ' I think he's finding it hard. He hasn't had any leave since he went out there.'

Florrie put her hand up to her ear. 'What? I canna hear you.'

'I said it's hard for him. I think they send them away from the line for a rest. Local villages a few miles away.' Florrie stopped her work and came over.

'Freddie has the same problem.'

'I'm sure. The only soldiers I see at home now are either

too wounded to fight or trainees from the camps.'

'I know what you mean. Ma's out of her mind worryin' about Freddie.' She stepped closer to Martha, both women sharing the same feelings of impotence and frustration at not being able to make things better for their loved ones. 'We haven't seen him for nigh on nine months. You'd think they'd enough soldiers for them to come home a bit more often, wouldn't yer.'

Martha put her face to Florrie's ear, shielding her mouth with her hand as she spoke.

'I don't suppose it's that simple. I wish we knew more. It's not easy to work out what's happening properly. The papers all say different things. Some of them say it'll all be over soon and others that we've a long way to go. George says there were a lot of casualties last week where he is. '

'How big is France anyway? They have these maps in the papers but it dunna say how big it is, does it?'

Martha didn't answer. She was staring across the vast warehouse.

'What's up, Martha?' Florrie gave her a nudge.

'What? I...I don't believe it.'

'What is it? '

Martha couldn't stop staring at the man who was walking across the shop floor. Her heart was racing so fast it was difficult to breathe. It couldn't be...could it?

'You'd best shut yer mouth else you'll be catching flies,' said Florrie, her voice flat. 'Good job your George isn't here. You'd have him right jealous.'

'Sorry?' Martha couldn't think straight.

'I said your George wouldn't like the way you're looking at his brother. What's the matter with you?'

'What's he doing here? He lives in Glasgow.'

'Well, whatever the reason, it'll probably involve a woman.' Martha turned to see Florrie's eyes flash as she watched Albert striding alongside the floor manager, Mr Castleton. He was using his stick, but she didn't think Florrie had noticed it as she tried to tidy her unruly red hair and tuck it beneath her cap.

Martha looked away, trying to concentrate on trimming the shell. Her hands were shaking. She needed to be more careful, she couldn't risk injuring herself or damaging the shell case. The men were already critical. The older men were the worst, laughing at their attempts when they first started training them, instead of guiding them. They seemed surprised when some of the women picked it up fairly quickly.

'He's coming over, Martha.' Florrie brushed herself down, pinching her freckled cheeks to add some colour, licking her lips to make them shine, her usual reaction whenever she was anywhere near a handsome young man.

Martha looked up to see Albert scooting through the rows and rows of rough shell cases lining the floor, waiting to be turned and milled. He was smiling and threw her a wave with his free hand. She lifted her hand limply in response.

'Martha, Martha. You look grand, lass. It's good to see you.' Albert held her at arm's length, his eyes scanning every inch of her face. She tried to look away but found herself held under his gaze. She noticed he was wearing an *On War Service* badge. The same as Mr Castleton's and the other men that worked in the factory.

'H...Hello, Albert. It's good to see you, too.' She felt the familiar burst of electricity shoot down through her stomach and swallowed hard, trying to gain some control.

'Hello, Albert'

Albert didn't respond to Florrie's interruption.

'I couldn't believe my luck when the job came up. I jumped at the chance of coming back. Canna imagine what it's going to be like working with a load of women though.' He let out a roar of laughter, finally looking at Florrie and the line of women behind her. 'I'll be spoilt for choice.'

Mr Castleton, who had chased after him, coughed deliberately into his hand. Martha wondered what he might have to say about Albert's actions. He wasn't known for being a lenient boss, and his face looked like he was about ready to explode. Her brother-in-law might find himself sacked before he'd even started properly. Albert apologised and rejoined his guide for a tour of the factory. 'Wait for me after work and I'll walk you home. Can't wait to see young William.' He turned his back before she had time to respond.

Florrie looked at the pink cheeks. 'I can see these girls are not the only ones who thinks he's handsome,' she said. 'You can tell me all about it when we take our break.'

'There's nothing to tell,' Martha snapped and picked up another shell, heaving it into position on the lathe.

'Of course there isn't,' said Florrie and turned away.

Martha felt as if she was standing naked in front of Florrie and the whole factory; her private life bared for all to see. She pulled at the collar of her overalls, her cheeks still burning.

'When did you get back?' Martha asked as they walked side by side. She was feeling uncomfortable and avoided looking at him as she spoke.

'On Friday. I got a train down to Darlington and then had to wait about two hours for a connection. Every station was packed full of soldiers coming down from Glasgow...on their way south for a connection to France.'

He seemed to tower over her and she struggled to match his stride.

'There are so many out there now. It seems like every family is missing someone. A brother, husband...son,' she replied, thinking of Florrie and Sarah. Sarah...it must be a couple of weeks at least, since she'd last seen her. She must go and visit as soon as she got a day off. There hadn't been any time since she'd started work at the munitions factory.

'It's bloody awful, watching them all go. I've been to join up five times with no luck. You'd think they'd have anybody by now. I only got this job 'cos your foreman was conscripted.

' Martha wasn't sure how to respond. Part of her was glad that he hadn't gone, part of her wondering if it might have been better if he had been the one to go and not George. Her thoughts filled with George's letter again. George was doing his best, and no matter how bad he was feeling at the moment, she knew he wouldn't let anybody down. As if reading her thoughts, Albert continued. 'How's George? Have you heard anything lately? Ma said to ask. She worries about him. Not surprising knowing his track record, is it?' He laughed out loud, grinning at her as she swung around to face him.

'Don't you dare say that. At least he's—' She stopped herself short, biting her tongue. Clenching her fists, she passed him the letter and marched ahead, leaving him standing in the street.

'Hey...Martha...' He caught her up outside her house. 'I didn't mean owt by it. I was just saying. '

'Well don't say anymore. George is out there fighting for his country. He's a good soldier, and I'm proud of him.' How dare Albert deride him? He'd no right...no right at all. 'I may not agree with this war, but while he's out there his family...All his family should be right behind him, Albert Hubbard, and if you're not ...I...I don't want to speak to you.'

She turned her back on him, fumbling with the key, trying to open the front door. Confused by the way she was acting. She felt out of control. Albert placed his hand over hers. She dropped the key as if scalded.

'Alreet, lass. Let me,' he said softly, bending down and retrieving the key. He opened the door and Martha flounced inside and headed for the little kitchen. She could still feel his hand on hers and rubbed it vigorously. The feeling wouldn't go away. She stood facing the hearth, her back to the room and him. Albert read the letter. 'I'm sorry for what I said. I'd no right... Martha?...Can we start again?...Please?'

Her shoulders relaxed a little. She could feel his eyes boring into the back of her head. She wasn't ready to turn around yet; her face pink and wet with angry tears; her hands still shaking from his touch. 'He...he's a good man, Albert. A brave man. He deserves your respect.'

'I...I know he does. It's...old habits die hard...I won't make the same mistake again. I promise.'

Martha warmed to the softness in his voice. 'I suppose you'll want some tea before you go back to your lodgings,' she said carefully, trying to control her voice. 'Where are you staying?' she asked as she lifted the kettle and walked over to the sink.

'Over on Wellbeck street. Not the best place I've ever stayed, but it's good to have a room to missel.' He half laughed, searching her face as she turned. 'It's not easy sharing a room with yer whole family. I feel like a sardine sometimes.' He pursed his lips like a fish and waddled around with his arms pinned to his side.

Martha couldn't help smiling and saw the sparkle in his eyes as he grinned back at her. He hadn't changed at all. He was still the big handsome man she tried not to think about. Her hand touched the soft curls of her hair as she felt self conscious and shy. Almost as shy as when they met for the first time all those years ago.

'You look grand, Martha.' His eyes shone and she knew he was remembering the same day.

'I...I'd better go and...and collect William. He'll be wondering where I am,' she stuttered, dashing back to the door. 'Make yourself at home. I won't be long.'

'Martha?...Martha wait...' The door slammed and she was gone.

Martha showed the part of George's letter where he mentioned the unexploded shells to Celia before she headed home. Celia promised to speak to Mr Grey immediately, although she suspected that the military would have been quick to inform all the factories. She also promised swift action by the group in ensuring the union was informed, too.

'Where's Uncle Albert?' asked William when they got home. 'I thought he was staying for tea?'

'He had to go,' answered Martha, reading the note on the kitchen table. 'He'll come another day. Now come and tell me all about school. Did you like it?' Martha's head was still full of Albert. His note was brief, the same untidy, scribbled handwriting she had seen several times before.

Have to get back to my lodgings. They don't like guests being late for meals. Tell William I canna wait to see him. I'll see you at work tomorrow. Yours, Albert.

She traced the last two words with her fingers. Yours, Albert? Was he just being polite? Of course he was, she chided herself. Don't be ridiculous. It's a note, nothing more.

'C'mon, William. You can help me lay the table.' She danced around the room as they worked together; her singing William's favourite song.

'Sweet and low, sweet and low
Wind of western sea,
Low, low, breathe and blow,
Wind of the western sea!
Over the rolling water go,
Come from the dying moon, and blow,
Blow him again to me,
While my little one, while my pretty one, sleeps.

Chapter 20

1910

Martha and George set off for Dene Street. They walked side by side, but Martha was miles away from him, lost in her own thoughts. She'd write a letter to Albert as soon as she got home. She'd tell him about the pregnancy. Tell him she'd be prepared to go to Govan. Marry him up there if he couldn't get much time off work. They could live with his parents for a while. She didn't mind how crowded it would be as long as they were together.

'What's up, Pet? You look as though you've the whole world balancing on your shoulders.' His tone was caring. Martha shrugged her shoulders.

'I'm trying to compose a letter to Albert. Ask him if he's settled in properly. That sort of thing.' She smiled weakly. 'It seems strange having to write to him. I'm used to him being around all the time.'

'Aye. It's strange at home with only me and Granda there now. I wish Walter was still here. I think I miss him more than Ma and Da in a way. I know it's been a while since the accident, but I think about it all the time. Still, no use dwelling on it. It won't bring him back.'

'I was so sorry to hear about it, George. You two were always together. It must be hard for you.' Martha felt guilty for thinking only about herself. 'I hope you get some comfort from your Granda being there.'

'It's alreet, but it wudda been better if he'd moved with them, then I wouldn't have to find so much rent on my own, but he won't budge.'

'It can't be easy for you. What would you do if he did move up there? Go with him?' she asked, glad to be changing the topic of conversation.

'No. I'd rent a small room somewhere. That's all I need. I want to stay here. Besides, Albert asked me to keep an eye on you. Make sure you were alreet.' He winked at her, grinning as he spoke.

'That's kind of you, George, but my parents do a good job of that.' She wondered what they might say about her going to Govan. She imagined how Da would be beside himself. Raging over what had happened. He'd probably insist on moving to Govan, too, rather than lose her... Once he'd come around to the idea.

Martha couldn't concentrate. Mrs Henry was not impressed with her for turning up to work in the same condition as yesterday. The other girls were obviously gossiping about her behind her back, all conversation stopping abruptly as soon as she had walked in this morning.

'You shouldn't be here, Martha. It's not very nice for our clients to have to look at someone as obviously bilious as you are. I've had a word with Mr Turnbull and he agrees with me that you should take the rest of the week off and return next Monday when you're fully recovered. Assuming you are fully recovered by then,' she said, looking over the top of her glasses as they perched precariously on the end of her long, thin nose.

She was sure that Mrs Henry had an idea of what was really wrong with her, but Martha's face didn't betray her as she answered as confidently as she could. 'I'm sure I'll be fine by tomorrow, Mrs Henry. It's must be something I've eaten,' said Martha, but she was grateful to leave a little early and get out into the fresh air. She gathered up her coat and hat as Mrs Henry re-iterated that she must not return until fully recovered and neither she nor Mr Turnbull expected to see her again that week.

Stepping out of the stuffy office and on to a busy Church Street, she was met by the clatter of horses hooves, the clanging of trolley buses at request stops, the rumbling of the trams on the lines and crowds of shoppers. She took a deep breath and filled her lungs. How long did this sickness go on for? She had no idea at all and there was no-one she could ask without giving her secret up. The queasiness began to subside and she found herself milling along in the crowd, passed the tailors and watchmakers, window shopping before coming to a halt outside Grace and Co Clothiers. She stared at the elegant, light grey suit in the window. She liked the simple cut. The hip-length jacket hanging loosely over the skirt. Her hand glided over her stomach involuntarily. Feeling inside her drawstring bag, she pulled out the letter she had written to Albert last night in her bedroom. Would he want her to go to him? Want to marry her? The suit wasn't too expensive and she did have some savings put by. Obviously, a white wedding was now out of the question, but a suit would be good enough for a civil ceremony at the registrars. Ma and Da would be appalled at the thought. She was sure of that, but what was the alternative?

She turned away and stepped off the kerb, so deep in thought she hadn't seen the automobile and nearly jumped out of her skin when the driver honked his horn at her. She dropped her handbag in a puddle in the gutter and burst into tears when she picked it up and found the letter inside it was soaked in dirty water. Pushing it into her pocket, she hurried away in the direction of the dockyard and George.

Martha had been standing outside the gates for around twenty minutes when she heard the horn sound the end of the shift. The mass exodus began almost immediately. Hundreds of men piled out of the huge wrought iron gates. The sound of their boots striking the cobbled road played a heavy rhythm that vibrated through Martha's body from the soles of her feet to the top of her head. It was quite a while before she spotted George amongst the heaving mass, his cap pulled down over his black hair, his jacket flung over his shoulder, engrossed in conversation with two other men. They were laughing and pushing each other in jest as they passed Martha.

'George,' Martha shouted as she stepped forward from the sidelines. 'George,' she shouted a little louder, standing on her tiptoes and using her hands to make a funnel. The three of them turned and saw her.

'Why aye. I reckon you've got an admirer. I wish our lass looked like that,' said one of the men, nudging George in the ribs.

'Ha'way, man. That's Albert's girl, isn't it?' said the other.

'Aye. It is. I'll see yer later.' George joined Martha and they moved away from the entrance. 'What yer doing here, Martha? I said I'd come over to yours when I found the address.'

'I...I thought I'd save you the trouble...I wrote the letter and brought it to work. I was going to go to your house tonight, but Mrs Henry sent me home early and...and then the man sounded his horn and the letter was in the puddle and...' It was all too much for her as nausea and emotion took over. She started to cry.

'Ha'way, Pet. Dunna cry...C'mon. Let's get you out of here.'

George led her away from the rush of workers and led her down a couple of side streets before emerging on Victoria

Terrace and back on to Church Street. 'Let's go to The Royal on the corner; it serves tea and biscuits at this time of day.' Martha followed his lead, grateful that someone was making decisions for her.

They found a table by the bay window in the hotel lounge. It was empty of any guests and Martha took her hat and coat off . A waitress appeared, as if by magic, offering a menu before taking the coat away and hanging it up on a coat rack near the lounge entrance.

'I...I'm sorry. I'm fine now.' She looked into George's concerned face. 'Really. I am. I've not been too well that's all.'

'Let's order tea and we can talk then. I'm not letting you go until you tell me what's wrong.' Martha was in danger of falling apart again as George's soft voice and sympathetic tone unravelled her composure.

'I'm not sure I can tell you, George. It's Albert I need to talk to.'

'You can tell me anything, Martha. You know how much I care for you. Let me help.'

Martha could see he meant every word. He had always been in the background since she had left school and started seeing Albert, trying to please her at every opportunity. Albert laughing at him, saying as how Martha was far too good for him and that he, Albert, was a much better match. Martha had been in love with Albert since the moment they met. She always felt a bit sorry for George but had only ever thought of him as a good friend. A good friend was exactly what she needed right now.

'Oh, George. I don't know what to do. I'm...I'm.'

'Expectin' Albert's bairn?'

Martha eyes were wide and her mouth went slack, dropping open. George took hold of her hand.

'I suspected as much yesterday when you dashed out to the netty. Does he know?' His face coloured and she could see a glint of anger in his eyes as he discovered something else he didn't like about his older brother.

'No...He was so excited about going. I didn't know how to tell him. I've written a letter but I dropped it and I'll have to write another tonight. What if he doesn't want me, George?'

'Course he will, Pet. If he doesn't, he's a fool and doesn't deserve you.'

'You're so kind. It— '

'Tea for two.' The waitress leaned between them, making them release their hold and sit up straight. Martha poured the milk and tea into two pretty china cups and passed one over to George.

'I like this,' he said. 'Me and you out for tea. We should do it again.'

Martha forced a smile. The tea calmed her and relieved the sick feeling. It felt good to have told someone her dreadful secret, had someone to share her problem with. 'Do you think he'll be cross with me?'

'I'll have summat to say about it if he is. He's to blame for this, not you. He shouldn't have taken advantage.'

'It wasn't like that, George. He and I...we...' Martha stopped herself. George's face was turning a deep shade of pink and he was pulling at his shirt collar as if he was too hot. 'I'm sorry. I shouldn't be— '

'I...I've been thinking...Say no if you like, but...Would you like me to write to Albert. Tell him you need him to come home. Say it's urgent...'

Martha grabbed the opportunity.

'Do you think that might work? You'd better not say why. I don't think he'd like me discussing something like this with you. Just say it's urgent and he has to come back. I can tell him when he gets here.' The idea of someone taking responsibility from her filled Martha with relief. Albert might be more likely to come back if George says it's urgent. He may think she was fretting over him again if she wrote. Maybe dropping the letter had been a good thing after all. Her Ma and Da always sorted things out for her and having to tackle something so big by herself had filled her with fear. Now George was there to help sort it all out. She reached out and put her hand on his arm. 'You've no idea how much this means to me, George. Thank you so much.'

'You leave it with me. I'll send a letter first thing tomorrow.

Chapter 21

Martha knocked on Florrie's door.

'Alreet. Alreet. You'll have the door down.' Florrie pulled it wide. 'I dunna know what yer thinkin'. There's folk still asleep. What's the 'mergency?' she asked, stepping outside into the warm morning sun. 'Eeh. It'll be a hot one the day.'

They both squinted at the round yellow ball, fierce and low in the early morning sky.

'It's going to be a beautiful day,' replied Martha, almost skipping along the pavement.

'Stop right now, Martha Hubbard. What's going on? Ah, I know. C'mon spill the beans. What happened?'

'Don't be daft, Florrie. Nothing happened. He had to get back to his lodgings for tea. William didn't even get to see him.' Martha tried to sound matter-of-fact, but Florrie was having none of it.

'Then why are you turning the same colour as my hair?' she asked, a grimace splitting the pale complexion.

'I'm warm. Like you said, "It'll be a hot one the day". C'mon, we'll be late,' she shouted back to her friend and ran to catch up with the lines of people heading up to Gray's.

They entered the gates and waited their turn to 'clock in. Hundreds of women and a few dozen men, all filing in to take their place and do their bit for the military machine of Britain's empire. It was impossible to hear what any one individual was saying, as the whole place was filled with hundreds of workers all talking, laughing and complaining at the same time. Martha was beginning to get the hang of lip-reading after more than a month of working in these conditions. It had been completely different at Turnbull and Tilley solicitors office. Only polite conversation with customers was allowed there. Many of the girls had come from local mills because of the better wages and working conditions. They were used to the hullabaloo and noise and were expert lip-readers already. Each week, more and more married women had taken the leap from stay-at-home mother to munitions worker, and they all seemed to be enjoying the freedom and sense of self worth. That and the extra money it provided, of course.

Martha and Florrie were soon at their stations and threw themselves into their work. It was obvious that action had been taken already. Extra women had been placed at each bench double checking each shell before it was moved on. One of the older men was walking up and down between benches, carrying out random quality checks. It pleased Martha that she had been instrumental in ensuring steps had been taken to improve things. She would tell George in her next letter. Martha kept herself as busy as possible. Mainly, to avoid Florrie's prying questions, but also to stop herself thinking about Albert. She chastised herself for even sparing a minute of her time to think about him when George was away risking his life.

'Slow down a bit. Yoos'll mek me look like a shirker, carryin' on like that.' Florrie came close to Martha to make herself heard.

'Sorry, Florrie. Busy thinking about what to make William for his supper tonight.' Martha didn't stop as she spoke.

'Ha'way, Martha. Do yer think I was born yesterday? I

know what...who yer thinking about. Yer can't kid me. C'mon, tell me. What's the history between you?'

Martha knew she wouldn't stop digging until she got the truth out of her.

'Albert's part of my past. We were seeing each other before George and I became a couple, that's all. I find it a bit awkward seeing as they're brothers.'

'If you'll take my advice yoos'll stay well clear of him. He's trouble, Martha. Allus has been. You'll only get hurt.'

Martha turned away. That was the second time Florrie had suggested that Albert was not a very nice person? What did she know about him? She sometimes found Florrie's ability to be so forthright and outspoken hard to take. Sooner or later she would worm the truth out of her. Her mind cast back to what Celia had said about her friend. Maybe she should tell her everything.

It was mid afternoon before she caught sight of him. He had been in the little wooden office at the other side of the warehouse all morning. Mr Castleton must have been going through all of Albert's duties and the rules and regulations, Martha thought. She had found herself constantly looking over and had seen a young girl of about ten or eleven go into the office. Now Albert was heading in her direction.

He stopped short of her and Florrie and spoke to a woman busy measuring one of the shells. The woman, who had smiled at Albert, suddenly put her head in her hands and Albert put his hand on her arm before leading her away. The woman was obviously crying and no-one needed to be told what had happened. Martha looked over to Florrie and they both nodded to each other, eyes shining with sympathy. Both women's thoughts turned to their own loved ones.

Martha didn't see Albert again and he wasn't waiting for her when she left work at six. She hurried to Celia's house to collect William before going around to visit Sarah. She wanted to hear that all was well with Edward but also to talk to her about George. Despite getting distracted by Albert's return, seeing that poor woman at work had made her anxious to see her dear friend who had done so much for her since her parents died. Sarah would know what to say to reassure her. So like her own mother, Sarah had a knack of putting things in perspective, making them seem less traumatic somehow.

'C'mon in, Martha. I'm reet glad to see yer...and you, young man.' Sarah took William's hand and led him in to the kitchen. Joe was sitting at the familiar wooden table eating a plate of potatoes and two large sausages. William's eyes glazed over as usual and Sarah laughed as she pulled out one the chairs. 'Up yer get then, lad. No need to ask what you want.'

'Honestly, William. I can't take you anywhere,' chided Martha.

'Nothing wrong with a good appetite. You sit yourself down too, and I'll dish up. There's enough for all of us.' Martha looked surprised. Sarah smiled and continued. 'I still canna get used to cooking for two.'

'You've done us both a favour; otherwise me and Ma'd be eating the same meal for two days in a row again,' Joe said, between mouthfuls.

'That's very kind, Sarah. Say thank you, William.'

'Thank you, Sarah. I had some cake at Daisy's as well. Have you got any cake, Sarah?'

'Don't be rude, William. I'm sorry, Sarah..,' she started to say, but Sarah and Joe were both laughing and William was grinning from ear to ear.

After the meal, Joe took William outside. 'Yer can help me clear up the stalls and put them away now you've grown a bit.' William nearly fell over his own feet in his rush to follow him.

'What's the matter, Lass? I can tell summat's troubling you.'

Martha passed Sarah the letter and waited until she'd finished reading it.

'I can see why yer worried. He must be somewhere on the Somme. I was reading about it in the Daily Mail. That's where all the fighting is concentrated at the moment. You need to have faith in him, Martha, he's sensible and he won't be taking any unnecessary risks. Not when he's got you and William to come home to. You remember that, and while you keep getting letters, you know he's alreet.'

'I wish they'd send him home for a spell. He hasn't been home for such a long time. I'm sure if he could get a few days leave, he'd brighten up a bit. He sounds so low in his letter.'

'Aye. I'm sure that's the answer, and he says he must be due some, although he's not hopeful he'll get sent back home. Keep yer chin up. He needs you to be strong for him. Tell him all about yer job and how well William's doing at school. That's what he needs to hear from you. Don't let on yer worried 'cos that'll only make him more low than he is already.'

'You're right, Sarah. I shouldn't be moaning at all. I need to let him know we're fine. I'll write to him tonight.' Martha fed on Sarah's suggestions. She could always make her see sense. 'Tell me about Edward. What's happening with him? What about the age thing?'

'He's alreet for the time being. He's in a camp away from the front line. They won't let him home though on account of him being nearly nineteen. He says he'll get sent back up the line as soon as he's had his birthday. At least it gives me a couple of months without worrying.'

'That's good news then...I think.'

'Better than nothing I s'pose. Tell me about Gray's. Do you like it?'

'I do. I feel as though I'm doing something to help and it's nice to have company all day. I've made a friend. Florrie Mason. She used to work on the butcher's stall.'

'I remember. Full mop of red hair. Bit of a loudmouth, but

a good lass all the same. Didn't she have a twin brother? Oh... and a sister whose parentage is a bit suspect. Aye that's the one'

'Her twin is over in France. He's a year older than George.'

'Aye, that's right. I'm not surprised George thinks you should make new friends though. Allus felt a bit sorry for her Da...Having to bring up someone else's child. '

'I think George is being a bit narrow minded.' Sarah had obviously not heard the other rumour about Florrie. Maybe it was only gossip after all. 'I'm not so sure it's true...Florrie doesn't think it's true. Poor Violet, it must be hard for her. Tell me about Joe. How's he getting on with the job?' Martha turned the subject away from the Masons, sorry she mentioned Florrie at all.

'He's doing a grand job and he can add up that quick. No-one'll ever pull the wool over his eyes when it comes to money,' she answered and Martha could hear the pride in her voice.

'That's good to hear, he always was a clever lad...You'll never guess who the new foreman is at work. Jack Gladstone got called up and they had to get someone else.' Martha thought it better to tell Sarah about Albert's homecoming before she saw him and then wondered why she hadn't said anything. Anyway, there was no reason why Sarah shouldn't be fully aware of his presence. There was nothing to hide.

'I think I can guess. Joe saw Albert going into the Star last night with some of the fellas from the dockyard.' Sarah looked intently at Martha's face before adding. 'Be careful, Martha. Be careful.'

'What do you mean? I...'

William and Joe burst through the door before Martha had time to think of an appropriate response.

'I told Joe all about school, Ma. He says I'm a good helper and I can come again. Look. He gave me a penny. All for me.' William held the coin up as if it were a fortune.

'Well, young man, it looks like you've earned your first

wage. We'll have to tell Da all about it in a letter, won't we?'

'Ooh. Yes, Ma. Can I help write it? Can I? We can tell him I worked hard for Joe. Didn't I, Joe. Didn't I? Tell Ma, Joe.'

'You did, William. You did.'

They all laughed, but Martha couldn't look at Sarah. She manoeuvred William towards the door. 'It's getting late,' she said.

It was after nine o-clock when they walked back home. Turning into their street, she could see the glow from a cigarette and the silhouette of a man leaning on the wall next to her door. She recognised Albert's face in the dull pool of yellow light from the gas lamp as she got nearer. He stood upright to greet her and William.

'I thought yer must be staying out the night,' he said. 'A bit late for you, lad.'

'Uncle Albert. I've been helping Joe in the market yard. He gave me a penny. Look!' he said pulling the coin out of his pocket and waving it about.

'Yer must have worked hard for that,' he said, squatting down to William's level. 'Yer Ma'll be reet proud of yer, won't she?' He looked up at Martha and her stomach made the usual, involuntary somersault.

'C'mon, it's time you were in bed, William,' she said opening the door.

They trooped inside and through to the kitchen.

'Can I stay up a bit longer, Ma? I need to tell Uncle Albert about school. Can I, Ma? Please?' he pleaded.

'I tell you what,' interrupted Albert. 'You go and get in bed and I'll be up in a minute to say goodnight and yer can tell me all about it then. Is that alreet, Martha?'

'I s'pose so. Go on. Up those stairs right now and don't be talking to your Uncle Albert all night.

'I won't, I promise.' William scampered up the steep stairs as fast as he could.

Martha turned to Albert.

'It's a bit late for calling. You'll have the neighbours talking.' She was trembling and hoped he hadn't noticed.

'It's a bit much if a man canna call on his brother's wife,' he answered, his rich tones spreading over her like a blanket. He pulled a small bottle of whisky from his pocket and placed it on the table. 'I'll go and settle the boy and be reet back.' His arm brushed against hers as he passed her and took the stairs two at a time. Martha took hold of the back of a chair as she felt herself grow faint.

'Where's your glass?' He asked, pouring himself a shot when he came back downstairs.

'I don't usually drink,' she answered. 'I don't like it that much. Besides I have to be up early for work in the morning.'

'So do I. C'mon, Martha. We can drink a toast to George. It's a peace offering for what I said the other day. Just a small one. It won't hurt.'

She didn't want him to think she was still cross and he was right. One wouldn't hurt. Then she could ask him to go.

She brought another glass and poured herself a very small drink. 'To George,' she said, raising the glass.

Albert poured himself another and followed her lead. 'To George. May he come home safely to his beautiful wife...and son. How old is William?' he asked as they tipped their glasses and drank.

Martha almost choked as the drink slid back, her throat burned so that she could hardly breathe. What had made him ask that? She coughed, gasping for air and coughing again.

Albert patted her back sharply, which made her cough even more. He took her glass and filled it with water. She grabbed it from his hands and drank deeply. Her cough subsided, but her eyes watered and her cheeks looked as if someone had given her a good slap.

Albert started to laugh. She glowered at him but soon found herself doing the same.

'I'll know better than offer you a drink again. You looked like you were going to explode like a tomato with stick a dynamite inside it.'

'Sssh! You'll be waking William up with all your noise.' She tried to chastise him but collapsed into a chair, laughing at the thought.

Albert held his stomach, bent double with laughter. All the tension between them was tumbling out and disappearing. The more she laughed, the better she felt.

'I haven't laughed this much since...since...' He stopped laughing and went over to her. Pulling her up from the chair he grabbed her face between his rough hands and kissed her. He tasted of whisky and tobacco. It took her a second or two to realise what was happening.

'Nooo...' She pushed him away as hard as she could, staggering backwards. 'Get out. Get out now,' she cried, turning her back on him.

'I...I'm sorry...I didn't mean...I thought that was what you wanted.'

'Of course not. George is my husband.' She stepped away from him.

'My mistake,' he said before leaving the room. She heard the front door slam behind him.

Martha brought her fingers up to her lips. She could still feel his lips on hers, taste him inside her mouth.

'Yer a bit quiet, Martha. Summat happened?' Florrie patted Martha's arm to get her attention.

'No...I...,' Martha was finding it difficult to speak. Her head was swimming from lack of sleep. How could she have let it happen? She loved George with all her heart. Albert had no part in her life now. How could he think...? Because she had behaved like a lovesick girl, that's how. Getting all flustered every time he looked at her... If it hadn't been for the thought of losing her job, she would have stayed at home today. She prayed he wouldn't come over and speak to her. The guilt would be plain for all to see. She was going to have to tell Florrie. That girl could sniff out scandal a mile off.

'I'll tell you later. Come to mine tonight. Make sure it's well after seven and I've had time to put William to bed.'

Florrie nodded.

'I'll be there,' she said.

There was no sign of Albert all day. Obviously he had made a good enough excuse not to be there. She kept her head down, ignoring any questions that Florrie threw at her. She didn't even go and sit down with the other girls in the canteen at lunchtime. They were bound to see the big sign that was etched on her forehead. The one that read *Adulteress.*

Martha flew downstairs. She glanced at the small round clock on the mantelpiece above the range. It was five minutes past seven. Florrie was obviously beside herself with curiosity, she thought, dashing to the door.

'About time. I thought you'd gone out.' Florrie marched in. She was still wearing her work overall. Martha had changed into a plain skirt and white blouse. 'Ooh. I didna think we were getting dressed up. Are we going out?'

'No...I always change after ...'

'Do you? I canna be mithered.' She poked her head in the door of the front parlour. 'Yoos've got it lovely, Martha. I wish I had my own place. Drives me mad. Never any peace in our house.'

'I put a bit away every week and get something when I can afford it. Come through to the back room. I always sit in there.' Martha led the way.

'This is reet cosy an' all.' She sat down and Martha made a pot of tea. 'C'mon then. Spill the beans.'

Martha was having second thoughts about confiding in Florrie.

'I don't know why I was making such a fuss this morning. It's nothing really. I...'

'It's about Albert, isn't it? Yer can tell me, Martha. I might be a loud mouth, but I can keep a secret.'

'He...well...he came round and... I'm sorry, this is a bad idea.'

'Look, Martha. I don't judge anybody. With a family like mine, I've no right. Sometimes it's better to get things off yer chest. You'll feel better and it'll stay between these four walls. You have my word.'

Florrie seemed genuine. It would make Martha feel better if she could tell someone. She couldn't tell Sarah. It would be like telling her own Ma. She didn't want Sarah to think badly of her. She hoped that Florrie was telling the truth and wouldn't tell anyone else.

'Albert came round last night.'

'Yes, you said. And? Go on.'

'He brought a small bottle of whisky with him...said it was to toast George...I don't know how it happened. One minute we were laughing and the next he...he...'

'Did he force himself on you?' Florrie asked holding her hand up to her mouth.

'No....No...Of course not. He...He kissed me.'

Florrie slumped back down in her seat.

'Oh...is that all?'

'Is that all? How can you say that? I'm a married woman. I feel so ashamed.' Martha's eyes filled with tears.

'Ha'way with you. I know lots of married women who've had a quick kiss from an admirer after a couple of drinks. There's nothing so bad about that...not unless you wanted him to...wanted more?' Her voice became more earnest, eyes darting as she tried to work out Martha's words.

'That's the thing. I don't know...we ...I was in love with him before...' Martha looked down at the table, unable to look at Florrie. 'He left me...George was so kind and gentle.'

'That's George all ower. Allus wanting to make things right. Is that why you married him? I knew he was in love with you. I used to watch the way he looked at you when you started going out with Albert. He were that jealous. Eeh, Martha. Do you still love him? Albert?'

'No...I don't know...I think so. How well do you know him? You keep saying what a bad person he is.'

'Oh...Not that well. Only from what George used to tell me. He...George...he was allus very kind to me too. Helped me through a bad time.'

Martha watched Florrie's eyes mist over. The girl must have cared for George very much at one time. She didn't feel jealous, only pleased that someone else knew his worth.

'I know better than most how kind he is. I love George so much. I can't hurt him.'

'What are you going to do now then? About Albert? Yer still going to work at the munitions, aren't you? I'd miss you if you left.'

'I need the money, Florrie. I don't know what to do? What do you think I should do?'

'Well, I think you'd better tell him not to come here again. You obviously can't trust yersel to resist him, can yer?' Florrie spoke in a low voice. 'You've got to forget him. You canna betray George. He doesn't deserve that.

Chapter 22

It was now a week into August and the weather was warm but cloudy. Light winds from the sea kept it cool enough to warrant a jacket or sweater in the evenings. The number of women coming to work wearing a black armband had exploded in the last couple of weeks as green envelopes were handed out in their hundreds, street by street, all over town. Martha prayed each night for George and Edward and even Freddie, so thankful that neither herself, Sarah nor Florrie were wearing one. The latest letter from George had dashed any hopes of him coming home on leave for the foreseeable future. Every man was needed at his post.

All the papers were full of the battles raging on The Somme, and it was fairly obvious that was where George was stationed from his descriptions of what was going on. There was a sense of desolation in his letters now, as though he had given up hope of ever living a life where peace reigned. There didn't appear to be anything left of the man who had come home on leave more than a year ago. His words were full of despair and grief for his fellow soldiers. Casualties were high and he had said there seemed to be no end in sight.

Albert had kept his distance and although she told herself it was for the best, she found herself searching him out whenever she could find a good enough reason. Florrie was as good as her word and never mentioned the situation and she was sure she hadn't gossiped to anyone else.

Florrie and Martha left work together and walked over to Celia's house to collect William.

'I'll be glad of a day off. Sam Pritchard's taking me to see a film tonight and we're off out for a day in Darlington tomorrow.'

Martha was glad Florrie's new friend had been given the opportunity to start work at the factory a couple of weeks ago. He had been honourably discharged from the army after being treated on the front line and eventually sent home on a hospital ship. His treatment in Hartlepool General had been slow and it had taken time before he was considered physically fit enough to return to civilian life. His disability made it difficult for the manager to find something suitable, but he proved his worth pushing the little trucks of shells from worker to worker, process to process.

'That'll be nice, Florrie. He seems a kind sort of a chap.'

He was a tall young man with a crown of thick black hair that never seemed to have even one strand out of place. He had a smile that showed off a set of tombstone teeth that were perfectly straight and even. Apart from an empty jacket sleeve, his injuries remained hidden from general view. Florrie had been so taken by him that he seemed to fill her thoughts night and day. He obviously had similar feelings towards her, always stopping to chat on passing her machine. Some of the other girls teased her about it and all the attention delighted her. While everyone was looking at Florrie, Martha felt less like a target for people's comments and she relaxed a little in her attempts to hide the fact that she blushed every time Albert came into view.

'He's a bit more than kind, Martha, and now that I've got used to him only having one arm it doesn't seem to matter. I allus make sure I'm on his left side afore I try and link up,' said Florrie almost singing out her words.

'There are so many coming home with limbs missing. It makes me angry and sad that some of them will never be able to work again.'

'Well Sam's not sad. Sez he'd rather be home with one arm than buried in a field in France where no-one'll ever find him. He's still as quick as a man with two hands though. I spend most of time trying to keep me blouse buttoned up in the picture house. Well...unless I'm in the mood for a bit of hanky-panky. Then I don't try quite so hard.' Her laughter rang out as they arrived at Celia's.

Martha grinned as she knocked on the door.

'Don't be saying things like that when William is with us. He'll be asking me all sorts of questions.'

'Why did Florrie go so early, Ma? I like it when she has tea with us. She makes me laugh,' said William as he undressed and slipped into his nightshirt.

'She's going out tonight.'

'Where's she going? Can we go out?'

'None of your business where she's going, young man, and no we can't. You've got school in the morning and I have to go to work.'

'Aah. We never go out. Can we go to Sarah's when you have a day off again? Please, Ma?'

'Only if you're a good boy and go straight to sleep.' She kissed him on his forehead as she tucked the blankets around him. 'Goodnight, William. Sleep well.'

It was still light outside, and the sound of older children playing in the street came and went as Martha stood by the stone sink, washing underclothes and William's shirts. By the time she had finished, and hung them over the drying rack suspended from the ceiling, it was growing dark and the sounds from the street had gone. She lit the lamp on the kitchen table and sat down to darn William's socks before turning in.

She must have dozed for a while and shivered as she woke with a start. She took the lamp and started up the stairs. What was that noise, she wondered. She could hear a droning sound somewhere off in the distance. By the time she was undressed and in her nightgown, the sound was much louder. Curious, Martha went to the window and looked out. The sky was black, clouds covering the moon. She was sure the noise was somewhere above her and then came the whining, whistling sound that she hadn't heard in nearly two years.

'William, William,' she screamed, running into his room. 'Get up. Quick.'

She dragged him from his bed, half asleep, and raced downstairs as the first explosion shook the house. They raced outside to see flames rising from somewhere in the next street. As they grew ever taller and lit up the night sky, the Zeppelin became visible high above them, a ship sailing through a black ocean. Another explosion echoed as a second bomb landed in a nearby field. They ran in the opposite direction. People were dashing out of their homes in whatever they happened to be wearing. Children were crying as they were dragged in their bare feet along the streets. The sound of the Zeppelin eventually grew quieter as it moved away. The battery guns over at Heugh peppered the sky with ground to air fire. People stood in the streets for a long time, huddled in groups, frightened to go home for at least a couple of hours.

As dawn slipped in and brought some comfort, people made their way back home again. Martha saw Albert waiting by her door. He threw his cigarette down and hurried towards her, picking William up and holding him close. 'Thank God. I thowt you must be safe, but I needed to see you afore I went home. Had to be sure,' he said.

'We're fine.' Martha was glad he was there. 'We've been waiting until we thought it was safe to come back.'

'Let's get you inside,' he said, ushering both of them

through the front door. It felt good to have a man looking after them, she thought. Albert lit the range and filled the kettle.

Martha warmed some milk for William before tucking him up in bed again and sitting with him until he had dropped off to sleep. When she came back downstairs, Albert was pouring the tea.

'It might be August but it's cold enough to be autumn at this time of a morning,' he said, trying not to look her full in the face. Martha sat down and cupped the mug in her hands.

'Thank you,' she said quietly.

'What for? It's only a mug of tea.'

'For...for being here when we got home. I wasn't looking forward to coming in on my own.'

'Aye, well...It were nothing. I was worried about William...and you of course. George wudna forgive me if I didn't look out for both of you.' He sounded so sincere. His brow was furrowed with worry and his eyes were misty.

'I'm grateful, Albert.' She reached across the table and touched his arm. 'Truly grateful.'

Albert placed his free hand over hers. 'I don't know what I'd do if anything happened to William...you, Martha.' She pulled her hand away, but he snatched hold of it again.

'I...I'm not sure we..,' she stuttered.

'I can't help it. I can't stop thinking about you,' he said, looking at the floor.

'We can't, Albert... I can't...its wrong—' and then he was leaning forward, kissing her and this time, she had neither the strength nor the will to pull away.

Albert pulled her onto his lap. He kissed her until she couldn't breathe and had to tear herself free.

'You...need to go now,' she whispered into his neck.

'I know...I know.' He stood up slowly, still holding on to her, pulling her to his chest. 'I love you, Martha Hubbard.'

I love you too, Albert Hubbard, she said to herself as he kissed the top of her head and left her standing in the middle of the kitchen, shaking from head to foot.

Chapter 23

'Would you like to play marbles again, Uncle Albert? I'll try not to beat you this time. I'm very good at it, aren't I?'

'You are, are you? We'll see about that,' laughed Albert as William took his hand and pulled him through the back door and into the shared yard.

She was suddenly aware of how much William had grown over the last few months; losing the last of his baby features. The plump cheeks and dimples had gone, leaving a narrow face. The chubby legs were now spindly and long, the arms wiry. Her baby had been stolen and replaced with a young boy.

'I'll shout you when dinner's ready,' she said as Albert looked back at her, feigned helplessness on his face at being dragged outside.

Her heart was pounding. They looked so natural together. William talking ten to the dozen about anything and everything, so glad to have a man about the place.

So what if people talked? There was no harm in a brother-in-law taking an interest in his nephew and his brother's wife, was there? She tried to convince herself that it was perfectly alright. They weren't doing anything wrong. He always left at a reasonable hour, making sure that the next door neighbours heard him go, heard William shouting "Goodnight, Uncle Albert" as he went. She was happy to have him near, watch him play with William, listen to his laugh, the laugh that stole her heart many years ago when they were so much younger. She could settle for this, she told herself. It was enough.

'That's cheating,' yelled William, jumping up. 'Ma, tell Uncle Albert. He's not playing fair and square. Tell him. You allus tell me I have to play fair and square.'

Albert held his hands up.

'You caught me out. I won't cheat again, I promise,' he said, winking at Martha as she looked on through the kitchen window.

'It's not about winning, Uncle Albert. It's about taking part. Isn't that right, Ma? Tell him.' William was standing, hands on hips, his face totally serious.

Martha stifled a giggle. 'You're absolutely right, William. You had better behave, Uncle Albert, or I might have to send you home early.' She wagged her finger at him to add effect.

'Aah. Don't send him home, Ma. He didn't mean it. Did you, Uncle Albert?' William's voice started to tremble.

'I didna mean it, Ma. I won't do it again. Please don't send me home.' Albert said in a squeaky voice, holding his hands up in a prayer position. Martha had to turn away before the laughter burst out.

'Well...just this once..,' she half coughed into her hand, her back to the pair of them. 'Dinner in five minutes.'

It had been quite a while since her last letter from George. The post mustn't be getting through, she thought. Angry with herself for not noticing sooner, her head always full of other things these days; other people.

'Have you heard anything from Freddie?' she asked Florrie, who was busy watching Sam wheeling his parts up and down the lanes.

'Aye. He's so tired. Can't sleep at nights or during the day. He sez everyone's had enough of it all. It's raining buckets all the time as well now that autumn's here.'

'I haven't heard from George for over a month. It was at the beginning of August when he last wrote. He didn't sound so good then.'

'I'm sure he'll be fine. They're all a bit down at the moment. Freddie had a spell when he didn't write, but he started again after a couple of months. Said he'd been a bit fed up.'

Martha wasn't so sure. His last two letters had suggested that he was very low. She wondered whether to write to his regiment and ask after him. She hadn't talked to Albert about it. She couldn't. It was too uncomfortable for both of them. He never mentioned George at all now. Except when William brought him up in conversation and then he would try and change the subject. It seemed the best way to ease their conscience. Out of sight, out of mind. Guilt crept through her, gnawing at her insides. What was she doing? She almost felt as if Albert was her husband. He was the one here. He was the one who took them out, who played with her son. He was the one who acted like a father to William, a husband... in all but one way. The one way that she craved now. Desperate for his touch, his kiss...his.. everything that constituted a marriage between a man and a woman. She was jealous of Florrie's relationship with Sam, jealous that her friend was free to declare her love openly. He had asked her to marry him and she now sported an engagement ring to confirm his intentions. How different her engagement to George had been. How unreal it had all seemed.

It was a fine Sunday in late October and they were enjoying a rare day off work, playing on the beach. It made such a pleasant change from the noisy and sometimes chokingly smoky atmosphere of the factory. Martha had developed a chesty cough over the last couple of weeks and was glad to be able to breathe properly in the fresh air. The camphor oil she had bought was also helping and she kept a woollen scarf around her neck to protect it. The crowds were out in force, making the most of the powder-blue skies. Not quite parasol weather, but warm enough for a stroll along the promenade or fishing for crabs and other sea-creatures in the rock pools.

The ice-cream seller had cycled over from the town square and parked up his brightly coloured cart to sell his home-made Neapolitan and vanilla cones. He sang Italian songs as he served each customer, twirling his moustache between his fingers; making the children laugh. Holding each little girl's chin in his hand, he effused over their beauty. 'Bella. Bella, little bambina,' he said in a kind voice when giving them a cone. The queue trailed back for almost two hundred yards.

Martha and William were sitting on the sand making castles while Albert stood in the queue.

'Is he nearly there yet?' asked William.

'About halfway I think,' replied Martha shielding her eyes as she looked up. 'He won't be long now.'

'Good. I'm thirsty.'

'Make sure you mind your manners, William. Say thank you when Uncle Albert comes back.'

'Yes, Ma,' he answered in a long drawn out tone. 'I allus use my manners. I'm a big boy now.'

'I know. I was only reminding you.' Martha looked up towards the promenade again. She could see that Albert was talking to someone. The light from the afternoon sun was too bright and she couldn't make out who it was. Turning back to William she helped him to create his castle.

'Let's try and finish it before the ice-cream comes,' she said and the pair worked furiously, shaping the castle and moulding turrets.

'Look who I found on the promenade.' Albert settled down beside her and handed out the three ice-creams.

'Sarah,' shouted William as he licked the drip off his cone. 'Look what I've done. It's a castle. Neddy is going to live in it.' He pulled his favourite little horse from his pocket and placed it inside the castle walls. 'He's the King's horse.'

'Hello, strangers,' Sarah panted, 'I thowt it was yoos two I could see down here, but it's that long since I've seen you, I couldn't be sure. Albert says yer all having a day out.' She raised her eyebrows, looking straight down at Martha.

'Y...Yes. Albert's been kind enough to accompany us.' Martha could feel a blush forming on her cheeks.

'That was kind of him.'

'Ha'way, Sarah. It's nothing. I'm only doing what anyone would do for his family. I'm only making sure nowt happens to 'em while George is away.'

'I'm sure,' she replied, still looking at Martha. 'How is George? You haven't been round much lately. What's the latest news?'

Martha glanced at Albert, what should she say?

'Da hasn't sent a letter for ages. Ma thinks there's summat up with the post,' piped up William between licks.

'I'm sure that's the answer,' said Martha quickly, but she could feel Albert's eyes on her.

'How long exactly?' he asked.

'I...I'm not sure. A few weeks, I think. It must be the post, else I'd have heard from his regiment.' She looked from one to another. 'It must be.'

'Aye, yer probably right, Pet. Dunna worry about it.' Sarah smiled at her. 'Yoos'll probably get six letters all in one go. That happened to a friend of mine. Nothing for eight weeks and then twelve all on the same day. It took her a week to read them.'

Martha forced a laugh that set her off coughing. Albert patted her back and she tried to wriggle free; embarrassed in front of Sarah.

'That's... what I was thinking... No...No need to worry for nothing is there?' she spluttered as best she could, her hand held against her mouth.

'Have you taken anything for that cough, Pet? It dunna sound reet good. Come round when you've got time. I've got some medicine that might help to shift it. I'll have to be off. Make Joe's tea...He misses young William and it's probably time we had a chat.' Sarah nodded at Albert and walked away, dragging her feet through the loose sand. All the weight she lost after Robert died seemed to have been put back on, thought Martha, watching Sarah fight her way back up to the promenade. She pretended to watch her for a while, shielding her eyes, not wanting to turn back to Albert.

'Why didn't you tell me?'

Martha turned to face him.

'I didn't want to worry you. What's the point of getting all het up if there's nothing wrong?'

'What if he's missing in action? What if he's injured?'

'Now you're talking silly. He can't be hurt or missing. I'd have known.'

'Is Da hurt?' William stood up and put his hand on Martha's shoulder. His bottom lip was trembling. His eyes starting to fill.

'No, William. We would have heard if he was. There's no need to get upset.' She hugged his waist to her. 'Is there, Uncle Albert?' she hissed through her teeth.

'No, lad. I was being silly. Yer Ma's right. Nothing to worry about at all.'

'Let's go home.' Martha coughed again as she stood. Albert reached out to steady her but she moved away. Sarah's visit had brought her crashing down to earth. She felt so ashamed she wanted to cry.

Chapter 24

Sarah spooned the mixture out of a large bottle and offered it to Martha.

'It's made from onions, honey and ginger. My mother taught me how to make it.'Martha set her face, squinting, ready for something revolting, as she opened her mouth. Memories of some foul concoction, her mother used to swear by, came to mind. Fiery hot with horseradish, it used to burn her lips even before it got inside her mouth and scalded her tonsils. The worst thing was that it never seemed to work and Martha would feel doubly, badly done to.

The metal was cold on her tongue as Sarah slid the spoon in. To Martha's surprise, it tasted sticky, quite pleasant and it warmed the back of her throat. The sharp pain and tickle was soothed almost immediately.

'Thank you, Sarah. It's good of you to come over.' Martha had guessed that Sarah would be knocking on her door within twenty four hours if she hadn't been across to her house. She had asked Albert to stay away and William wasn't too happy. He liked to spend time with Uncle Albert and had complained bitterly when it was time for bed and he hadn't seen him at all.

'Now then. Let's get down to it. What are you playing at?'

'Sorry? I don't know what you mean?' Martha turned back to the clothes she was folding. She had a slight fever and her head was feeling light and spinning a little.

'I'll spell it out then, shall I? What's going on with you and Albert?'

'He told you. He's looking out for me and William. There's nothing more to it than that.' Martha felt her temperature rise a little more and opened the door to the yard. The cold night air blew in and Sarah wrapped her shawl tight around her.

'Yer'll catch yer death, girl. Shut the door. Do you want pneumonia?'

'I'm too hot. I need some fresh air.'

'Stop changing the subject.' Sarah slammed the door closed. 'It'll come to no good yer know. What about George? What happens when he gets home?'

'He'll be glad I had Albert here to look out for us. That's what,' Martha snapped before a coughing bout had her bent double.

'Martha, Pet? Yer not well. You need to be in bed.' Sarah's tone softened as she took the laundry from her and placed it on the table. 'Ha'way to yer bed. I'll bring you a hot toddy up. Go on, I'm not arguing with you.'

Martha hadn't the energy to fight back and did as she was told. Sarah put the kettle on and took some honey and a small bottle of whisky from the basket she had brought with her. It was going to be a long night.

'Can I stay at home with, Ma?' asked William, wolfing down the last of the bowl of porridge.

'Sorry, lad, no. Daisy'll be here for you in a minute. She'll tek yer to school as normal and I'll stay here to look after your ma.' The knock at the door came soon after and William left with Daisy to go to Celia's.

Martha had been listening, glad Sarah had made William

go to school. She didn't want him around her for a while, didn't want him to catch whatever it was she was suffering from. She heard Sarah coming upstairs. Her head ached and she felt weak as she tried to sit up.

'Lay down, Lass. Yer won't be going anywhere the day.'

'I've got to send a message to work. I can't stay in bed.' She tried to sit up again, but her head started to spin and she fell back on the pillow. 'I'll get the sack. Someone needs to tell them.'

'Joe's gone. He came looking for me last night. I told him I'd be staying a while 'til you were fit.'

'I'm sorry to be a trouble to you, Sarah. Where did you sleep?' she asked, not noticing the pillow and blanket on the floor at the end of her bed.

'Dunna worry about that. You get yersel well again. Yer were out for the count last night. Dripping wet. I had to change the sheets twice.'

'Really? I don't remember anything.'

'Yer were shouting out in yer sleep as well. Crying and such.'

'What...What was I saying?' Martha asked.

'Nothing I didn't already know,' she said, 'I'll be downstairs if you need me.'

Martha lay still and closed her eyes. She could hear the huffs and puffs of Sarah going back downstairs. The familiar smell of hot water and carbolic soap wafted up and around the bedroom. She should have known she'd be washing the sheets. Such a kind person, she didn't deserve her.

The thought of Sarah being disappointed with her hurt as much as it would have if she'd been her real mother. Her head was bursting with the pain of fever and emotion; Fear, shame, guilt, all raining down on her. She buried her head in the pillow, trying to block it out, and sobbed herself to sleep.

Something... some noise had woken her. The room was dark.

The sound of someone knocking on the door was followed by hushed voices, then William shouting.

'Uncle Albert.'

She could picture her son racing to greet him and then Albert would pick him up and twirl him around. Exactly has it had been every night for the last few weeks.

'Hush, William. Yer ma's sleeping.' Sarah's voice sounded brusque as she chided him.

'Sorry, Sarah, it was my fault,' replied Albert. 'I was calling to see how she was. Joe said you were having to stay. Is she reet bad?' Martha felt her heart flutter as she heard the concern in his voice.

'I'm not asleep,' she called but her voice was barely a whisper. Her throat burned and she felt herself drift away as the room turned black again.

The next time she woke it was light...so bright that it hurt her head to look. Closing her eyes again, she half remembered Sarah sitting over her...bathing her forehead with a cool, damp cloth. She remembered Sarah's voice, soft and calming. There was another voice? Who was that? He was whispering to Sarah. She couldn't make out the words. She remembered the taste of the onion and honey and ginger, soothing and warm. She remembered William shouting "Uncle Albert" and opened her eyes again, wincing and blinking.

Martha struggled until she was sitting up. The throbbing across her forehead was almost unbearable, as if someone had pushed a nail in and was hammering it into position.

Sarah appeared in the doorway.

'I thought I heard you moaning. Dr Bartholomew came last night. Yer were that poorly, I sent Albert to fetch him. He's coming back this morning to see how you are.'

'Albert?'

'No. Dr Bartholomew. He reckons it's probably influenza. Apparently it's rife in the trenches and it's spreading across the country. I told Albert to leave you be until yer up an' about again. Yer dunna need him pesterin' while yer on yer back.'

Martha didn't respond. She was in no fit state to argue and she wouldn't anyway. Sarah was who she needed, the one who she wanted right now, the one who would look after her and William properly.

'Do you think you could manage a bit of soup, Lass? It'll do yer good?'

'Maybe when my head stops hurting.'

'Here, the doctor left some aspirin for the pain,' Sarah answered, picking up the small packet on the little table next to the bed. Martha opened her mouth as Sarah opened the sachet and poured it onto her tongue. She passed a glass of water as Martha's lips pursed at the bitterness. Sarah laughed. 'He wanted to leave something stronger, but I sent it back with him. Dunna want yer getting addicted, do we?'

Martha remembered her ma taking something from a bottle that Dr Bartholomew gave her when she had a tooth abscess. He'd said it was strong but would definitely kill the pain. It had made her all woozy and she sounded drunk when she talked. She wouldn't be taking any of that.

'I'm glad you sent it back, Sarah. I couldn't chance William getting hold of it.'

'Get yer head down again and I'll bring the soup up in an hour when that powder's had time to work.'

Martha slid down under the blankets again, surprised at how tired she was already. She'd only been awake a few minutes. She was grateful for Sarah's presence. This time she fell asleep with a smile on her face.

Martha woke with a start. It wasn't a noise that woke her this time. It was a sudden feeling that she had heard George calling her. It was dark apart from the glow from the street lamp outside. She shivered. She was sure he had spoken to her from somewhere very far away, like an echo from a deep mine. Da used to tell her how he could hear the other men when they were working on different seams, in different tunnels. He said their voices carried like whispers through the thick darkness. He always knew when someone was in trouble, long before anyone else. Her Ma said he had a sixth sense about these things. George was in trouble. She knew it as certainly as she had known her Ma and Da were dead before she'd been pulled up by Billy Mason that terrible morning of the bombardment.

Chapter 25

1910

Martha had arranged to meet George by the lake in Ward Jackson Park. It had been windy and raining over the last few days, but today was another bright and crisp autumn morning. The park paths and expanses of grass were filled with golden beech leaves that dazzled her eyes; yellow sycamore leaves mottled with brown spots like a brown trout; the bright red Acer leaves that always reminded her of delicate finger shaped lace; all frosted and crunching under her boots as she made her way across the park. Families were walking the path on the lake's edge, some feeding the ducks and swans, others enjoying an ice-cream, a group of boys were playing football on the grass and they came running as the ball shot across her path. She didn't notice any of them. There had been enough time for Albert to have replied and she shook with nervousness and anticipation. Would she be packing for a life in Scotland? Whatever the outcome, she would have to tell her parents soon. Her Ma was definitely becoming suspicious of her excuse of an upset stomach. She had already insisted that Martha go and see the doctor on

Monday if things hadn't improved. She had felt her mother's eyes following her around the house, a pained look on her face. She was almost sure it was because her Ma knew what was wrong but was too afraid to ask.

George was already sitting on the bench as she approached. He stood and kissed her on the cheek and they sat down together.

'Hello, Martha. How are you today? A bit less sickly?'

'Definitely a little better. Have you...'

'I have...I got a letter yesterday...I'm sorry, Martha but it's not good news.' He took hold of her hand to steady her as she stared at him; her eyes glistening; her body shaking.

'What did he say?' It was difficult to speak. Her voice trembled as much as her body.

'It seems he's met someone else. Love at first sight. He sez...I'm not sure I can tell you what else...it wudna be fair. He's a bloody fool.' Martha put her head in her hands and sobbed. George put his arm around her shoulders and held her until she could compose herself. Passing couples stared at them, but Martha was oblivious, she could only see that her life was over. She could only feel grief for the loss of Albert as if he had died. She could only know shame for her and her Ma and Da for what she had done.

'He's not worth it, Martha. I'll sort it out for you. I'll make it reet, I promise.'

'How? Wave a magic wand? Turn back time?' she asked him, angrily. 'No-one can make it better. No-one.'

He stayed beside her, neither of them showing any sign of being ready to leave. Eventually, she spoke again, without looking up.

'I need to go and tell Ma and Da,' she muffled from behind her hands. 'They need to know.' She started to stand, but George held her fast, grabbing her hand.

'Sit down.' She tugged her hand, but he pulled her down beside him. 'Please...wait a minute...I might have the answer.'

She looked at him. Hoping. Willing him to give her a

miracle. Save her from this dreadful predicament.

'What is it, George? What?'

'Marry me...I know you don't love me, but ...Marry me.' he was looking into her eyes in earnest. She couldn't speak for a minute. 'It could work...the family resemblance would be there...You know I've allus loved you...I could make you happy.'

'It...It's a sweet idea, George, but I couldn't do that to you. You'll meet someone who truly loves you one day. I can't take that chance away from you.' She stroked his cheek. 'Thank you for being so kind. I'll never forget it.'

'I dunna want anyone else, Martha. I've allus wanted you. Even if you say no, I'll never marry another. Think about it. Please.'

Martha wished Albert had been as keen as George to marry her. Why couldn't she have fallen for George? He cared for her so much, but she loved Albert. She would always love Albert.

'Oh, George. How could you even think about marrying a woman in my condition? I'd bring shame on you as well as my family. Your friends would pity you.'

'Not if we said the baby was premature. How far gone are you?'

'I...I'm not sure. Not long. I don't know. No...It's ridiculous. I can't do it to you.'

'You'd make me the happiest man alive, Martha. Don't you see? Having you as my wife is all I've ever wanted. Please. Please.' George dropped down on one knee just as another couple were passing. They stopped to watch, both smiling with pleasure at being witnesses to such a momentous event.

'Martha Palmer. Will you please do me the honour of becoming my wife? I haven't got a ring reet now, but we'll go shopping the minute you say yes.'

Martha looked down at him, not knowing what to do or say. The couple were waiting for her to respond. He said she would make him the happiest man alive. He said he had always loved her. Could she learn to love him? He was a good man. He looked so sweet down there, his eyes pleading with her. He'd look after her. He would look after her.

'Yes, George. Yes. I will marry you.' She'd said it out loud and there was no going back.

Chapter 26

Martha dragged herself out of bed and was surprised to find Sarah, fast asleep on the floor. Her face looked so tired and worn as she slept; her complexion grey; her eyes flickering as if her mind was taking on all the world's worries even though her body was supposed to be resting. Martha resolved to lighten her load, at least as far as her own and William's welfare was concerned. Sarah had enough to do without taking on their problems on top of her own.

Taking a blanket from her bed she laid it over Sarah as gently as she would a small child, desperate not to wake her. She stepped over her dear friend carefully and pulled a shawl around her own shoulders before slipping out of the room and downstairs. Although still feeling quite shaky, she certainly felt much better and the headache was now barely a dull throb.

The kitchen was warm and when she opened the firebox on the range, the embers needed only the smallest whisper of breath to awaken them. Sarah must have stoked it before coming to bed. She placed a few pieces of kindling on the baby licks and watched them grow, stretching into long fingers of flame reaching up to the roof of the box and curling out of the open square. Martha fed some coal on top of the sticks and closed the door. Rubbing her hands together, she brushed off the coal dust and put some water on to boil before Sarah and William stirred.

She had made porridge and laid the table when Sarah appeared, her eyes black from lack of sleep.

'What are yer doing out of bed? You should be resting.' Sarah's voice was thick with tiredness.

'I couldn't sleep. I'm definitely feeling better this morning,' replied Martha.

'Well sit down and let me— '

'No. You sit down, Sarah. I'll make your breakfast this morning. Honestly...I feel fine.'

'Well...if yer sure?' Sarah sat down and sighed. 'I am a bit tired.'

'I'm not surprised, sleeping on the floor. You must go home today and sleep in your own bed. William and I'll be fine now.' Martha put on a brave front, lifting her head and holding herself upright. 'In fact, you can go and sleep in my bed after you've had your breakfast. Make up what you've lost afore you go home.'

'I'm fine. I'll see how you are by lunchtime and if you still feel alreet, I'll go home then.'

'If you must, but you're not to do another thing. Is that clear?' Martha tried to sound stern, but her voice was so weak, she practically squeaked her order out.

Sarah chuckled and tucked into her porridge.

'Yes, miss.'

Martha went to wake William. Bending over him, she kissed his forehead and stroked his hair. He'd been so good while she had been ill; coming to sit with her when he got home from school; telling her what he had learned that day; reading his letters out loud; showing her the latest scrape or bruise from falling in the playground. His presence had barely registered with Martha for the first few days. Daisy had brought him home each night. Sometimes she brought some fresh baking. Mrs Finch had been teaching her now that Celia was hardly ever there. Cakes and pastries were put in front of Martha in an attempt to get her to eat but it usually ended up on William's plate when she couldn't face it.

'Good morning,' she said softly.

'Morning, Ma.'

He sat up and rubbed his eyes. 'Ma, you're up? Are you well now?' He hugged her waist.

'Much better. Now you be a good boy and get dressed and come down for breakfast.'

'Yes, Ma,' he answered, jumping up and climbing into his clothes.

Daisy arrived half an hour later.

'Oh, Martha. It's good to see you up. We've all been worried about you. Mrs Clarke will be that pleased to hear you're better.'

Daisy was turning into a beautiful young woman and Martha could see she'd be quite a catch for some man one day. Her black hair shone like coal and her deep cobalt eyes flashed when she smiled. Martha asked after Celia.

'She's that busy up at the hospital, I hardly ever see her now, but Mrs Finch sez she's enjoying life again. Has a purpose like. Helping all those poor wounded soldiers and that. I'm reet glad for her. She was so sad before.'

'I know, Daisy. It's good to find a purpose in life.' Martha had felt much the same since she had started work at the munitions factory. She was providing for her family, George, and feeling more like an independent woman every day. That was, up until she had become ill and Sarah had been looking after her. Still, she was better now and life would go back to normal. Back to work and ...her tummy somersaulted...back to Albert coming around for tea or taking them out. She'd missed him this last couple of weeks. It occurred to her that Florrie hadn't been over to see her. She hoped her friend hadn't been ill as well. Sarah had said there were a lot of people with all sorts of illnesses at the moment. Not least this new strain of influenza. Spanish Flu some people were calling it.

When Daisy and William had gone, Sarah told Martha how Joe had come over one night to have his supper with her and William. How he had seemed particularly interested in Daisy when he saw her there.

'The poor girl didn't know where to put hersel, he were gawping at her that much.' Her eyes were alight with mischief as she relived the incident. 'I told him to stop staring at her. He were that embarrassed and red as a beetroot. He mumbled summat about having to go and nearly fell ower his chair as he made a dash for the door.'

'I couldn't think of anyone nicer than Daisy for him,' said Martha, chuckling at the picture of poor Joe in her head...

'Me neither,' added Sarah. 'She was handing out leaflets for the cause with me before you got ill. Wants to better hersel and Celia sez she'll help her once this war's ower. Quite a strong headed girl when you get to know her.'

'Good for her. Since I started work at the munitions, I've started to think that are lots of things I could do, even though I realise just how hard the work is. It takes a lot of effort for the women to keep up with the men but we all manage it. We've got to show we're worth the same money.'

'Yoos've changed yer tune lately. There was a time yer wouldn't have a word said about taking ower men's jobs and the like. Eeh. My Robert would have had summat to say about it all.' Sarah laughed but a wistful gaze washed over her face.

'Have you heard from Edward?' Martha asked, trying to bring Sarah back from her thoughts.

'I got a letter last week. He sez the fighting is slowing down a bit. He's got a job at one of the clearing stations. Fetching and carrying for the doctors and nurses. He's in stores of all places. Dishing out bandages and dressings. Boil washing the old ones as well. Trying to get all the blood out so they can re-use them. He isn't seeing much action back there, thank the lord, but he sez there are so many soldiers with horrific injuries.'

Martha shivered involuntarily. Where was George?

The answer came much sooner than she expected. A letter arrived later in the morning when Sarah was about to leave.

'There's a letter for you. Pet. I said it wouldn't be...'

Martha looked up from where she was sitting at the kitchen table mending one of William's shirts. The look on Sarah's face made her blanche.

'What? What is it? Ouch!' she yelped as she stabbed herself with the needle in her rush to get up.

'It's my Edward. That's my Edward's hand? Addressed to you?'

'I don't understand?' Martha took the letter from Sarah and ripped the envelope open. Her hands trembled. 'It's dated 3rd November. That's over a week ago.'

She read it out loud.

Dear Martha,

I know you won't be expecting a letter from me but I am writing it on behalf of George. I discovered him in the casualty clearing station that I am working in. I was carrying drinks around to the patients when I spotted him. I have been assigned here due to a small injury to my leg and it's slowing me down a bit. I'm told there's some infection. There's a chance I might get a few days home while it heals proper but it's not certain. I told Ma I was working here permanently so's she wouldn't worry, so please don't tell her. I can break the news if I get home.

'The little devil. I'll give him a right piece of my mind when he gets here. I canna believe it. I'll see my son again.'

Martha continued...

You could tell her to send me a food parcel. We're half starved out here. Not much in the way of food supplies getting through. George is not dying so no need to worry yourself too much. He is a bit under the weather though and can't seem to hold a pencil to write or even a cup to take a drink. I had to help him drink his tea. He's not talking very much, can't get his words out without stuttering and stammering all the time, and he stares quite a lot. Not at anything in particular. It's like he doesn't see much at all. The doctors say they're not sure whether he's putting it on a bit so's he doesn't have to go back to the front but I don't believe it. George wouldn't do that. Some of the other soldiers are being a bit rough with him, saying he's a shirker. Doctor Rose is kind though. She came out a couple of months ago. She's been working at a hospital near Edinburgh where there are quite a lot of soldiers with the same problem. She says he is in some sort of shock and it's called neurasthenia, (she wrote that down so's I could copy it) but it seems like only officers are likely to get that. That's according to the high and mighty top brass and most of the other doctors out here. They say that us ordinary soldiers are just looking for a way to get home to blighty. Typical of them.

Anyway, she says she'll try and get him some home leave so that he has a chance of recovery in his own surroundings.

A strange thing happened last night. Remember that song you always sang to William when you were staying at our house? You know the one Sweet and low, sweet and low. Wind of the western sea. *Well, I sang it to George last night and he seemed to recognise it. Stopped shaking for a while and even smiled. Isn't that the oddest thing?*

I told him I would write to you and explain and I think he understood. His eyes lit up when I mentioned your name.

Anyway, I thought I should write. Try not to worry and I'll let you know if I hear anything before I go back up the line. I'll ask Doctor Rose to write if nothing has happened by then.

Please tell Ma and Joe I'm doing fine and I miss them.

Edward Colby

Martha's hand dropped and the letter floated to the floor as she stared at the ceiling with tear filled eyes. Poor George. Here she was safe and sound and thinking about another man when her dear husband was lying in a strange place all on his own.

'He's in the best place, lass. Sit yersel down afore you fall down.' Sarah helped her back to the chair.

Chapter 27

Albert had arranged for Martha to do a job that didn't involve too much heavy work. She was to operate the magnet crane, moving the heavy shell casings from one part of the building to another. Sitting in the small box, high above the shop floor made Martha feel small and isolated from the rest of the women. It seemed an awfully long way down and sometimes made her quite faint and dizzy. It was a much lighter job but it was a lonely job too, with no-one to talk to all day. It gave her time to chew and worry over what the other women were saying about her. Time to worry about George and what was happening to him. She knew there had been talk of favouritism. Quite a number of women had been ill with the influenza exactly as she had, but none of them had been given light duties on their return to work. Martha tried to explain that she only got the job because she had asked first, but she knew that no-one believed her. She thought about the comments she'd overheard earlier that day when she'd gone for her lunch break.

'That's her. Too pally with Albert Hubbard for my liking,' said one girl. 'I bet they don't give the job back to our Nancy when she's better. That's if she does get better. She didna look good the last time I saw her.'

'Aye. Just 'cos he's her brother-in-law, it dunna mean she should get special treatment.'

'Special's the right word I hear. Allus round at her house. I wonder what her husband'll say when he gets home? Poor lad, fighting for his country and her swanning about with his brother. Shameful. That's what it is.'

'I heard he canna keep his hands to himself whenever he sees a pretty face. I saw him slap young Mary Carter's bottom the other day. She didna seem to mind it either.'

'Aye. Miss high and mighty is in for a shock if she thinks she's the only one he's got eyes for.'

Martha remembered him always being playful with other girls when she was walking out with him all those years ago. It didn't mean anything. "Nothing wrong with a bit of fun." he would say. He couldn't help it if all the ladies were fond of him and wasn't she glad he'd chosen her out of all of them? Martha tried without success to push the thoughts away as she lowered the shell cases by the exit to the train yard.

The word "Shameful" was echoing in her ears and she was sure the whole factory was staring at her. She'd speak to Albert tonight. Tell him what they were saying about him...about her. Ask him to move her back to her old job. Besides, she missed working alongside Florrie and the other girls on her side of the giant warehouse. She had made friends with quite a few of the girls who were living at the Raglan Hotel. Since it had been turned into a hostel, there were young girls from all over the country coming to Hartlepool to work in the factory. It seemed that most of them jumped at the chance to earn decent money. "We can make ten times as much as when we were in service" said quite a few of them. They all seemed to be having a good time, making the most of their freedom from the drudgery of looking after the upper classes. Martha wondered if their families knew what they were up to.

'Mary Carter? Take no notice of them. You know me. Anything for a laugh. She means nothing.' He looked at her like a naughty schoolboy who'd been caught out. Flashing an innocent smile. ' Don't be cross with me. Anyway, what do you want your old job back for? I was only looking out for you. I dunna want you overdoing it. You're already looking like you haven't been fed for months. There's hardly owt left of you. There'll be nowt to get hold of soon.' Albert reached across the table and clasped her hand. She pulled it back quickly in case William noticed from where he was playing on the floor.

'Please, Albert,' she whispered. 'This is serious. The other women are talking. Putting two and two together and saying we're a couple. I can't have tales getting to Sarah or ...' She nodded in William's direction. 'It wouldn't be right.'

'Alreet, but you have to promise to take it easy. I know everyone's switched to piece work now, but I dunna want you breaking yer back trying to make a decent wage. I like a bit of meat on my women.' He winked and grinned again.

'I won't. I'll take my time. I promise. I don't know why they want everyone to do piece work. People'll drop their standards to make sure they make more money.' Martha worried about faulty shells leaving the factory. Hadn't the total massacre of soldiers been enough for them to improve standards?

'I organised the piece work. Mr Castleton thinks it's a good idea. The checkers won't be any less careful; they only need to work faster at it. You shouldn't be worryin' yer little head over things like that. Leave it to the management to sort out.' He reached over and stroked her cheek. A flash of annoyance went through her. He was treating her like all the other men.

'I'm capable of having useful thoughts. Don't treat me like an idiot, Albert.'

He smiled and put his hands up in defence.

'Sorry. I'd best watch my tongue in the future.' He stuck it out and crossed his eyes trying to look at it. Martha had to smile and the annoyance subsided. At least she would go back to her old job.

Hopefully, the talk would die down soon if they didn't spend time together openly. She needed him to be the strong one. The one who was cautious and sensible. Her feelings for Albert always seemed to win the battle with her conscience. He only had to touch her or smile and she followed his lead like someone who had been put under a spell or a dog who obeyed every command its master made, adoring and desperate to please.

'Have you heard anymore about George? He canna be so bad else he'd be back home by now.'

'I don't know. Edward seemed to think he was bad enough and that Doctor Rose was trying to get him some sort of sick furlough. George wouldn't put it on. It's not in him to do such a thing.'

'Uh! Dunna kid yersel. He was allus putting it on when he were younger. Owt to get away with not going to work.'

'He's a grown man now, Albert. Not a child,' Martha snapped, as angry with herself as she was with him. 'Give him some credit.'

'Aye. Well.'

Martha dished up a couple of potatoes for each of them and a little gravy. Thick slices of bread were used to mop up any excess. Thank goodness there was no rationing on bread, she thought, otherwise there wouldn't be enough to fill them. The meat ration wasn't anywhere near enough for three of them, but she couldn't claim for Albert. His landlady claimed his share.

'C'mon, William. Time for supper.'

They ate quietly and with little conversation, only speaking when necessary, Martha's guilt and anger hanging heavy in the air. She took William up to bed soon after the meal, tucking him in and staying a while, not wanting to go back down, not wanting to fight over what George was or wasn't doing. Surely Albert could see that it must be something serious, or else Edward wouldn't have written to her. A short while later she heard Albert leave and went through to her own room. Looking down from the window, she watched him walking away under the street lights, hands in pockets, head and cap pulled down against the damp night. She wanted to open the window and call him back. George might be home soon and there would be no more time alone together. She wished she hadn't been so sharp with him. She wished she could stop herself having feelings for him.

'I'm reet glad to have yer back. That woman from Middleton Street were a right misery. Moaning about anything and everything she were. "Oooh, me back hurts." one minute and then "Aaargh, me feet are that sore standing here all day." I could've lamped her one.'

Martha laughed out loud as Florrie mimicked the woman's actions. She made the day pass easily with her chatter and sense of humour. There hadn't been much opportunity to speak to each other since returning to work while Martha was up on the magnetic crane. Florrie had been off sick for as long as Martha and her face was looking even paler than its usual pasty self. In contrast, the freckles on her cheeks stood out like tiny splashes of red clay and the fuzz of hair sticking out from her cloth cap seemed so bright. It looked like a halo of fire.

'I hope Sam came around to look after you while you were ill,' said Martha.

'He did. Fetched and carried for me. Brought all sorts of things to whet my appetite. Not that there was much I fancied, but it were appreciated. Nothing were too much trouble to him. What about you?' Florrie nodded towards the office on the other side of the warehouse. 'Did his lordship look after you?' She sounded angry.

Martha continued trimming the shell carefully. Florrie

must have been listening to the gossips.

'No. Sarah came. She stayed for days. Like a mother hen. I don't know what I'd do without her.'

'That's good. She's a kind woman. I wish my ma was a bit more motherly. It's allus me that has to be there for her and Da and the kids instead of the other way round. They love us, but they've never been what you call dependable. Like a drink or two if yer know what I mean. That's how come there's so many of us... Bloody Hell... What's our Violet doing here?'

Martha watched as Florrie headed for the manager's office, starting to run, her mouth open wide but no sound coming out. Martha hauled the shell case on to the workbench and followed her friend, dread already filling up inside her.

Florrie was sitting in the manager's chair, still clenching the green envelope and letter in her hands as Martha knelt down in front of her. Violet was standing with her hand on Florrie's shoulder, not sure what to do, the tears making grubby tracks down her face.

'Da clattered my ear. Said I were lying when I read out the letter to 'em,' she hiccupped, still sobbing. Martha reached out to her.

'It was the shock, Violet. He didn't mean it. C'mon. I'll take you both home.' She stood up. 'Is that alright, Albert?'

'Course. Stay with 'em if you like. I'll make it right with Mr Castleton.'

'It ain't fair. Why my Freddie?' sobbed Florrie as Martha guided her and Violet across the factory floor. Sympathetic eyes followed them as they made their way out of the factory. This scene had been witnessed a hundred times over the last few weeks, but it never got any easier.

'It says he was fighting bravely when it happened.' Martha was reading the brief letter and explaining the contents to Florrie's mother, trying to find some comfort in the words. 'It says you should be very proud of your son's sacrifice.'

Mrs Mason keened and wailed, head in hands, rocking back and forth on the rickety chair by the open grate. The fire was dying but nobody made a move to stoke it or put coal on. Mr Mason was nowhere to be seen.

'He's gone to the pub. He said he needed to drown his sorrows,' said Frank numbly from where he was sitting next to his Ma's feet, Violet beside him, both staring into the smouldering embers, both shivering. Shock or cold? Martha wondered. Probably both.

'About all he's good for,' snapped Florrie, her face twisting as she realised the horror of it all. 'We can't even bury him. He'll be in some hole that'll get bombed again and again. Tearing him into little pieces 'til there's nothing left.' Her voice rose in the air, thinning and growing fainter. Mrs Mason's wailing turned into screams and Frank and Violet started to bawl.

'I can help you sort out a service for him,' Martha said, her voice trembling with pity for her friend. She took hold of Florrie's hands. 'I'll talk to the vicar, make arrangements.' She didn't know what else to say. She wondered what it must be like to lose a twin sibling. Losing a brother would be dreadful enough...but a twin? It must be like losing part of yourself. Half of the whole. It was all too dreadful to think about.

'Th...Thank you Martha. Yer a good friend. I won't forget this.'

Sam arrived soon after, and Florrie flew to him, wrapping her arms around his neck. Martha built up the fire and made hot, sweet tea for them all. Giving Florrie a hug first, she turned to Sam.

'That's the last of the coal. Do you think you could get some more for them.'

Violet stood up.

'Shall I go down the beach and collect some?' she asked.

'Leave it to me...I'll sort it. Thanks for all your help, Martha.' Sam's hand touched her arm as he spoke.

'I'm happy to help,' she said and left to collect William

from Celia's.

'Is there anything I can do?' Albert asked when Martha came down the stairs that night. William hadn't wanted to go to sleep when she had put him to bed. He talked about Frank going home from school early and she tried to explain what had happened to his brother, Freddie. The fear on his face as he wondered if his Da was going to be alright unsettled Martha. The scene at Florrie's had been hard to bear. Everything was beginning to feel a little too close to home.

'I think Sam's capable of taking care of everything. I'll call on the Vicar after work tomorrow. Perhaps you could call in to see them and say she needn't rush back to work?'

'I canna do that. Everyone else'll want time off to grieve. I dunna think the company'd be too happy if production went down.'

'It's not right. A person needs time to come to terms when they've lost a loved one.'

'We've all got to carry on, Martha. There are thousands of people who have lost someone. The whole country would come to a standstill if we all stayed home to grieve. The soldiers can't stop fighting when their pals are dropping down dead around them in the middle of the battle.' Albert screwed his face in anger.

Martha knew how much he hated being at home when all his friends were out there giving up everything. 'You're right, of course. I wasn't thinking straight. It's when you see someone you care about suffering.'

'I thought it was me you cared about,' he said suddenly taking hold of her and pulling her close. 'Florrie Mason can take care of herself.'

The warmth emanating from his chest and through his shirt comforted her, made her feel safe in the world they were creating for themselves. It was wrong, but they hadn't crossed the final line. She'd been strong and hadn't succumbed to the one thing she knew he desired more than anything else. Electricity rippled through her body, taking her by surprise, as they clung to each other, she gasped. How could this happen? How could they fulfil each other's deepest want without doing anything except hold on to each other? Martha marvelled at what was happening inside her. He kissed her desperately, his tongue probing deep inside her mouth as she arched against him, exploding again and again.

They stood silently, waiting for it to subside, breathless and stroking each other gently, slowly until they felt able to part. Martha couldn't look at him. She felt shy, embarrassed, shamed?

'Martha...I...I'm not sorry. You wanted it as much as me...' He reached out and lifted her chin. 'Open your eyes. Look at me.'

Martha blinked. He was smiling, his eyes sparkled with pleasure, his pupils fully dilated. 'I...We..,' she muttered.

'We need to tell him. When he comes home, we need to tell him. Your mine now, Martha Hubbard. You and William. I want to shout it to the world.' He pulled her close again.

Her voice cracked, almost a whisper. 'We can't...I can't. William...'

Albert held her at arm's length. 'What about William? You've seen how we get on. He's fond of me. I know he is. I'll make a better da than George. You both belong to me.'

Martha pulled herself free. What on earth was she doing?

'We can't. I can't take William away from George. No. It's not right. You'll have to go, Albert. Please.' She pushed him towards the door. 'Please. I mean it. Go. Go.'

'I...I don't understand...Martha?'

Martha opened the front door. She had to end it. 'Go, Albert. I don't want to discuss it anymore.'

He stepped out into the street, his cap in his hand. 'You know you won't be able to stay away,' he said turning from her. 'We'll talk about it tomorrow.'

She didn't watch him as he walked away. Pushing the

door closed she slid down behind it and cried until there was nothing left.

Picking herself up, she walked through to the kitchen, poured ashes on the fire and went upstairs to bed.

Chapter 28

20th November 1916

The papers were full of reports about the German army pulling back from the Somme as the battle seemed to have reached a stalemate, neither party gaining any ground in the worsening winter weather. Martha hoped it meant that George would come home for a while.

William kept asking for his Uncle Albert. 'Why hasn't he been, Ma? Is he sick like you were? We should go and see him. We can—'

'Hush now, William. Uncle Albert is busy at work...that's all. He can't spend all his time here.'

'But—'

'No buts. Daisy'll be here any minute. Get your cap and scarf. The winds are biting out there today... See. That must be her now.' Martha went to answer the knock on the front door.

It took a couple of seconds to recognise the young soldier smiling down at her.

'Edward. When did you get back? Does your ma know you're here? Come In. Come in.'

Martha made way as Edward removed his cap and

stepped over the threshold.

'Come through and warm yourself.' Martha sidled passed him and beckoned him into the kitchen.

'Do you have to kill Germans?' asked William, gazing up at Edward in awe. 'Do you shoot a rifle or do you have to fire one of those big guns on wheels? I've got a big gun on wheels. Does yours have horses to pull it. Mine does. I can show you if you like?'

'William...that's enough. Go get your cap and scarf.' Martha tried to steady her voice. What was he doing here? Was it bad news? She must get William out of the way before he told her.

'Tea, Edward? I've just made some. Sit down. You must be tired. A long journey...'

'I'm fine, Martha. I came to say that— '

'News? News can wait a few minutes. William's about to go to school...you can tell me when he's gone.' Martha breathed a sigh of relief when the second knock landed on the door. 'I'll go and hand him over to Daisy. I won't be a moment. Sit down...Please...sit down.' She ushered William away and opened the front door to the waiting Daisy.

'There's a soldier in our kitchen, Daisy. He's called Edward. He's...'

'Sorry, Daisy, but I can't chat this morning. I'll call for William later.' She hoped Daisy could sense her urgency to have William away from the house.

Daisy looked puzzled but took William's hand.

'I...I think Ma is a bit busy this morning, William. You can tell me all about it on the way,' she said as they set off up the street.

Martha closed the door and leaned her back against it. Taking a deep breath, she went back into the kitchen.

'Is it George?'

Edward nodded. 'He's alreet. I've just got back and I wanted to let you know before I go home. George will be shipped out in a couple of days. It were a shame he couldn't come with me, but they had to sort out his paperwork at the clearing centre first. He should be home quite soon.'

'Oh! Thank God. Thank you.' Martha hugged her messenger. 'I...I'm sorry. I thought you were here to tell me...'

'I know. Anyway. I must get home. Ma'll be so surprised to see me.'

'Of course. Sarah'll be over the moon, Edward...Off you go.' Martha rushed back to the door and opened it. 'I wish I could be there to see her face.'

'Aye. It'll be a picture.' He laughed and sped off to find his family.

'He'll be here in a day or two. Isn't it wonderful, Albert?' Martha stood in Albert's office spilling out her good news. Albert got up out of his chair.

'I suppose. I'm not looking forward to telling him though.'

'Telling him what? What do you mean?' Martha felt her insides begin to churn.

'About us of course. It'll be hard, but it's better done quickly. Sooner rather than later.' He came round from behind the desk and took her hands. 'Finally, we'll be able to be together. The way it should be.'

Martha snatched her hands away, her eyes wide.

'Albert...No...There is no US...There never can be.'

'You know you want to be with me. You canna keep fighting it, Martha. We have to be together. You know I'm right.' He took hold of her hands again, pulling her towards him. Martha couldn't help herself. She hated herself. She fell against him, pressing herself as close as she could. Needing him so much. How could he have this hold over her? She thought about what it would do to George. How could she hurt him so badly, be so cruel?

'He's ill. I can't tell him something like that. What if he has a breakdown? I can't take that chance.'

'He's already had the breakdown by the sounds of it. We

can't let his illness change what we want. We have to tell him.' His voice sounded hard. Immune to any feelings of guilt about what he was doing.

'No...I won't do it. He needs me right now and I'll look after him. It's the right thing to do.' She moved away from him, trying to collect herself; face up to her duty as a wife.

'And what about us? What's the right thing for us?' Albert's face was twisted in anger.

'I...I don't know, Albert.' She didn't want to hurt him either. Her heart was breaking. 'Give me a little time. Please, Albert. Enough to see that he's alright. A couple of weeks.'

His face softened, relaxing enough to fill and smooth the creases of anger.

'And then you'll tell him?' It took a while for her to say the words.

'Yes. I'll tell him. You'll have to let me tell him in my own time though. Give us some privacy until I think he's strong enough.'

Martha left him leaning against the desk as she made her way across the floor and over to her workstation.

It had only been two days since the memorial service and Florrie was back at work. There wasn't much conversation between them. Florrie performed her duties physically, but her mind was somewhere totally different. Her eyes were dulled by the pain of her loss, no longer shining with laughter and mischief. Martha tried to keep a line of chatter going, but the simple 'yes' or 'no' answers made it difficult. She hadn't the heart to tell her that George was coming home. It didn't seem appropriate at the moment when Florrie's nightmare was still ongoing. She would try to have a quiet word with Sam when he came down the line. Get him to tell Florrie when he thought the time was right. Ask him how things were at home. The other girls on the line started up a chorus of *It's a long way to Tipperary* which, along with other popular war songs, was fast becoming a favourite way of putting some rhythm into the job they were doing. Martha didn't join in and

Florrie didn't even seem to notice or hear it.

'Is he back?' asked Albert. Martha held the door open and stood with her back to the wall. William ran to her side, eyes wide with expectation at first but then his shoulders dropped as he realised who it was.

'I thought you were Da, Uncle Albert. Where is he, Ma?'

'He won't be long, William. I know it's been a few days. Maybe tomorrow.'

'But, Ma.'

William plodded back into the kitchen, chin down and arms hanging limply down his sides.

'I thought we agreed you were going to stay away until I let you know?' Martha whispered to Albert.

'It wouldn't be surprising to anyone that a man wanted to see his brother when he's been away such a long time, would it?' Albert held her back in the hallway, planting a kiss firmly on her mouth. Martha felt her insides stir but pushed him away gently, her resolve already melting.

'Wait until he's in bed.' She smiled and stroked his cheek before following William.

'Time for bed, young man. I want you bright and breezy for school in the morning.'

'Aaw, Ma. What if Da comes? Can't I stay up and wait for him? Please, Ma.'

'Ha'way with you. Your Ma'll shout up to you if he comes. Won't you, Ma?' said Albert laughing as he picked the boy up and swung him around in a circle. 'Your Da wudna like it if you were up late on a school night.'

Albert stopped in mid flow.

'Da, Da.' squealed William, wriggling to get down.

George stood in the kitchen doorway, looking dishevelled in his crumpled uniform. His face, lined and hollow, had at least three days' stubble casting a dark shadow over it. He looked ready to fall down. The impact of William flying into his legs and wrapping his arms around them nearly toppled him and he had to fight to keep his balance.

'George. Oh, George.' Martha could hardly believe this skeleton of a man was her husband. She took his arm and guided him to a chair. He slumped down, letting his kit bag slide to the floor.

'Hello, M-M-Martha,' he said, looking up into her eyes.

Martha poured another kettle of steaming water into the galvanised bathtub. She had thrown his infested underwear into the fire and put his uniform outside the back door. It had almost seemed alive with the armies of lice running all over it. The range was topped up and the room was cosy with heat.

'What on earth?'

'B-B-Barbed wire. We have t-t-to crawl under it,' he said in answer to her shock when she saw the state of his back. She took a deep breath and sponged him, trying to lift some of the dirt without catching the half healed sores and wheals that patterned his skin; a map that had been scratched out of his flesh, criss-crossing its way from the top to the bottom of his back. His swollen feet were a dull blue-grey colour. Martha had heard a lot about trench foot from the women at work whose husbands and sons had trouble walking or even ended up having a foot amputated. George's seemed to be intact, although badly blistered, and she washed them, massaging them at the same time to encourage blood flow. What sort of hell had he been through? The tears trailed her cheeks.

'The-The nurses d-d-dunna have time for cleaning us up,' he mumbled. 'Too busy helping...' George's eyes welled up and he tried to swallow but ended up having a coughing fit.

'Don't talk now. You need to rest.'

He closed his eyes while Martha sponged and rubbed, lathered his hair and poured warm water over his head. This wasn't the man who came home on leave eighteen months ago. That man was strong and held himself tall. Her mind drifted to that day at the fair, how proud she had been, linking his arm, watching him lift William up and on to the rides. How they had laughed. How happy they had been. She helped him out of the tub and dried him down carefully. His body seemed all corners, angles...hips...bones protruding from under his skin. His legs were thin, the muscle wasted and she knelt down and dried them as gently as she could. Frightened he might break.

Eventually in his night clothes, she led him upstairs. He lay under the covers, staring at the ceiling as she undressed and climbed in beside him. He turned his back to her as she spooned him, her arm over his waist, cradling him like a child. She could feel his body shaking and held him tighter to let him know he was safe. It seemed the most natural thing to do as she sang softly in his ear.

'Sweet and low, sweet and low
Wind of western sea,
Low, low, breathe and blow,
Wind of the western sea!
Over the rolling water go,
Come from the dying moon, and blow,
Blow him again to me,
While my little one, while my pretty one, sleeps.'

'Are you sure you're going to be alright?' Martha was worried about leaving George alone all day while she went to work.

'I...I'm fine...dunna worry...it's alreet.'

'There's been a lot of changes. To make the shells safer. I like doing my share, George. I've joined the union. I'm putting money away as well...for when it's over...' Martha stood behind George's chair and stroked his back. 'Are you sure you're going to be alright? I can ask for time off?'

'I'll be f-f-fine. You go.' George gazed into the fire. 'I can sit here all day. I-I-I like the quiet.'

'You can help yourself to some bread and dripping when

you're ready, can't you?'

'Yes,' he said absently.

'I haven't told Florrie your home yet. Not with her grieving for her brother.'

'Florrie? I thought I asked you not to get involved with her family.' He sounded agitated, his voice snapping at her as he tried to stand up.

Martha flinched. 'And I thought you weren't so unkind, George Hubbard. Even if the story about Violet is true...and I don't believe it for one minute...it's no reason for you to look down your nose at them.'

'V-Violet? '

'About her not being Mr Mason's. What other reason could you have? Don't tell me you've been listening to the tattle about Florrie having a baby out of wedlock. I'd never forgive...'

George looked down at the floor. 'N-No...of course not. I'm s-sorry...I shouldn't have...'

'No, you shouldn't. Florrie's my friend and I won't give her up over people's prejudices. Goodness me, George, she has nothing but the kindest words for you. You're usually the last person to throw stones.'

George took Martha in his arms. 'I'm such a f-fool. T-T-Take no notice. You go to work.'

George sat down.

Martha kissed his cheek, anxious to smooth things over. 'Perhaps we can do something with William tonight? Walk over to Sarah's?' He was gazing into the fire again. 'George? What do you think? They'd all love to see you.'

'What? '

'I said it would be nice to see Sarah. Take William over.'

'I'm f-f-fine here. Dunna worry about me.'

'Could you at least try a little harder with William? He doesn't understand what's happened to you. He thinks you don't care about him anymore...George?'

He was no longer in the room; his mind was somewhere.

Like Florrie. Florrie wasn't the same person since Freddie's death and now...She felt as if she had lost George to this blasted war even though he had come back. He had barely spoken in the three days he'd been home. It was as if he didn't want to be home, to be with her. Martha felt out of her depth. How could she get through to him? Poor William had been so desperate to see his father, but George had barely acknowledged him.

She pulled her coat on, pinned her hat and went outside. There was no wind today but the sky was dark and thick with cloud. The morning seemed to reflect the mood in her home and in her husband's head. She yearned for the sun and the lightness of the dreams and hopes she had as a young girl. When her Ma and Da were alive, when life was simple and everyone was safe and happy in their own little world. She cursed the war and everything it had taken away from her.

Chapter 29

Daisy walked into Church Square with Martha and William. She was wearing a warm woollen coat that Celia had given her. Underneath the coat was a plain white blouse and a grey wool skirt that finished above the ankle showing off the new boots she had bought last week with the money she had been saving all year. She had pinned her hair up and the broad-brimmed hat with the feather trim cast a shadow over her face, making her look more mature than her sixteen years.

'What do you think, Martha? It doesn't look too old on me does it?' she asked, referring to the hat.

Martha smiled. 'Of course not, Daisy. You look a picture. I'm sure Joe will be delighted.'

'Why can't I go to the picture house with Daisy?' asked William as he scooted along, holding on to Daisy's hand and swinging it up in the air.

'Because she's going with Joe, and we need to get home to Da after we've been to see Sarah.

'I don't want to go home. Da's no fun anymore. I want to play with Uncle Albert. He's funny.'

'That's enough, William. Don't say such things. You know

Da's not very well at the moment.' Martha felt embarrassed when William spoke like that. He didn't understand why his Da wasn't the same person who went away. How could he. It was awkward and the long silences were difficult to fill. Sarah would know what to do. Sarah always knew what to do.

The shops on Lyn Street were as busy as usual. Rationing may have curbed the variety of food on sale, but it certainly hadn't stopped people shopping, especially all the young single women working up at the munitions factory. They strolled around in small groups, wearing their latest fashion purchases, arms full of bags. So much money and no family commitments seemed to have made them all behave completely differently. They had suddenly found a whole new world in which they were free to think and behave in any manner they saw fit. Not only did they fill the shops, but they were beginning to fill the pubs as well, at least during the hours that women were allowed in.

'You'd think they'd donate to the hospital fund if they've so much money to spare,' sniped Daisy. 'All them poor soldiers up there and not enough beds or medicine for 'em.'

'Maybe they think it's not their problem being as a lot of them are from out of town.'

'They complain about only being allowed in the pubs at certain times. They think that's a problem. A few have joined us at Celia's and are desperate to rally about that. They don't seem to be interested in the bigger picture.' Daisy voiced her disapproval. 'Some of them talk like men, even blaspheming sometimes.'

Martha changed the subject. 'Are you helping with the fundraising, Daisy?'

'I am. Me and Sarah were standing outside The Empire last Saturday, but only local folk put money in the tin. Are you and George coming to the football match? I'm in the women's team. It's such fun, Martha. You should join in. We're playing your lot from the munitions factory.'

Martha laughed. 'I can't imagine running around a

football field, showing off my legs to the world. I'd be too embarrassed.'

'All the money's going to the hospital for the Thanksgiving Anniversary next month. They reckon we'll have raised more than two thousand pounds by then. We're trying to beat last year's total but it'll be hard. Two thousand three hundred pounds it were. Can you imagine it? I don't know how many years' wages that would be. I couldn't earn that much in all my life.'

'Just think of how much good it'll do, Daisy, and how much you helped. You should be very proud of yourself. Giving up all your spare time to help our wounded soldiers.'

'Aye, well. Are you coming then? To the match?'

'I...I'll have to see how George is on Saturday. It might do him some good to get out.'

Martha remembered her Da going to the football whenever he had the chance. She couldn't believe it was only two years ago since her parents died. It seemed like a lifetime. So much had happened.

Martha spotted a couple of the newly-appointed policewomen patrolling up and down the street; monitoring the women; making sure they behaved in a lady-like manner. There had been public outrage and several complaints about women getting drunk and encouraging men to act inappropriately towards them. She remembered reading in the Echo about it. Some women were arrested for being drunk and disorderly. It said that the local government had appointed women supervisors at the Raglan Hotel hostel to ensure that there were no men visitors late at night. It seemed that this war was changing everything and everybody. She couldn't help wondering what Mrs Wicklow would make of it all. Would she approve of women drinking? After all, women could do anything that men could, couldn't they?

Joe's face lit up when he saw Daisy, and he grabbed her,

pulling her back out of the door. 'Come on. We'll be late. The picture starts in ten minutes.'

It reminded Martha of how Albert would look at her whenever they met. If only life could be that simple again. Her stomach turned at the thought of him coming over tonight. He had insisted and nothing she said could put him off. She'd better not stay too long. It was important that she was home before he arrived. The fear of him blurting something out made her sit on the edge of her seat, clock watching while she drank her tea. William was sitting on Edward's lap listening to all his tales about being a soldier.

'What is it, Lass?' Sarah had been watching her fidget.

'I need to be home soon...Albert's coming over to see George. I don't want him upsetting him.'

'Why on earth would he do that? He'll be glad to see his brother, won't he?' Sarah set her cup down. 'What's going on, Martha?'

'It's...It's Albert. He thinks George might be putting it on. The illness. I'm sure he'll see that it's real when he sees the state of him.'

'It'll be fine. I know Albert's a bit of a hard man, but he wudna turn his back on his brother.'

'No. No. you're right. It's ...It's not easy, Sarah. I don't know what to do half the time. George's so quiet one minute and shouting the next. I can never be sure what sort of mood he's in.' Martha felt her lip start to tremble.

'Have you had a word with Dr Bartholomew? He'll be able to advise you a bit better than I can. I don't know much about this sort of thing.'

'I think Ma's right,' interrupted Edward. 'He might have summat he can give him. Calm him down like.'

'I s'pose. I'll go down on my day off if he's no better. When do you go back, Edward?'

'Monday after the football match. It's not long enough. I feel like I've not even settled in. Still, the leg's nearly as good as new now it's had Ma's attention for a few days.'

'Not well enough for going back there.'

'Stop it, Ma. I canna stay home, yer know that.'

'Do you like being a soldier, Edward?' asked William.

'How could I not like it, William? I get to play in mud all day. Hide in big holes. Shoot rats.' His voice quietened. 'It's just like I imagined.'

'Do you eat the rats for your dinner?'

'Oh no. I get to eat little boys for my dinner.' He started tickling William and pretending to bite big chunks from him. William squealed with laughter. Martha made her excuses, finally managing to tear William away, and set off for home.

Albert stepped into the hall. 'Where is he?'

'By the fire. You'll have to be quiet. William's in bed. I don't want him waking... George is a bit...Be gentle with him.' Martha followed him into the kitchen.

'Hello, George,' he said cheerily. 'How are you?'

George looked up from his chair, his eyes dull, before turning his gaze back to the fire. Albert looked at Martha, his face beginning to flush.

Martha took control. 'Sit down, Albert. George is a bit tired. He's fine. Thank you for asking.'

'Yes, I'm fine. M-Martha and me are f-fine when left to ourselves.'

'No need for that.' Albert started to rise, but Martha put her hand to his shoulder, pushing him down again.

'I'm just dishing up. You'll join us for a bite won't you?'

'Thanks, Martha. That'd be good.'

'What about you, George? Can you manage a bite?'

George looked at Albert. 'W-What are you doing here, Albert? Have you c-come to see me? ' He struggled to his feet. 'I'm s-sure you must see enough of M-Martha at work,' he said before sitting at the table.

'Albert's come to see if you're alright. Haven't you, Albert?.'

Albert grunted confirmation.

George picked up a spoon. His hands were shaking as he dipped into the food on his plate. Half the vegetable broth splashed on the table and most of the rest down George's shirt.

'Let me help you,' said Martha, taking the spoon from him.

'Thank you, P-Pet.'

'It's a pleasure, George.'

'M-Martha. I've missed you so much. It's good to be home.' Martha let him finish speaking. He was obviously uncomfortable with Albert here, trying to keep her attention focussed away from his brother.

'It's good to have you back. Let's get some more food down you. You need building up.' Martha wiped up the mess on George's shirt, feeding him as if he were a baby.'Surely he can do that for himself,' Albert snarled. 'Stop acting the bloody fool, George. Yer embarrassing yersel.'

George cowered at the sound of Albert's raised voice, putting his hands over his ears.

'Stop shouting, Albert. It's not helping matters.' Martha's eyes pleaded with Albert, willing him to be more understanding.

'Martha...can't you see he's pretending. Putting it on so's he won't have to go back.'

'He's doing no such thing. He's ill. He needs help.' Surely he couldn't put on such an act, she thought. Albert had only seen him for a few minutes. He couldn't possibly understand. 'Let's not argue about it. You'll be waking William.' Martha spoke quietly and calmly but it made no difference.

'I reckon I best go now,' he said, standing up and bringing the conversation to a halt. Putting his jacket and cap on, he added. 'We need to talk about this again.'

'Dunna worry about m-me. I'll be b-back up the line and out of yer w-way soon enough. T-Tek care of yersel,' George mouthed between spoonfuls.

Albert turned away and started for the door.

'I'll see you at work tomorrow,' he called before the door slammed behind him.

'That's it. One more spoonful. You're doing so well, George.' Martha bit down on the blister that had formed on her lip earlier, the taste of blood warm and metallic on her tongue. Does he know? 'Enough? Let's get you ready for bed then, shall we? You must be tired.'

'Aye. I'm glad the shooting's stopped for a while.'

'So am I,' she responded, helping him to his feet and guiding him upstairs.

Martha lay on her side, watching the rise and fall of George's chest. The light from the gas lamp outside seeped through the thin curtains; enough for her to make out his features. His face was unlined, peaceful, his breathing calm and even. He looked...what? Normal? Could he be acting, like Albert said? Surely not? He couldn't be so cruel to them all, could he? It was odd how he could behave as if he didn't want to know her one minute and then act all loving the next. She had climbed into bed with George later when she'd taken William upstairs around half past seven. He had been shaking again and she held him close, singing to calm him. He'd held on to her and kissed her, pushing against her, wanting what was his right as a husband. That surely meant he knew what he was doing, didn't it? He had been so gentle, like he'd always been; telling her how he couldn't believe his luck; amazed that she was his; amazed he was allowed this privilege. Martha felt guilty for pretending it was Albert touching her, stroking her, kissing her. It allowed her to give herself up to the surging force inside and let it out, slowly at first, teasing, delicate and then...rising, building up to the crescendo she longed for. She'd almost called out his name as the release came.

Now she longed for sleep, but it wouldn't come. Sliding out from under the blanket, she dressed and tiptoed downstairs. It was barely nine o-clock and her mind was full of Albert. She was disgusted with herself for thinking that way about him. A glass of hot milk didn't help to make her sleepy, so she decided to bake. Throwing herself into the task took her mind off things for a short while.

The droning sound didn't register at first. It was floating at the edges of her mind, steadily getting louder. Rapid anti-aircraft fire brought her back to earth. She looked out of the front door to see torches from Heugh battery searching the night sky. It was another Zeppelin. The whining started, the whistling, the crash and bang of an explosion somewhere nearby. Martha raced upstairs and grabbed William before looking for George.

He wasn't in his bed? Where was he? 'George. We've got to get out. George,' she screamed running downstairs and outside.

The street was bustling with men and women and children. Some had their emergency suitcases with them and they were hurrying away. Away from the flame lit sky.

'Wait here, William. I'll go and get your Da.'

'No, Ma. No.' William grabbed his mother's hand.

'I won't be long. You be a big boy for your Ma.' Martha pulled herself free and ran back inside. 'George. Where are you? George.'

Running upstairs, she looked again into both bedrooms. She was about to run back down when she heard the whimpering. It was coming from under the bed. She dropped onto her knees, lowered her head and saw him, curled into a ball; hands over his ears; crying like a baby.

Martha gasped. 'Come out, George. Come to me.' She spoke calmly, stretching her arm out to him. 'I'll look after you. It'll be alright. Hush now. Give me your hand.'

Slowly and timidly, George reached out to her, grasping her hand so tightly she thought he'd crush it. She coaxed him until he shuffled his way out. Flinching with every bang and flash of light.

Helping him to his feet, she led him downstairs and out onto the street where William was shivering and crying. He ran to her and buried his face in her skirt. She put her arm around him and held George's hand.

'Right then, you two, let's get you both somewhere safe,' she said dragging two pairs of unwilling feet along the road as another shell whined before exploding over in the direction of Middleton Road.

Albert appeared, running towards them. 'Thank God you're all safe. I'm glad George got you both out,' he said taking William from his Ma and picking him up. 'You did a good job, George.'

'Da didn't get us out. It were Ma. She had to go back in and get Da.'

'What the hell? What's got into you, George? You bloody idiot. They could have been killed.'

George didn't answer. He was shaking violently, hanging on to Martha as if his life depended on it.

'Yer bloody lily livered piece of work. Call yersel a man. You should be ashamed. Yer a coward, George Hubbard. A bloody coward.' George cringed at the onslaught, holding tighter to Martha's hand.

'That's not going to help, Albert. Can't you see the state he's in,' Martha said as calmly as she could.

'Don't shout, Uncle Albert. I dunna like it.' William was bawling. Martha stroked his back as he clung to Albert, his legs wrapped around the big man's waist.

Chapter 30

Martha's family had watched the Zeppelin from the market yard with Sarah and Joe. The sky was lit by anti-aircraft fire and the massive torches that were hunting it out. As it was travelling so low, they could see the actual shape of the giant gondola. George had huddled by the fire in Sarah's kitchen. Bombs were blasting somewhere over in the Middleton Road area, and Albert, along with Edward, went to see if they could be of help. Martha, George and William didn't see either of them again that night. They eventually went home and had all lain in the same bed. William cradled in his mother's arms; George shaking and twitching beside them.

Martha had left George in bed when she set off for work the following morning. She couldn't face another minute watching him cower at the slightest noise. Was she a bad person? Wasn't she the one who had defended people who were afraid to fight when Mrs Wicklow had been handing out white feathers? She didn't know anymore. This war had changed everything; changed her. All she knew right now was that being at work helped things to feel a bit more normal.

There was a lot of talk about last night's attack in work.

Some of the girls from the hostel had been watching everything from Church Square. Crowds had dashed out from the pubs and restaurants to see what was happening. The morning newspapers were filled with pictures, telling the story of the attack. It was lunch break and Martha was reading a copy she'd bought on her way in. Apparently the Zeppelin had dropped several bombs during its journey over the town; mainly in Elwick before a couple had landed in Ward Jackson Park and then it emptied its final load on Middleton Road. Quite a few people had been killed or injured and the hospital was full. Cheers and roars went up from the crowds when the Zeppelin had eventually been hit; bursting into flames and dropping in to the sea where it slid slowly into the dark water.

'What a carry on. Me and Sam took the kids up to the church. Ma and Da refused to move. Said if their time were up, it were up,' said Florrie, shaking her head.

'We went over to Sarah's. Standing in the yard; watching it all happen. Not sure where we could have gone to be completely safe to be honest. Perhaps your Ma and Da did the right thing?'

'Aye. Mebbe yer reet. It must have been hard for George thinking he'd left it all behind. Sam told me he was back. You should have told me, Martha. I must come round to say hello. Anyway, I've got some exciting news, me and Sam have named the day. Last night we decided. We might as well. We could be dead afore we get round to it if we wait for the war to be ower. '

Martha hugged her friend. 'I'm so pleased for you, Florrie. He's a good man. I don't think you'd find better.' She'd be so hurt if she knew George's opinion of her.

'I know. He's been so good since...Freddie. He sez he'll still help with the little ones as well. I couldn't leave them. Frank needs me. Ma and Da are worse than useless.'

Her fondness for Frank made Martha wonder if the rumours were true after all.

'When is it? Soon?'

'Not for a couple of weeks. Certainly not before Saturday's football match. Sez he couldn't miss all them young women running about in shorts,' she laughed out loud. 'He's a right one. "As long as you only watch 'em" I said to him.'

Martha saw how happy she looked when she talked about Sam. How she envied her friend that feeling. Being able to talk openly about the man she loved must be wonderful.

'Daisy's in the team. She asked me to go and watch,' Martha said, setting a shell on the checking bench.

'We can go together. You and George and me and Sam. We're taking the young uns. Frank's that excited. Bring William.'

'I will. That'd be nice.' Martha wondered what they'd make of George's behaviour.

'You will if yer can get the coward to leave the house.' Albert had joined them. She hadn't seen him coming over. 'Can I have a word in my office, Martha,' he added before walking away again.

Martha's cheeks were burning with embarrassment. Why did Albert say that in front of them? As she followed him, Martha looked back to find the girls in a huddle, deep in conversation.

'How could you? Now they'll all be gossiping about it.' Martha was furious with Albert. How could he be so cruel?

'It's about time everyone knew what a snivelling little coward he is. He were crying like a bairn, last night. I were ashamed to be with him. And dunna tell me he's ill. He were an embarrassment, hiding behind yer skirts every time another bomb landed. Some bloody use he'll have been on the front line.

'Don't say that. It's not true. He's ill.' Martha was crying. She didn't know what was true anymore. She didn't understand what was happening to George but she couldn't believe he was what Albert was saying.

'Martha, he doesn't deserve you. Look how you had to be the strong one last night. Yer could have all been killed in yer beds if it hadna been for you. Leave him. Come with me. I'll find us a little house somewhere. I'll look after you. At least I could make a better job of it than him.'

'Like you did when you left me?' she snapped at him. 'It was George who looked after me then.'

Albert turned on her now. 'Well, what did you expect? I wasn't about to come back after what you did, was I?' he yelled at her, his face sour with anger.

Martha stopped in her tracks. She couldn't believe what she was hearing. 'What I did? You were the one who left without a backward glance. I was the one left to cope. You had better write me a leaving certificate. I can't work here anymore,' she yelled at him and marched out of his office and back to her workstation.

'No need to worry about having to work alongside me. I'll be leaving as soon as I can find another job.' She stared at the women, daring them to say anything.

'If you believe him ower George, you're a bigger fool than I thought. He's worth ten of that one.' Florrie turned from Martha and set about trimming another shell.

'Wait, Martha. Wait.' Albert chased after her, catching her arm, pulling her to a stop. 'Let me walk home with you. I need to know what you meant.'

Martha pulled away from him and quickened her pace. She had tried to get out of work without him noticing. All day she had been going over what he had said. "*What did you expect?*" She didn't understand? She was the one left behind. She was the one left to face the consequences. It didn't make sense. Did he think she had tried to trap him? He should have stayed. Not leave George to pick up the pieces.

'What I meant? About what? You're the one talking in riddles.'

'Me? You know what you did. I thought you would wait for me. At least for a few months. But you'd already started making your plans before I left. It took me a long time to forgive you. But I did and I thought we...I thought we could make a go of it.'

Martha stopped and turned to face him. Her blood was boiling. 'Forgive me? I wasn't the only one in the relationship. It takes two.'

'Don't I know it. You could have told me before I left.'

'What? And have you feel sorry for me? Pity me?'

'Pity you? Now why would I pity you?'

'It was as much your fault as mine. George said you would never come back and he was right. He was prepared to marry me. We hadn't time to wait. You must see that?'

'Of course I could see it. You deserve each other.'

Albert stormed off leaving Martha shaking with anger and frustration. She was well rid of him. What a fool she'd been. He wasn't worth a second more of her time and energy.

On the way back from Celia's, William had complained about not being able to go and see his Uncle Albert or even to go and see Edward and Joe over at Sarah's.

'I dunna want to go home. Please, Ma. Please can we go and visit Edward and Joe? They play with me. They make me laugh.' Martha was still angry with Albert, and their conversation whirled around her mind. She would never speak to him again, she promised herself. George didn't deserve any of this. She'd been a fool, but now she'd concentrate on helping George get better.

'We need to get back for your Da, William. He'll be getting hungry.'

'He's not my Da,' snapped William. 'My Da doesn't cry like a baby. My Da's big and strong. He lifts me up on to his shoulders. Like Uncle Albert. Why can't we live with Uncle Albert? Then they won't be so mean to me.'

'What do you mean, William? Who's being mean to you?' Martha stopped walking and looked down at him. She squeezed his hand. 'Tell me. What is it?'

'Horace Bickerdyke said no-one should talk to me on account of my Da being a coward.'

Martha felt her chest tighten. Now William was bearing the brunt of Albert's outburst as well. She tried not to sound too upset as she remembered Bessy Bickerdyke dashing out of their house across the road last night during the Zeppelin attack. She and her family would have seen the state of George as she brought him out of the house. Witnessed Albert screaming at his brother. She was always gossiping about someone. There was many a woman at the factory that had been on the receiving end of her bad mouthing.

'Horace Bickerdyke ought to know better at his age. Ignore him, William. Words are nothing. They can't hurt you.'

William started to cry. 'He said that they shoot cowards in the army. He said Da should be shot. Then they all started shouting *Shoot him. Shoot him.* And I couldn't get away. Frank kept telling them to shut up but they wouldn't. I was scared, Ma. Mrs Appleby took me inside. Will they shoot him, Ma? Will they shoot Da?' Martha squatted and pulled him close.

'Of course not. I've a good mind to go round to Bessy Bickerdyke's and give her a piece of my mind. Don't worry now, Ma'll sort it out.'

'I wish we lived with Uncle Albert. Uncle Albert isn't a coward. I dunna want to live with Da anymore.'

'You don't mean that, William. He's not very well at the moment. Don't be angry with him. He'll soon be back to his old self, you'll see. He'll be telling you stories before you go to bed like he used to do. You loved his stories. They were always funny.'

'I don't remember any stories.' He sniffled, trying hard to stop crying.

'That's because you were quite small before he went off to France. You just don't remember them. It'll be nice when he's better and he can do it again, won't it?' she said, trying to soothe him. It seemed to help and they walked on in silence for a while.

'Did he really tell stories, Ma?' William asked as they neared home.

'Yes he did. He loved to tell you stories.' The memory made her smile. 'We shouldn't upset your Da with all these awful things people are saying. It might make him even more ill. We need to look after him, don't we? You won't say anything, will you, William? Let's keep it to ourselves, shall we?'

'Yes, Ma,' sighed William.

'Have you eaten?' Martha asked George, taking her coat off .

'Yes. I've had the b-broth you left.'

Martha saw the dirty bowl on the table. Bending down, she unbuttoned William's jacket. He approached his Da.

'Da?' he asked cautiously. Martha's heart beat a little faster, wondering what sort of response her son would get. 'Da? Can you tell me a story tonight? Ma sez you used to tell me stories before you went away to war? Will you?'

The room was so quiet. Martha held her breath as George turned to look at his son.

'I...I'm not sure I can remember any. Let me think s-s-son,' he replied, turning back to watch the flames spark. Martha let out a sigh.

'There. Da'll think about it. That's good, isn't it, William?' she said brightly. 'Are you going to set the table for me? That's my big boy.' William went to the drawer and got the cutlery out. Poor bairn, thought Martha. He's so quiet, frightened of what George'll be like. What his mood will be. It's not right. He shouldn't have to be like this.

The evening meal passed in silence. Martha watched William looking at his father all the time, waiting to see if a story would be forthcoming. Frightened to ask again. By the time he was ready for bed there had still been no mention of it and William went to say goodnight.

He knelt down in front of the range and looked up into George's face.

'Have you remembered a story to tell me?' George was gazing into the fire, not moving, not blinking.

'Da.' William spoke a little louder and put his hand on George's knee. George jumped from his seat pushing William to the floor.

'I can't. I canna stand it no more. Get away,' he yelled before throwing himself on the floor and crawling under the table.

'George! For goodness sake,' shouted Martha, running and picking William up. 'It's alright, William. Da didn't mean it. I'm so sorry.' She hugged him to her.

'I don't like Da. Make him go away, Ma. Make him go away.'

Martha took him upstairs and laid him in bed. She climbed in beside him and cradled him close.

'It'll be alright soon. I promise.' She comforted him until he slept, rocking him back and forth. She had no idea how she was going to make things better, but she'd think of something. She had to.

Chapter 31

Martha had never felt so alone before. Faces turned away with every step she took to her workstation. Words wormed their way into her ears as she tried in vain to shut them out. Whispering voices filled her head.

'She must be shamed to have a husband like that.'

'My Harry sez he saw lots of 'em out there. Bloody cowards. They shoot 'em you know if they run off.'

'Wouldn't want the likes of him watching my back. Frightened of his own shadow I've heard.'

Martha looked straight in front of her, holding her head high. She was determined not to run away. Enough that her husband's name was dragged through the mud. She wasn't to blame. Neither was he. They'd see that he'd been ill. Once she'd worked out how to get through to him. Brought the old George back.

'Tek no notice. I dunna care what they say, George is no coward. Never in a million years. He's ill that's all.' Florrie squeezed her arm. 'My Sam sez it could happen to anyone. You stand yer ground. Yoos've done nowt wrong. I bet there's a few of 'em in the same boat as you if they'd admit it.'

'Thank you, Florrie. It's good to know I've one friend in this factory. I can take it. It's when they start taking it out on my son. What's he done wrong?'

'I'm so sorry, Martha. Our Frank told me what they'd done to him at school. He sez Mrs Appleby gave 'em what for. He sez she collared Bessy when she came for Horace and had a word with her too. I dunna think they'll be doing it again.'

'Will you tell your Frank I'm very grateful to him for standing up for William. It was brave of him. I've asked Daisy to stay at school until he goes inside this morning. Make sure he's safe.'

'I will. Our Frank'll take care of him. He knows how to look after his own.'

The other girls in the row had ignored her, but now they started chatting loudly.

'Hey, our Jessie. Tell us again how your Tommy killed fifteen o' them Germans single-handed.'

'He shot all the cowards who wudna go ower the top wi' him first and then wiped out the Huns with grenades and mortars. He's bound to get a medal.'

'He did reet shootin' all them cowards. They deserve no better.'

'Ha'way yoos lot—' Florrie started to say but Martha stopped her.

'Don't, Florrie. It'll only make them worse.'

Martha gritted her teeth and got on with her job. She steeled herself to all their comments, singing songs in her head to shut out their bad mindedness.

Sam came by with his little truck of shell cases. 'I'm looking forward to the football match,' he said loudly. 'And to meeting your George. I've heard a lot about him.'

'So have we,' one of the girls called over and the others laughed.

'Some folks ought to look in their own backyards afore commenting on someone else's,' he shouted, winking at Martha. Martha smiled at him gratefully and Florrie mouthed a silent "Thank you" to him to show her appreciation of his kindness to her friend. Sam gave Florrie a quick peck on the cheek and continued on his rounds.

This was all Albert's fault, thought Martha. Not only had he deserted his brother, he'd made sure that the whole factory thought ill of him too. Martha waited until she saw the floor manager, Mr Castleton, leaving the office and marched across. She would have it out with him. She didn't care that everyone was watching her. She didn't care what they were saying. She didn't even knock on the door before she threw it open and slammed it shut behind her.

'Happy now? You've ruined my life and George's. My son was bullied at school. He's five years old. All because of you. You disgust me. Why? How could you?'

Albert looked up from the ledger he had been writing in. His face betraying the regret he was feeling. 'I'm sorry, Martha. I didn't mean for you or William to get hurt. I heard what happened to him. I don't know what I was thinking. Blurting it out in front of all your friends. I was so angry...'

'You were angry? You'd no right to do this to us. You've made it impossible for me to stay here now. What'll I do for money?' she screamed at him, her heart aching to turn back time. Make everything as it was. Wake up from this nightmare.

'Come here,' he stood up and held his arms open. 'Come here. I'll make it alreet again. I promise... Please.'

Martha hated herself as she dissolved in his hold. Holding on to the person who had caused all her hurt; still loving him after what he'd done. Her tears soaked through his shirt and wet his skin. He cupped her face and kissed her eyes, her cheeks, her mouth.

'We need to talk properly. Sort this out.' He let go of her and pulled his jacket on. 'Come with me.'

The couple walked out of the office and he guided her back towards her workstation. He removed her cap and handed her coat to her before heading for the exit.

'He's after takin' her home. Poor man must be that embarrassed, having a family like that,' she heard one woman say as they passed. She could feel Florrie's eyes burning into the back of her neck.

Albert didn't take her home. They walked across town and he took her into Mrs Haw's dining rooms on Lynn Street. The smell of warm cakes and freshly-made sandwiches reminded Martha of the day George had taken her to The Royal. Almost the same circumstances, but this time she would be discussing George with Albert rather than the other way around. The floral print wallpaper with its great blousy roses made it seem cosy and small, but the well-polished silver teapots and cruets suggested a high class establishment, not like the family-friendly hotel she and George had gone to. Martha felt out of place in her work overall and kept her coat buttoned high as two ladies at the table by the bow window stared at her. They went and sat in a corner, well away from them, pouring over the menu. A young waitress in a starched white cap and matching pristine apron came over to take their order.

'Can I help you, Sir?' she asked slowly and politely, ignoring Martha. Her employer had obviously told her to try and lose the local accent. It reminded Martha of when she worked at Turnbull and Tilley.

'We'll take tea and a small selection of sandwiches.' Albert tried to sound as if he'd done this dozens of times.

'Yes, Sir. Would madam like me to take her coat?' She seemed to be looking down her nose at Martha, who straightened her back and responded in the same manner.

'One is feeling a slight chill. Perhaps a warmer environment might have helped.'

Albert grinned widely as the waitress turned on her heel and marched away. 'Good for you, Pet. Snooty little madam.'

Martha forced a smile in return before dropping her shoulders and slumping back down in her seat.

'Oh. What's the point? This is a mistake. We've nothing to discuss here. I may as well go home.' She started to rise but Albert grabbed her hand.

'We need to clear the air, Martha. I canna bear us being at loggerheads with each other. I need some answers. When I left...all those years ago... I need you to tell me why you were seeing George at the same time as me? I thought you loved me.'

'What makes you say that? I wasn't seeing George until after you left. He helped me. I didn't know what to do.' He didn't seem to hear what she had said, continuing as if she hadn't spoken. He was looking down at the table, playing with the salt cellar.

'I canna understand why you let him...You know...You were mine— '

'What? I should have known... How could you say such a thing...I never...only ever with you... I wished I hadn't.' Her face was beetroot with embarrassment.

'You don't need to lie to me, Martha.' He sat up, eyes flashing dark. 'George told me how you couldn't help yourselves. You shudda put me straight before I left.'

'What are you talking about? I don't understand.' Why was he saying all these things? Hadn't he hurt her enough without all this?

'George wrote to me. Said how you were...you know? How you'd fallen in love and it had started when I was doing extra hours at the shipyard. How lonely you'd been on your own every night. He said you had to get married quick afore you started *showing*. '

'You're lying. George would never have said that. He wouldn't.' She couldn't take it all in. George wouldn't do that, would he? She'd turned to him for advice. He'd been a good friend. "I'll write to him" he'd said. "Tell him he has to come home. It'll be alreet, Martha. I'll sort it out," he had said to her and she'd believed him. Trusted him. No... Albert must be lying. 'You're making it up. Trying to get at George. I hate you, Albert Hubbard.' Not caring if anyone was looking at them, she left him sitting there and ran to the door.

'Ask him if you don't believe me,' he shouted after her as she left the teashop. She didn't stop running until she was back on Tankerville street. Her chest heaved, her breath rasping in her throat as she struggled to fill her lungs with air.

After calming herself down she opened the front door.

'No, George. I've told you. I've come to see how you are. Not to ask for money. Put it back in yer pocket.'

Martha stopped in her tracks. Florrie?

'I f-felt that guilty w-when I had to stop. I-I couldn't split the allowance. It went d-direct to M-Martha.'

Martha crept into the parlour and held the door ajar so that she could listen. What was happening?

'Don't be silly. I understood. You could hardly ask Martha to give me money for Frank. '

Martha began to shake. Now it all made sense. The rumours about Florrie. George asking her not to have anything to do with her. Frank was George's son. George was no better than his brother. Poor Florrie. How could George have left her that way?

'Look...I'd best go. I thought Martha would have been home.' It took all Martha's willpower to stay put. She was ready to storm in there and let them know their secret was out. Demand that George explain himself.

'Where is she? Didn't she leave with you?'

Martha held her breath.

'No she left...she left early. Said something about going to Sarah's. I canna remember what for.'

Martha closed the door softly as Florrie came passed and left the house. Martha breathed a sigh of relief. Why hadn't Florrie told him that she had left with Albert? Why had she covered for her? If George had left her expecting a child and then married someone else within a year, she would have hated that someone with a vengeance. Why hadn't she grabbed the chance of splitting them up?

She waiting a few minutes then crept outside the front door. Taking a deep breath, she pushed the door open and stepped inside the hall. 'I'm home. Sorry I'm late.' She took her coat off. 'Went by Sarah's to say hello but she was out.'

Martha didn't go to work the next day. She couldn't face anymore gossip. She couldn't face seeing Albert. She had left George asleep and gone downstairs to make William's breakfast. She had readied him in a daze, unable to shake the weight that was dragging her down, overpowering her mind. Barely remembering the walk to school and home again, she dropped into a chair and laid her head on the table between her arms. She had lain awake most of the night thinking about what she had overheard between Florrie and George. How could she broach the subject with either of them without revealing that she had been listening to their conversation? It seemed impossible to her that George could treat anyone that way, let alone Florrie. The girl must have felt so alone. She wondered how she had managed to hide the fact from people as her size altered. How had she covered it up until she handed him over to her parents to raise as their own? She obviously hadn't been too successful. The rumours had spread enough for it to become a topic for gossip even now after several years, although no-one seemed to be aware of who the father was. And George? He had kept it secret from her all this time. No wonder they were always short of money. He had been lying to her for years. Maybe he had lied about the letter too. Maybe Albert was telling the truth about that. The only redeeming thing from this whole mess was that George had actually supported his child financially. Maybe he thought she wouldn't have married him if he'd told her about Frank and Florrie? Had he been so frightened of losing her? It occurred to her that was what Florrie must have meant when she said that Frank knew how to look after his own. Frank and William were related. More closely related than she had ever suspected. She wanted to have it out with George, but she feared it might have a negative effect on his recovery. He was still so delicate and, regardless of how angry she was with him, she couldn't bear the thought of upsetting him.

Her first priority, she finally decided, was to get some help for George. She would wait and see what the doctor could offer in terms of treatment. The last thing she could do at the moment was to ask him about Frank or whether Albert was telling the truth about that letter. He wouldn't know what to say if she asked him in his current condition. Getting him better first was the answer. She would ask him when he was well again. If she found out that it was true it would change everything. She couldn't support someone who had betrayed her in that way? She couldn't continue to live with such a person. She searched her mind for answers but only came up with more questions. Had George sent the letter to make sure that Albert would never come back to her? Because he was frightened of losing her? Would he stoop as low as that to get what he wanted? Albert would have been left with no choice. He would have felt humiliated. Hurt beyond belief that she had gone with another man, his own brother... No... It wasn't true, it couldn't be. Had he kept Frank a secret because he loved her? Had his love removed all sense of duty and decency? Had she known him so little? It didn't make any sense at all.

George had done nothing but love her all their married life, and no matter what she thought she felt for Albert it could never match what she and George had. Albert was lying. He must be. But Florrie? She was so confused.

The knock on the door brought her back to the present.

'Doctor Bartholomew. Thank you so much for coming.' Martha stepped to one side and let him in.

'Daisy said that George is unwell. What symptoms is he showing? He'll be susceptible to all sorts of illnesses and infections after a stint on the front line. We'd better have a look at him, poor man,' he said, heading for the kitchen. He put his bag down on the table and started to open it.

'He's got lots of sores and his feet are in a mess, but it's not that. I can't explain it properly. He doesn't seem himself since he came back. Edward...Sarah Colby's son, said he'd been in a sort of hospital near the front line. Casualty clearing station? Yes, that was it. He's confused sometimes. Thinks he's still out there and his hands shake all the time.' Doctor Bartholomew closed his bag again.

'I see. Sounds like a touch of hysteria to me. I suppose we'd better have a look.' The change in tone was clear. From someone eager to treat his patient, Doctor Bartholomew now seemed indifferent to George's condition.

Martha followed him upstairs. George was still in bed. 'I left him to sleep this morning, doctor. He's been having some sort of nightmare most of the night. Like he's back out there. Screaming sometimes. Talking out loud.'

'Yes. I was right. Some men find it difficult to cope out there. Start behaving in a peculiar fashion. The best answer is rest and quiet for a few days, and then he should be fit to go back. When does his leave end?'

'A week on Thursday. Doctor...he's been like this for over two weeks. It can't be this hysteria thing.' Martha was confused. The doctor seemed to think it was something and nothing. Trivial.

'It does present itself as something quite serious, but the army assures me it's something the men can get over quite quickly once they are back on the front line. They don't have time to worry about things out there. Too much going on for them to stop and think and build it all out of proportion in their minds. I've heard of some even admitting it was simply fear that had taken hold, but once they were back with their pals they soon bucked up their ideas. After all, their fellow soldiers depend on them, don't they?'

'But... Edward said that a Dr. Rose at the hospital said he needed treatment. I can't remember what Edward called it...neuro something? She said there were treatment places—'

'A woman doctor, you say?' he stopped her mid flow. 'That explains it. They have a tendency to over dramatise the lady do-gooders I'm afraid...no offence, Martha. You'll see. A few more days rest and he'll be right as rain. That's right isn't it, George? You don't want to let all your pals down, do you? You want to do your duty, don't you?' He turned on his heel and went back downstairs without waiting for a reply.

Martha followed him.'There must be something you can give him? Please, Doctor. He's so tired.'

He opened his bag and pulled out his prescription pad and scribbled a note.

'Take this over to the chemist. They'll help him sleep,' placing his hand on her shoulder, he added. 'Stop worrying, Martha. He's a strong lad. He'll cope as long as you don't keep pandering to his woes.' He left her feeling more confused than ever.

Chapter 32

'I like you bringing me to school instead of Daisy. Can you bring me every day now, Ma?' William asked as they arrived at the school gate.

'For a little while, William. Until we get your Da better anyway.' Martha had made the decision not to go back to the munitions factory. She couldn't get another job, not without Albert signing a leaving certificate; no-one would employ her without it. She had some savings and they could live on those for a while. Concentrating on caring for George was the most important thing at the moment. He seemed pleased that she was going to stay at home with him. Perhaps she should have stopped work as soon as he'd come home?

'Will you come and collect me after school?'

'I will. Off you go.' She kissed her son and he ran into the playground just as Mrs Appleby rang her bell. The children stood in their appropriate lines and she watched them all start to troop inside. She smiled as she saw William and Frank elbowing each other out of the queue in turn as they disappeared through the large wooden door. Frank would make sure he was alright, and Mrs Appleby would be watching them like a hawk. Martha turned to say good morning to a group of women standing outside the playground. The minute she caught their eye, they all turned away from her. Martha wasn't surprised. News travels fast, she thought and set off for home.

George was laughing. He seemed to have come round a bit since Dr Bartholomew had been to see him earlier in the week. He was certainly sleeping well. It was as if his mind was improving as the wounds on his body healed. He was talking a bit more. Saying he was feeling better. She wasn't sure if it was the tablets or what the doctor had said. Either way it was at least one tiny step in the right direction. She was reading the newspaper to him. Only the local news. She thought it better to avoid any mention of the front. She had been telling him about a woman that had been so drunk in the town she had thought the policewoman arresting her was a man and had been flirting with her all the way back to the station, even attempting to kiss her.

'The judge sentenced her to a month in prison for propositioning a police officer and said she might find some of the women prisoners more receptive to her deviant tendencies.' Martha's eyes were watering as she laughed with him, picturing this poor policewoman trying to fend off the advances. 'Can you imagine it, George?'

'I bet the drunken w-w-woman had a shock the day after when she was told what she'd done.'

This was more like it, thought Martha. She decided it was a good time to mention the football match.

'Daisy's playing in a ladies football match on Saturday. To raise funds for the hospital. I said we'd go...Would you like that?'

'I...I dunna think so, Martha. It'll be n-noisy...L-Lots of people.' The laughter in his eyes has been replaced by a look of fear, she thought as she held his hand between hers.

'I'll be with you... and William will be there too. We won't leave you on your own. Not for a minute.'

'People'll be staring. P-Poking fun. Maybe next time. I still canna stop my hands shaking.'

'Please, George. Florrie's fiance'll be there. Sam. You remember. The one I told you about. Lost an arm in France. Folks are more likely to stare at him than you.'

'I dunno...Do we have to go with F-Florrie? I-I dunna f-feel...'

Martha interrupted him, her voice sharp. He hates the thought of Florrie and me talking to each other. 'Can you do it for William? He's looking forward to it. Daisy's playing and she needs our support after everything she's done for William.'

'I...mebbe.'

'Thank you,' she said, trying to keep her voice even as she leaned over and kissed his cheek. 'That's the spirit.'

'And you'll stay with me all the time?'

'I'll stay with you all the time. I can't wait to tell William. He'll be so excited.' Martha picked the flat iron up and spat on it; she pulled George's shirt down from the drying rack and started to press it. 'You'll enjoy it. You wait and see.'

'I s'pose.'

Martha's hopes started to rise. He's definitely improving. Perhaps Doctor Bartholomew was right after all. A day out is exactly what he needs. She wondered how he would react when he saw Frank.

'So I wondered if you were coming too,' Martha asked Sarah as she joined them for some lunch. Joe and Edward were wolfing their food down. Martha wondered how long it would be before Joe was talking of joining up. He must be nearly seventeen now.

'We are. Edward has to go back on Monday, so we thought we'd all go and cheer Daisy on. Joe will be cheering louder than anyone. Won't you, Joe?'

'Give ower, Ma.' Martha noticed the blush rising on his cheeks. She pretended not to see and carried on talking.

'I'm so pleased you'll all be there. I've managed to talk George into going, but I think the more support he has around him the better. He's nervous about how people will treat him. I think having Edward walking alongside, as well as Florrie's Sam, will give him some confidence and it might stop the gossipers from saying something that would upset him.'

'Is Albert going to be there?' Edward asked.

'I shouldn't think so,' Martha said quietly. 'George doesn't need his sort around right now. He reckons that George is putting it on; too scared to go back out there and fight.'

'The man's a fool and a bully. I didn't think he'd sink so low as to turn his back on his own brother.' Sarah sounded angry. Martha cringed. She still didn't want to think too badly of Albert, but after the lie he'd told her she couldn't reconcile her feelings for him anymore.

'I won't tell him that you're all going to be there. He might panic and change is mind. William is excited about having a day out with his Da again. I hope it reassures him that George is on the mend.'

'Has Dr Bartholomew been to see him yet?' Edward asked. 'He may need to go to one of them hospitals I was telling you about.'

'Yes. He came a few days ago. He says it's a bit of hysteria and George needs to get back out there and join his pals.'

'What? The man doesn't know what he's talking about. Did you tell him what Dr. Rose had said?'

'I did, and he says that she's prone to over exaggerating, her being a woman and all.' Martha hadn't been too happy about the doctor's patronising view of women and it was obvious in the way she answered Edward.

'Ha'way with him. The cheek of it.' Sarah's voice was high with indignation. 'He's probably afraid she'll do him out of a job. Arrogant little—'

'Now then, Ma. No need for that language.' Edward stopped her in mid flow. 'I'll have a word with Dr Rose as soon as I get back, Martha. I'll ask her to write to Dr. Bartholomew for you. George is in no fit state to be going back yet.'

'Thank you, Edward. It's very good of you. But you'll have to be quick. He's due to go back next Thursday.'

'I've made a plate up for him, Martha. Tek it back with you.' Sarah handed her a large plate of potatoes and rabbit stew.

'Thanks, Sarah. You're all so kind to us. I'll take a bit off it for William's tea. Now that he's not getting fed up at Celia's. Do you see anything of her? I haven't had sight of her since I started at the munitions factory. She's always up at the hospital when I collect William.'

'Not much. She's lost a lot of weight. Thin as a sparrow these days. Daisy sez it's because she doesn't eat proper. Too busy looking after all them poor wounded soldiers, but I've heard she and Mrs Wicklow will be at the match. They're having a day off to help collect the money for the hospital. It's only me and Daisy who go out canvassing for now. We're organising a protest about women's rights to go into the local pubs whenever we want. It's ridiculous that men can drink every hour they're open and we can't. Not that I've time to drink all day, mind. I only want what's right. Like the right to vote...One day,' she said wistfully.

'Maybe sooner than you think. The papers reckon they'll make Lloyd George prime minister before Christmas. He'll be looking at votes for women at the same time as he sorts out the soldier's rights to vote.'

'I hope so. I'll believe it when it happens. Mebbe you can help us a bit now you're not working?'

Martha thought about it for a minute. 'Do you know, I think I will. I'll have to fit it around caring for George and picking William up from school but,Yes, I'd like that very much. It seems to me that women definitely need a voice when people like Dr Bartholomew can't even support a fellow doctor's opinion just because she's a woman.'

Sarah laughed out loud. 'Finally, the woman can see sense. Hallelujah!'

Martha left feeling better than she had for quite a long while. The cold weather didn't dampen her spirit as she strode home carrying the basket with the plate of food for George, humming along to *Oh I do like to be beside the seaside* as she walked briskly towards home. She hadn't thought of it for such a long time. It brought a picture of her and Ma and Da on the beach when she was around fifteen years old. The day had been hot and sunny and it seemed as if the whole town was down there, paddling in the water and playing games along the sands. The tune had been playing on a big steam organ on the promenade. Da had grabbed Ma and they had danced a jig. She'd been embarrassed until a dozen other couples had joined them. Martha remembered thinking they looked so happy and it made her feel happy too. William was always happy when she and George were laughing together. What she wouldn't give for such happy days again. She would do her best to make life at home like that again.

Martha collected William from school, always nervous now as she thought about what sort of day he might have had. As long as he stayed by Frank when he was in the playground he would be alright, she hoped. She found herself comparing the two boys. Frank definitely had Florrie's hair and eyes, but what about the mouth? She thought she could see something of George's smile but she wasn't sure. She half hoped Florrie might come to pick him up, she missed their chats and the way they laughed together at work. She was disappointed when she saw him leave with Violet, even though she knew it would be almost impossible for Florrie to get a day off before the wedding.

William was smiling as he ran to her, seeming a little

brighter than on previous days. 'Mrs Appleby made me stay in class with her at playtime again. She said it was better if I spent more time learning my letters. I think I'm getting better at it, Ma. I canna do the *q* very well. I keep forgetting that its little tail kicks out straight on the little one and it's curly on the big Q. Frank wanted me to play out with him, but Mrs Appleby said I couldn't but he could come and learn his letters at the same time if he wanted.'

'And did he want?' asked Martha.

'No. He said anything was better than learning his letters.'

Martha laughed and said a silent thank you to Mrs Appleby as they walked along. Thank goodness she's taking the bullying situation seriously, she thought. At least I won't be worrying what's happening when I'm not there.

'Frank said to tell you that Florrie misses you at work and she wants to know when are you coming back? You're not going back yet are you , Ma?' Martha was pleased that her friend felt the same way as her.

'No, I'm not going back yet. We've got to look after your Da, haven't we? He was laughing today, William. I think he's starting to feel a lot better. Those tablets that the doctor gave him seem to be helping. We'll soon have him telling you some stories and playing games .'

'I s'pose. When will Uncle Albert come to play games with me? I miss him.'

'I don't know, William. He's a bit busy at the moment. He's got so much extra work to do now that I'm not there anymore.' It was the only answer she could think of.

'That's not fair. He'll have to get someone else to do your job , won't he? What about Mrs Clegg who lives next door but one? She doesn't have any children or a poorly husband. She'd be able to go and work.'

'I think Mrs Clegg's a bit too old to work there. She has got children, but they're all grown up and fighting the war like your Da.'

'How old is she? Is she as old as you, Ma. You aren't too

old.'

'No. She's as old has your Da's Granda was when he died.'

'That's very old, isn't it, Ma.'

'It is, William. Very, very old.'

'Like dinosaurs. Mrs Appleby says dinosaurs are very, very old.' He seemed to have totally forgotten about Albert.

'Yes, that's right. Like dinosaurs.'

'I'm going to tell Da about dinosaurs,' he said. 'I'll tell him that they are very, very old like Granda and Mrs Clegg.

'He'd like that, William. He'd like that very much.

Chapter 33

'Come on, Ma. Can we go now?' William was jumping up and down at the thought of going to his first football match. It didn't matter to him that girls were playing and not men.

'Hold your horses, young man. We've got to wait for Florrie, and your Da needs to get ready. He has to finish shaving and then he'll get changed into his uniform.' Martha was so pleased that George had felt able to wash and shave and get himself dressed. He had been doing more and for himself over the last few days.

'I canna wait for Frank to get here, then he can play horses with me. Is Sam coming? Frank sez Sam's a nice man. He likes him.' The revelation that Frank was coming with Florrie didn't seem to have affected George at all, or he was hiding his feelings very well.

'He is a nice man. He's meeting us there. He's on the early shift at the factory this week.' Martha had hoped he'd be able to walk up to the ground with George. Give him a bit of support, but never mind. At least he'd be at the match.

William went and stood next to his father's chair as he looked into the small mirror. It was propped up on the kitchen table against a mug of hot water. George swished his razor in the hot liquid before slicing it through the white beard of soapy lather that started above his mouth and ran all the way down his neck.

William looked at his Da's contorted face and spoke to his reflection through the glass. 'Why do you pull that face when you're shaving, Da? Does it hurt?' he asked, concern in his voice.

George stopped what he was doing and looked down at his son. 'Cos I'm trying to be c-careful. The razor's sh-sharp and if I dunna move my face so that the blade goes over the s-skin all smooth, it'll tek a piece of my chin off. Then I'll b-b-bleed all over this clean vest that you're Ma washed.'

'When will I have to shave? I dunna think I'll like having to do that.'

'You won't mind when you're older. It's s-summat all men have to do if they dunna want a hairy f-face. I only have this moustache 'cos the army s-sez I have to, otherwise I'd whip that off as well as the beard that's starting to grow.'

William continued to watch his father through the mirror, copying his actions; twisting his own face as he drew a pretend razor down over his chin in short bursts and then sticking his chin out, sliding the imaginary blade up his neck and back over the curve of his jaw. He pretended to wipe his blade on a leather strap as his Da was doing on the real one that hung down over the edge of the table.

'That'll be Florrie and the children,' Martha said as someone hammered on the door, making George flinch and nick his cheek. 'Christ!' he yelped and William backed away from him.

'George,' snapped Martha. 'Don't shout.'

George grabbed a facecloth and held it to the blood that was running freely from his face.

'It...It's alreet, lad. No need to be f-feared. I'm not cross with you.' George held a hand out and William went back to him.

Martha painted a smile on as she opened the front door, expecting to see Florrie.

'Albert. What are you doing here?' She almost lost her balance as he pushed his way in.

'Have you asked him yet?'

'No...I'

'Asked me what?' shouted George from inside the kitchen.

'If it was alright for him to come to the football match with us.' Martha jumped in quickly, not giving Albert time to say anything. 'Look how well he's doing, Albert. He's feeling much better aren't you, George? As long as he doesn't get any sudden shocks to set him back, he's going to feel better every day. Isn't that right, George?' Her jaw was set as she spoke, keeping her eyes fully on Albert, jamming her words home. Her eyes flashing as they told him to keep quiet about the letter. She wasn't going to have the day ruined.

'I...Aye, that's right. Yer dunna mind if I come do you?' he growled in response.

'Course not, Uncle Albert.' William flung his arms around Albert's legs. 'I've missed you. Will you sit me on your shoulders at the match? Ma sez there'll be a lot of grown-ups there and I won't be able to see.'

Martha saw the look of disappointment on George's face as he turned back to the mirror and wiped off the remainder of the soapy lather.

'Your Da might want to do that, William... If he feels strong enough. Let's wait and see shall we?' George got up and disappeared upstairs.

Another knock at the door heralded Florrie's arrival. Martha let them in. Frank was the first through the door, shouting for William, and the pair flew upstairs to play with William's precious farm set.

'Where's Violet? I thought she was coming with you?' asked Martha as she ushered them through to the kitchen.

'She's got hersel a Saturday...Oh, hello, Mr Hubbard. I didn't know you were coming as well.' She looked to Martha, her face showing surprise at seeing him there before continuing. 'She's got a job at Wiley's where I used to work. First day today so she daren't miss it.'

'That's a shame...Not about the job, that's good news...I mean about not being able to come to the football.'

Albert offered a short nod to Florrie, forcing a brief smile before he stood with his back to the range, hands clasped behind his back. Martha felt his eyes watching her every move.

George came downstairs with a clean shirt on. He barely looked at Florrie as she said hello to him, leaving Martha wondering if he was finding the whole situation difficult. She had laundered and pressed his serge trousers, carefully picking out any remaining lice from the seams. The boys followed him down and raced about between the grown-up's legs, slapping their thighs as if on horseback.

'Take it easy, our Frank, dunna want you knocking someone ower afore we've even got out of the door.' Florrie grabbed his collar as the boy knocked George's legs, jolting him to a stop.

George put on his uniform jacket before pulling his cap down over his head. Martha fastened the top button, straightened his collar and kissed him on the cheek. The feelings inside her made her clumsy as she wondered what Albert was going to do while checking to see if George was trying to steal glances at his son or Florrie, or Albert for that matter.

'Are we all ready then?' she said nervously. 'We're meeting Sarah on the other side of Hart Road by the allotment gardens. We can all go across to the ground together from there.

The weather had been kind and it was a bright and dry day for late November. They made their way along Sheriff Street, crossing over Murray Street and onto Lowthian Road. There were other families, looking forward to a great day out, heading in the same direction; all falling into step with each other by the time they reached Hart Road. Martha linked George's arm, trying to ignore Albert who was bringing up the rear and holding William's hand. They all talked excitedly at the prospect of watching a lot of young women running about and kicking a ball. A group of soldiers from the training camp were standing outside the Lion pub. They seemed particularly effusive, making a few lewd comments about bare legs and some of the girls not always wearing the appropriate underwear that allowed certain parts of their bodies to jiggle about quite a lot. Florrie giggled as they passed, finding it all very funny, but Albert stopped and asked them to 'mind their mouths' when ladies were out and about. Albert walked on quickly, pulling William along in order to catch up with the others. The sound of the soldier's laughter followed them up the street.

Hart Road was heaving with folks on their way up to the football match. A great mass of people crossed the road and cut through Throston Street and on towards the gates of the Victoria grounds. Martha and her group kept themselves tightly to the right, so as not to miss Sarah and the boys when they passed the allotments.

William spotted Edward who had climbed a fence and was waving his soldier's cap at them furiously in order to get their attention. Joe was waving alongside him.

'Edward...Joe,' he shouted, leaving go of Albert's hand and pushing his way over. Albert followed quickly, so as not to lose sight of him in the river of supporters.

'Hello, Albert,' said a surprised Sarah. 'Didna think you'd be here.' Her tone sounded her displeasure at the sight of him.

'Bad penny me,' Albert snarled. 'Allus turning up. William wants me here, don't you, lad?' he added, lifting the boy up on to his shoulders.

Martha made her way over and hugged Sarah. 'I'm glad you could make it. It's fair busy, isn't it?'

'It is, Pet. We best keep moving afore they knock us all ower.' Sarah had packed a large basket of food and drink, as she had promised, and she passed it to Florrie. 'Yer dunna mind carrying this do you, Lass. It's breakin' my arm.'

'It's my pleasure. I was feeling a bit peckish,' said Florrie, laughing.

Sarah placed a hand on George's arm. 'It's good to see you, lad. Welcome home.'

George nodded and Martha could see how agitated he was becoming being pushed and shoved by passing people. She linked his arm again.

'Come on, Sarah, grab George's other arm will you. We need to get inside the grounds and find a spot away from this lot.'

Edward and Joe took it in turn to carry William through the tightly packed throng. Martha prayed the day would go well. Albert looked in the mood for a confrontation and she was worried about what he might do. Why couldn't he accept it was over? Carrying on with this lie about a letter wasn't going to make her believe it.

The Clarence Road stand had been hit by the latest Zeppelin attack, but the local council had started to erect a temporary wooden stand until a new one could be built. It wasn't finished yet, so the crowds jostled for space near the edge of the pitch. Some of the money raised today would be donated towards a new stand, although the bulk would still be going to the Hartlepool General Hospital for all the help it gave to the people of Hartlepool after the bombardment.

'Is it alreet if me and Joe take William nearer the front so he can see better? ' Edward asked Martha.

'I can take him,' said Albert, reaching out for William's.

'I want to go with Joe and Edward.' William grabbed hold of Joe's hand and smiled up at him. George's breathing was fast and he looked about ready to keel over. She nodded at them grateful that they should look after him for a while.

'Thank you, Edward. That would be good. George and I are going to stand at the back somewhere. It's too crowded for him.'

Albert rolled his eyes. 'Mustn't let anybody knock the poor man. He might fall ower. Make sure a puff o' wind doesn't catch him by surprise.'

Martha glared at Albert but didn't respond. She turned and led the way, keeping tight hold of George's hand as she pushed and elbowed her way through the wall of supporters. They moved slowly towards the back of the crowd until they found room to move, air to breathe.

'C'mon, George, let's go over by the fence where it's quieter.'

They found a spot far enough away and Martha laid down a small blanket that she had brought with her. The blanket was about thick enough to fend off the cold and damp feel of the grass beneath it. They heard a roar go up that she assumed meant that the lady footballers were coming out on to the pitch. Daisy's team, The Domestics, were playing The Munitionettes and the wolf whistles made Martha think that the shorts they were wearing must be living up to their name. She couldn't imagine herself showing so much leg. Not even to play a sport.

'I'm bloody useless, aren't I?' said George when he managed to get his breathing under control.

'Don't say that. You're tired. I shouldn't have brought you. It's too much.' Martha felt guilty for pushing him into it. She had only thought of what William would want.

'I'll be alreet when I've rested a b-bit. It's all the noise and everyone p-pushing. It's like I'm back...' He turned his face away from her.

'Tell me what it was like, George. I want to understand what's wrong with you. I feel useless when I don't know how I can help.' She stroked his hand as she spoke; her heart reaching out to him.

'There's nowt to tell. L-L-Like you said, I'm just t-tired, that's all.' He sat upright, straightening his back and smiling at her. 'See. I'm feeling better already.' Martha looked at his hand as she felt it start to quiver under hers. She had tried several times to get him to open up, tell her what was bothering him. It seemed like it was too painful to remember; as if by talking about it he would have to relive it again and again. Every time she asked, he went inside himself and the shaking would get worse. She changed the subject as she looked over towards the crowds.

'Look. Florrie's coming over with Sarah. They obviously can't stand the noise either.' Martha waved at them; she could see how red Sarah's face was as they got nearer.Florrie put the basket down as Martha got up and offered her place to Sarah.

'Sit here. You look a bit puffed. Are you alright?'

'Fine, fine, but I won't say no,' she replied, lowering herself clumsily on to the blanket with Martha hanging on to her arm, supporting her as best she could.

'Celia's ower the other side. Handing out leaflets with old sour face...Mrs Wicklow.'

Martha laughed. 'Now, now, Sarah. That's not very nice is it?' she said in mock anger. 'She can't help the way her face got stuck from frowning all the time.'

'Why do you call her sour face?' asked Florrie.

'We don't usually call her names. Sarah's being silly. It's just that it seems to take a lot to please her. She's always very serious.'

'Eeh. Life's too short for that. 'Specially while there's a war on. Leave her with me for a couple of hours. I'll teach her how to laugh.'

'I'm pretty sure you would, Florrie. You can always make me laugh.' Martha smiled, remembering some of the things she joked about at work. She was still finding it difficult to comprehend Florrie's closeness and friendship under the circumstances. 'What time will Sam be here?'

'He reckons he should make half-time, but we'll see.'

Martha looked over towards the crowds again. 'It's a shame Celia's over on that side. It would have been good to see her. It must be months.'

'What are you waiting for? Get yersel ower there.' Sarah was digging in the basket for something to eat.

'I don't want to leave George...'

'George is fine where he is. Aren't you, George? Would you like a sandwich? Beef and pickle?' beamed Sarah as she offered him the doorstep slices of bread and meat; slivers of onion circles hung out of the sides like large cart wheels.'

'I'll have it if he won't,' said Florrie, eyes wide as she sucked up the saliva.

'Hold yer horses. There's plenty for everyone,' said Sarah, pleased at Florrie's response. 'The lads'll be ower for theirs at the break. I assume Albert'll be with them, Martha?'

'I suppose so.' Would he say anything else to George, have another dig, she wondered? She hoped not.

Martha was waiting for George's response to what Sarah had said. He looked up at her.

'You go, Pet. I'll be f-fine here. Go and see yer friend.' The smile was tight and false, but she knew he meant it.

'Yes, go on. Me and George can catch up a bit, talk about old times.'

Martha looked for George's reaction to the idea, but he was watching her, not Florrie. Was he too ashamed to acknowledge her in front of Martha?

Florrie didn't seem to be put off as she handed George the sandwich. 'Here. Get that down you. You need building up a bit. Your all skin and bones.'

Martha bent down and kissed his cheek. 'I won't be long. I promise.'

Setting off to find Celia, she put George out of her mind and felt her mood lift slightly. It would be good to see her friend again. Thank her for everything she had done for her and particularly for making Daisy available to look after William.

'Martha, how wonderful to see you. Have you come to help?' Celia hugged Martha in welcome. A loud cheer went up and both ladies wondered which team had scored.

'I'm afraid not, Celia, I'm with family and friends, but I couldn't miss the chance to say hello. We've been like ships in the night. Always missing each other.' Celia looked terribly thin, thought Martha. Sarah had said so but it was a shock to see her looking so pale and stick like. 'How are you?'

'Oh, I'm fine. Tired but fine. The same as every other volunteer. Gladys...Mrs Wicklow, the dear lady, is over there doing her bit. I don't know how she does it. She must be at least twenty years older than me, but she's made of such sterner stuff. Nothing seems to stop her.'

Martha's eyes followed Celia's gaze until she spotted her old enemy. Mrs Wicklow looked exactly the same. Tall and straight, holding her leaflets in those thin bony hands, waving them at passing people. Shouting out to them.

'Votes for women. Votes for women. Stand up and be counted fellow sisters. Stand up for your rights.'

Martha couldn't help but marvel at her commitment to the cause. Since Lloyd George was likely to become Prime Minister very soon it was looking more and more like women would get the vote after this dreadful war was over. She'd read that he had lots of opposition in parliament with regards to lifting the status of women, but he had replied that what the fairer sex had done for the country could not go unrewarded.

She spotted a couple of scruffily dressed fellows heading towards Mrs Wicklow. They looked as if they might have had a drink as they staggered and swayed in her direction.

'I won't be long,' she said to Celia and headed over, running when she heard one of the men start to shout.

'Ger off yer soap box, yer silly old cow. It's the likes of you that's been giving my wife ideas. Allus wantin' to come to the pub with me. It's no place for women.'

'Yeah. Bet gack...bet ba...go home to yer husband and do

what yer fit for,' said the other, slurring his words and dribbling from the corner of his mouth.

His companion nearly fell over laughing as he stood on the wooden crate and put his face right up to Mrs Wicklow, belching loudly and spraying her with his spittle.

'It's women like you who put ideas in my wife's head, and then I have to go and knock it out of her again. Remind her who's in charge.' He prodded her chest, his thick fingers permanently yellow from years of smoking. Mrs Wicklow stepped back and fell off the box, flat on her back. The drunk lost his balance and fell directly on top of her. Martha heard Mrs Wicklow cry out as she reached down and started yanking the drunken man off the poor woman.

'Get off her, you animal. Get off!' she screamed at him. He was too intoxicated to offer much resistance and rolled over onto the grass before vomiting. His friend slumped down beside him, laughing and coughing. Two policemen arrived followed by Celia.

Martha knelt down onto the grass. 'Don't move, Mrs Wicklow. Are you hurt?'

'It...It's my wrist. I think it may be broken.' Her voice was faint and she was obviously in shock.

'Oh, Gladys, you poor thing,' said Celia, lifting her skirts and kneeling down beside Martha. 'The first-aiders are on their way. We'll soon have you sorted out.'

Mrs Wicklow clasped Martha's arm with her good hand. 'Thank you so much for coming to my aid. I'm very grateful.' She smiled weakly and Martha was sure she saw a glint in her eye as she added. 'Of course...I would have boxed his ears if I hadn't lost my balance.'

Martha grinned. 'I'm absolutely certain you would have, Mrs Wicklow,' she said smiling widely.

'Gladys. Please call me Gladys.'

'If you wish...Gladys.'

Martha and Celia stayed with her until the first-aiders arrived with a stretcher. They attempted to lift her but the independent woman shook them off.

'I'm perfectly capable of standing on my own,' she said putting her weight on the good hand and trying to raise herself.

Martha jumped up and helped her to her feet.

'You can put that thing away, young man. I'll walk to the first aid tent on my own two feet .'

The half-time whistle blew. Martha turned to Celia. 'I better get back. I'll come and see you soon, Celia. When might you be at home? Take care, Mrs Wicklow,' she called after the injured woman, half laughing as she watched the two first-aiders running along behind her, trying to keep up.

'I'll let Daisy know when I'm likely to be free. Give my regards to your family.' Celia kissed her cheek and followed the two men with the stretcher and her friend. Martha made her way back around the pitch to her family. Albert would probably be on his way over to Sarah and Florrie...and George. She was frightened he might upset George by accusing him and spreading more lies. Her stomach lurched as she allowed herself, just for a moment, to wonder what she would do if George had said all those things in his letter. What she would do if he'd been the one who had kept her and Albert apart.

'How's Celia? Did you think she was too thin?' asked Sarah, handing her a sandwich as she sat down next to George. Albert was sitting by Joe and she purposely ignored him.

'I did, but we didn't have much time to speak to each other. Some drunks set about Mrs Wick...Gladys Wicklow and knocked her down. One of them fell on top of her.'

Sarah and Florrie cracked out laughing.

'He'd not get much change out of her. It'd be like squeezing a lemon,' said Sarah. 'I can just picture it.'

'It wasn't funny, Sarah. She's badly shocked and she might have broken her wrist.'

'Ha'way? I didn't realise. I'm sorry.' Sarah's attitude changed immediately. 'I didn't mean any harm.'

'I know,' Martha's voice softened. 'Celia's going up to the hospital with her.'

'Why did they hurt her, Ma?' asked William, his eyes wide.

'Because they were drunk and didn't know what they were doing. She'll be alright, William. No need to worry.'

'Daisy scored a goal, Ma. She can run as fast as any boy. Everybody cheered. I cheered very loud. Edward said I was the loudest,' he said, smiling again.

'You were the loudest.' Edward ruffled William's hair. 'Right in my ear.'

Martha and George laughed but she couldn't help noticing that Albert's face was like thunder.

'Why didn't yer Da put you on his shoulders? Why did he sit back here out of the way?'

Albert was bent on starting an argument, thought Martha. 'Because his Da's not feeling too good as you well know, Albert,' she said pointedly, looking him full in the face.

'More like 'cos he's scared of any little noise,' Albert mumbled under his breath.

'Albert Hubbard...' Martha felt the blood rush to her head.

'No, M-Martha..,' George interrupted. 'He's right. I d-don't know why that is. I didn't ask to f-feel like this.'

'I know why it is. It's 'cos yer a bloody coward. No wonder they sent you home to rest. Yer a liability.'

Martha jumped to her feet. 'William. Come with me and your Da. I think it's time we went home.' Albert had gone too far. She couldn't bear the sight of him anymore. He seemed to have become ugly through hate and bitterness. She couldn't stand how cruel he was being to George.

George eased himself up off the ground.

'Well I never! Shepherd, it's you. I canna believe it.' Sam had arrived without anyone noticing and dashed over to where George was now standing and started shaking his hand vigorously.

George looked confused.

'What are you talking about, Sam?' Florrie looked puzzled.

'This is him. Shepherd. The one with the dog.'

'That was George?' Florrie's mouth fell open.

'Yes. If I'd known that it were you, Shepherd, I'd have been ower to see you afore this.'

Chapter 34

'You mean my Da saved your life?' William's face was shining with delight and pride. 'That means he's a hero. My Da's a hero.' He started to sing as he ran from Sam to Sarah to Florrie and back to George. He almost stopped to sing it to Albert but changed his mind and moved on.

'He certainly is,' said Sam. 'I wudna be here the day if it hadn't been for your Da. Not only me, William. There's a lot of soldiers out there who owe their lives to the Shepherd. He was well known for being the one who allus came looking. He and that little dog of his wudna leave anyone out there if there was the slightest chance of them surviving. It got so we allus asked if the Shepherd were on duty when we knew we were going ower the top.

'N-No more than any other s-soldier would have done,' mumbled George. 'Yer all m-m-missing the second half. Go and watch the game.'

His face was grey and Martha was concerned. She watched Albert who was standing back and listening to what Sam had to say. He looked on edge, hands stuffed in his pockets, scratching his arm and turning away as if looking for something else to focus on instead of his brother. Martha was disappointed that he hadn't made a fuss of George like the others. Surely he had to realise how wrong he had been about him. He could at least say sorry for saying such unkind things. She knew he wouldn't be able to bring himself to do that. He was far too stubborn to admit he was wrong about anything. Martha felt guilty for having had some doubts, for almost believing his pathetic lies. Now everyone would know the truth. George was truly ill. He wasn't a shirker. He was a hero.

'Will you tell me more about what Da did, Sam?'

'Mebbe after the footie. Come with me and Florrie to watch the second half and we'll have a chat later. How about that?'

'Alreet. You can tell me and Frank. You'd like that, wouldn't you, Frank?'

'I would that, William. You're lucky to have a Da that's a hero.'

Martha swallowed hard. Poor little thing thought his useless grandfather was his Da. It wasn't right. It wasn't right. Her eyes stung as she turned from the child.

'I'm sure you're Da was a hero when he were younger, Frank. He's gettin' on a bit now. Not as young as he used to be.' Sam tried to reassure him.

Frank wasn't convinced. 'Was he, our Florrie?'

'Your Da was definitely a hero.' She sounded bitter as she looked over to George.

'Do you all mind if we get off home? I think he's had enough for one day.' Martha linked arms with George.

'You get off, Lass. One of us can bring William home later. Dunna worry yersels. Go and get some rest.' Sarah took charge as they all went back to watch the match.

Albert hung back until they were all out of earshot.

'I'll come by later. We've still got some unfinished business to discuss,' he said before walking away.

'We've nothing to discuss,' Martha said firmly.

'W-What does he mean, Martha?' asked George as he

watched his brother go.

'Nothing for you to worry about. Some lie he's concocted. Never mind about that. Let's get you home for a rest.'

George seemed to drag his feet as they went back through the streets. It was unbelievably quiet. The whole town must be at the match, thought Martha. The distant roar of the crowd broke the silence briefly as they crossed Murray Street. Another goal. She was surprised at George's response to Sam. Not even being called a hero had lifted his spirits. The old George would have been cock-a-hoop to be the centre of attention. Martha wondered if he would ever truly recover from this...What did Edward call it? Neuro something. She couldn't remember.

There was a letter on the hall floor as she opened the door. Martha stooped to pick it up. The postmark said Glasgow.

'It looks like Edith's handwriting. Do you want to read it or shall I?' Martha asked as she took her coat off and went to stoke the range.

'Can you do it? I'm a bit tired.' George sank down in his chair by the fire.

Martha made them both a hot drink before sitting down with him.

Dear Martha,

I hope you are well and are enjoying fine weather down there. It's so cold here and all the roads are covered in ice all the time. I still miss living next to the sea even though they've seagulls on the Clyde. It's not the same.

Baby Percy is getting big. Thank you for the little jacket and mittens you knitted for him. I don't know how you find the time when you work so many hours. It won't fit him for long. He's growing so big but it'll come in handy for the next one. It's hard to believe I've caught again so soon after this one. John says he wants a big family. All boys. I told him we don't get to choose these things but he said that his Ma had seven boys so it runs in the family.

We don't get out much on account of the cold and me being scared to death of slipping and breaking my neck. It's not much better in the tenements either. Damp creeps up the walls but there's no use in complaining. The landlord says we know what we can do if we don't like it. He can soon fill the rooms. One day we'll have a proper house John says but rents for those seems to go up every week. There's talk about another rent strike like we did last year but I'm not sure if I'm brave enough to join in this time. I think it was only because John and his pals laid down their tools at Beardmore's and some of the other men on the estate from Fairfield's that we got our way. The government made them freeze the rents and stopped them evicting us but as I told you back then, it didn't make the landlords improve the living conditions even if they weren't allowed to increase the rent unless they did.

Thank you for letting us know that George got home safely. I'm sorry to hear he's not well. Ma and Da are not in the in the best of health as you know and they are worried about him. Albert never tells us what's going on so I said that we would come and get the latest straight from the horse's mouth so to speak. John and I would like to come down and visit while he's on the sick. Some fool dropped a weight on his foot and he's on crutches at the moment. He gets a bit of an allowance from the union on top of his pitiful sick pay but it's not much and it's hard to make ends meet. John will tell you more about it when we get down there. We should arrive soon after you receive this letter. Don't worry about beds. We can sleep on the parlour floor if necessary. Anywhere'll seem like luxury after here.

There's also a private matter I need to discuss with Albert so could you let him know when we are coming. Tell him he'd better be around or he'll have me to answer to. Tell him it's very important.

See you soon
All our love
Edith

'Won't that be grand, George? It'll be so nice to have a bairn in the house. William'll finally get to meet his cousin.' Martha was already looking forward to their visit. 'The postmark is three days ago. They'll be here any day. I can put a couple of blankets on the parlour floor for comfort like she suggests. I'll ask Sarah if she's got any spare. It'll be so nice to meet John at last, won't it?'

She looked up to see that George had fallen asleep in the chair. Covering him gently with a rug, she went upstairs to see what bedding she had. The tin bath would do for the baby to sleep in as long as she lined it well. She had forgotten that Albert said he would come around later.

It was around a quarter to six when the hammering on the door woke George. He dived to the floor in one smooth motion.

'It's alright, George. It's only the door,' said Martha, putting her knitting down. He looked up at her, his eyes blank for a second or two. 'You're home. It's safe.' Recognition came and he pulled himself up and sat back down as the hammering started again. 'For goodness sake,' said Martha as she made her way to the door. 'What's so urgent?'

Albert stood with his hands in his pockets. He wobbled a little and the words coming out of his mouth were slightly slurred.

'Wilbian...William.' He burped loudly. 'He's gone for his teeee. Sarah's. She did...didn...' He shook his head from side to side. 'I can't go. I'm not Saint bloody George...am I? Can...Can I come in?' He staggered backwards but managed to stay upright. Martha had never seen him in this state before.

'Not in that condition, you can't. Come back when you're sober, Albert.'

'I...I'll go when you...when you ask him.'

She closed the door on him and locked it. How could she have thought she was in love with that?

'Who is it, Martha?' George called.

'It was Albert,' she replied, walking back into the kitchen.

'Well? W-Where is he?'

'He's outside.'

'What?' George looked at her, his eyes questioning.

'He's drunk.' Martha sat down and picked her knitting up.

'Why didn't you l-l-let him in?'

'Because he's so drunk, he can barely stand. I don't want him...' The hammering started again. George winced.

'You can't leave him b-banging on the door, Pet. You'd better let him in,' he said. 'I canna stand the n-noise.' He held his hands over his ears, screwing his face up.

Martha threw her knitting down, marched back to the door and swung it open.

'Yer think he's a good man. He's...I'm not lying, Mar...Mar.'

Albert fell forward, flat on his face in the hall and passed out.

'You'll have to help me move him, George. He's blocking the doorway.'

George helped her to pull him into the parlour and they left him lying on one of her latest acquisitions from a big house sale in Darlington, a small square of brightly coloured, finely-woven, Persian carpet that she had spread proudly in front of the tiled fireplace. The room was now well furnished but, without a lit fire, very cold.

'Let him sleep it off there,' said Martha firmly as they came out and she slammed the door. 'Perhaps the cold'll bring him to his senses.'

William was asleep on George's knee and Martha was busy knitting a blanket for baby Percy when Albert staggered through from the parlour. He was shivering as he edged his way between their chairs and stood in front of the range. Martha looked up at him and almost felt pity. His face was grey and drawn and his eyes were bloodshot. Her stomach had been churning the whole time he had been lying in the parlour. Could he be telling the truth? She'd searched

George's face a hundred times in the last couple of hours. He hadn't shown any signs of being worried that Albert might say something he wouldn't be comfortable with. He hadn't shown much interest when Albert had said he had unfinished business to discuss with them; although...he had been very quiet on the way home.

'I see they brought the lad home. What time is it?' he asked, turning and squinting at the clock on the mantelpiece.

'Time you went home,' said Martha, a forced sharpness in her voice.

'Give the l-lad a drink afore he goes,' said George quietly, trying not to disturb William who had stirred at the sound of his mother's voice.

'No need. I'll get one back at the lodging house. I'll see you both tomorrow.' He was looking directly at Martha.

'Edith's coming down with John and the new bairn. She said to tell you she wants to speak to you about something important,' Martha said matter-of-factly, her voice almost monotone.

'Edith's full of her own importance. Tell her I'll see her if I have time,' he said, heading for the door. He didn't say goodnight as he closed it quietly behind him.

'I don't know w-what's gotten into him,' said George. 'I've never seen him that f-full of drink afore.'

Martha took a deep breath. 'He's been trying to tell me that you sent him a letter...when he left... It said that you and I had...Oh never mind. It's all lies. He's only trying to cause trouble between us.'

Martha kept her eyes focussed on her knitting. She daren't look up, daren't see his response to what she had said. The silence seemed to last an age before she heard him say...

'Better get this one up to his b-bed. I'll turn in myself. It's b-been a long day.'

George lifted William up in his arms and carried him upstairs. Martha felt her heart thump and tear a little as her fingers lost control and the knitting came straight off the needle.

Chapter 35

'Surprise.' Edith was standing on the doorstep.

'Edith. Come in. Come in.' Martha hugged her small sister-in-law, trying not to crush the bairn that was wrapped up and cradled in her arms. The musty smell of Edith's grubby clothes assaulted Martha's nose but she refused to allow herself to react. It was what she sometimes came across when she was out shopping. It usually belonged to someone from the tenements on the far side of Hartlepool. It was disgraceful how people had to live in such appalling conditions and all because they were poor.

Edith's dull brown hair, thin face and pinched cheeks were barely recognisable. The last time Martha had seen her she had been a child and now, here she was, not only grown and a child of her own but another one on the way. The tiny bump would have gone unnoticed if Edith hadn't mentioned it in her letter. Life would be hard for her and her husband.

'This is John.' Edith proudly presented her husband to Martha and George who had come through to the hall at the sound of her voice. Martha saw John's crutches and the way he was holding his bundled foot up off the cold pavement. He was shorter than she had imagined but well built. He made Martha think of a bulldog.

'Edith, Pet. It's g-grand to see you. I canna believe it's you, you've g-grown that much.' George stroked his sister's cheek. His voice was soft and filled with emotion. Martha knew how much he missed her and his parents.

'Not that much,' she said measuring the top of her head against his chest with the flat of her hand. 'I'm sure I was nearly this high when we left Hartlepool.

'Come in out of the cold. Let me close the door before all the heat seeps out.' Martha led the way back through to the kitchen. 'I've made up the bath as a bed for little Percy. I hope it's alright.' Edith saw it laid out in front of the hearth, lined with a thick grey blanket.

'Ha'way, Martha. It's better than the drawer he sleeps in at home. Thank you,' she said, laying the sleeping baby down and covering him with the little blanket Martha had stayed up all night to finish.

Martha hadn't gone out and bought bright coloured wools for the blanket. She had used all the oddments of grey, brown and green that she had left from making socks and vests for George while he was overseas. She had finished it early this morning, lining it with an old pair of cream-coloured bloomers she had cut up to make sure the coarse wool didn't aggravate the baby's delicate skin. She thought it looked fine for a boy.

'It looks a lot grander than I remember. It allus seemed much smaller and cold when we lived here with Granda. You've made it look so cosy, Martha. Haven't they, John?' said Edith gazing around the cosy little room.

'Aye. There's nae danger of it being as bad as our clatty wee rooms.' Martha and George looked at each other.

'Yoos'll get used to it,' laughed Edith and the sparkle in her dark eyes suddenly lit up her face, making her appear much prettier. 'Ma and Da say I talk all Scottish now but I canna hear it. Well mebbe for a wee bit.'

'Sit yourselves down. I've had a pot of broth simmering all morning and I'm sure you'll be ready for something to eat after your long journey.'

'We are that. My mouth has been fair drooling since we came in.' Martha was glad it was a large pot as she watched her in-laws tuck in as if they hadn't eaten for a week. 'Where's young William? It's about time I met my nephew,' said Edith between mouthfuls.

'School. I was about to go and get him. Make yourselves comfortable. I won't be long. I need to call round at Sarah's for those blankets, George. Maybe I'll catch Edward before he goes back. Say goodbye and wish him a safe journey back to France. I'm sure you and Edith have a lot of catching up to do.'

Martha put her coat on and left them to it. She hoped there would be something left for herself and William to eat when she got back. She looked in her purse and her ration book. It's a good job bread isn't rationed, she thought. They'll have to eat a lot of that to fill up on while they are here. She was glad they had arrived. It eased the tension between her and George. He had barely spoken to her today. Was that guilt? She was too afraid to bring the subject of the letter up again.

'Now then, Sarah. He needs you to be strong for him. Remember what you said to me when George joined up. How pathetic I was instead of supporting him. You told me to pull myself together.'

'I know but he's only nineteen, Martha. I canna bear losing him all ower again.' Sarah buried her head in her hands. William stroked her back.

'He promised to be careful. He promised he would come and see me as soon as he gets back. Edward won't break his promise,' the child said solemnly. Martha wanted to hug him for being so thoughtful.

'He most certainly will not, young William.' Edward came

downstairs with his kitbag slung over his shoulder. 'You listen to what he says, Ma. I made a promise to come back and that's what I'll be doing, so stop yer blubbin' and come and give me a hug.'

Sarah wiped her eyes and stood up to hug her son. He was head and shoulders above her. 'Make sure you eat properly and keep wrapped up else you'll catch yer death.'

'I will, Ma. Do I get a hug from you, Joe, or are you too much of a man now?'

Joe fought back the tears as he hugged is older brother. 'I'll be joining you next year,' he said quietly.

'It'll all be ower afore then. You wait and see.' He turned to Martha. 'You look after George. I hope he feels better soon. I won't forget to have a word with Dr Rose for you.'

'Take care, Edward. We'll all miss you,' said Martha as she ruffled William's hair when she saw his eyes filling. 'Especially this little one.'

'Now don't you start blubbin'. I thought you were a big lad now. ' He held his hand out and William shook it, smiling through his tears.

Sarah walked him to the door and came back inside.

'I best get you those blankets,' she said and disappeared upstairs.

'Well, if you're sure it's not too much of a bother, Martha. That would be warmer for the wee babby,' said Edith as they all sat around the fire.

'No bother at all. I've put William in our bed. He can sleep with me, and George says he's happy to be on the bedroom floor.' Martha had worried about how cold their guests might be on the parlour floor as she pictured Albert shivering with cold when he came out of there on Saturday night.

'I feel bad about George being on the floor.' Edith looked at her brother.

'I'm used to sleeping on the f-floor,' said George. 'Sort of feels more n-natural these days. They dunna have b-beds in the trenches.'

'Whits it really like oot there? I wouldnae want tae be in your shoes.'

'He's asking you what it's like in France. He doesn't feel comfortable aboot still being at home when so many have gone out there.' She turned to her husband. 'You don't have a choice, John. You're on war work building them ships.'

'It's not easy,' was all George managed to say before changing the subject. 'Tell me more about M-Ma and Da. I miss them a lot.'

'They're the same as they allus are. When do you have to go back?'

'Th-Thursday.' His hand started to tremble slightly.

'Not if I can help it,' Martha chipped in. 'He needs more rest before he goes anywhere. He's not well enough to go back.'

'You know I have to, Pet. It's no good thinking any d-different.'

'He sounds alright now, Edith but you should have seen him when he first got home. There's a Dr Rose out there who says he's got a condition that needs treatment. She talked about a hospital up in Edinburgh that help soldiers who have it. I can't remember the name of it but there are quite a number of soldiers who seemed to have the same symptoms as George.'

'What did the doctor here say?' asked Edith.

'He said he needed a few days rest and then he'd be right as rain. Fat lot he knows.'

Edith didn't look convinced as Martha tried to express how worried she was. 'I'm sure the doctor knows what he's talking about. He looks fine to me. A bit tired, but as well as any man...apart from the stammer. Stop worrying yourself, Martha.'

Martha raised her voice. 'You weren't here when he came

home. We'll wait for word from Dr Rose before he even thinks about going back. Won't we, George?'

'I canna do that, M-Martha. They'd charge me with desertion.'

'Let them. If they threw you out, you'd be home for good then.'

'In a b-box? Is that what you w-want?' George looked at Martha, his eyebrows raised, questioning what she had said.

'What do you mean? Don't be silly. You're ill. They'd understand that.' Martha was the one shaking now. Surely they would understand? Dr Rose would speak up for him.

'What does he mean?' asked Edith looking at Martha.

'They sh-shoot deserters in times of war,' George said.

Chapter 36

They had little sleep that night; the bairn cried most of the time; Edith traipsed up and down stairs. John snored so loudly that burying their heads under the pillows made no difference. Martha had gone down to see if she could help Edith settle Percy. His thin legs jerked up and down as he screwed up his little face and screamed.

'Probably trapped wind,' she said taking hold of him and putting him on her shoulder. She patted his back gently and hummed softly into his ear. A few tiny burps later and Percy fell asleep.

'You're a miracle worker,' said Edith, relief flooding her face.' Show me how it's done, will you. I'm that tired. He's like this most nights.' Martha hoped they wouldn't be staying too long. The two women dozed in their chairs, waiting to see if the lull was permanent.

He slept for an hour before the tirade started up again. She showed Edith how to relieve him. 'You can get some gripe water from the chemist. That usually helps them get their wind up,' she said and then went back to bed.

'I'm too tired for school. Percy kept me awake all night,' wailed William the next morning.

'Sssh now. You don't want to upset them, do you? They'll think we don't want them here,' Martha said softly as she fastened a scarf around his neck and pulled his cap down.

'W-W-Would you like me to walk to school with you and Ma, William?' asked George. 'Give Aunt Edith and Uncle J-John a bit of privacy while they get up and dressed?'

'Oh, yes please, Da.' His spirit lifted and he smiled up at Martha. 'I can tell all my friends that Da's a hero.'

'Yoos'll do no such th-thing,' said George. 'Come on now, we dunna want you being late.'

Martha knew he was desperate for a bit of peace. He had been on edge all night, listening to the bairn going on and on. Even when asleep found him, he was shouting out. It was as if he was back in the trenches again. Reliving whatever it was that had made him so ill.

'Mr Hubbard. How nice to see you,' Mrs Appleton said cheerily. 'Young William has been telling us how you saved Miss Mason's fiancé and many more of our brave soldiers. I'm very proud to be able to meet you.' She grabbed his hand without waiting for a response.

George pulled away, pink with embarrassment.

'He isn't one for blowing his trumpet, Mrs Appleton.' Martha linked George's arm. 'We're in a bit of a hurry I'm afraid. Family visiting.' They turned tail and headed for the gate where the women were also keen to pay their respects.

'Hello, Mr Hubbard. Glad you're out and about again.'

'I'm fair proud to say I know you.'

'My Clarence said he'd seen you out there. He talked a lot about the Shepherd. Shall I give him your regards?'

They all tried to speak to him at once.

Martha stood in front of George, her face red with anger. 'It's a pity you didn't try as hard to speak to your children about bullying our son.'

'We...we're sorry for that,' said one woman. 'We didn't know.'

'That didn't make it alright, did it? '

'No... We...'

'Leave it, P-Pet. It doesn't matter.' George took Martha's hand and led her away. 'None of it m-matters.'

'Of course it matters,' argued Martha as they walked home. 'William was so upset.'

'Martha.' He squeezed her hand as he stopped and turned to her. 'There are thousands and th-thousands of men dying out there. William has gotten ower it already. The f-families of those men will never get ower it. Those women are entitled to be angry s-sometimes if they think their l-loved one died for nowt and someone got the ch-chance to come home 'cos they ran away.'

'You didn't run away. You're ill.' Martha was appalled that George thought of himself in that way.

'No...But I came home first ch-chance I got. Some of those women won't have seen their men folk for over t-two years. Some'll never see them.'

Martha thought about what he'd said as they continued to walk. Thousands and thousands dead. It was inconceivable. She couldn't imagine so many people. So many women left to grieve. When would this terrible war end? When would the killing stop?

They had barely got their coats off when Albert arrived. 'I'll not be put off any longer,' he said brushing past Martha, following George into the kitchen. 'It's time we had this out in the open.'

'Albert, please...don't...Edith...'

'Edith? Is she here?' Albert looked around the empty room then towards the little staircase. They must have gone for a walk, thought Martha, half relieved, half sorry she wasn't there. Her presence would have stopped his outburst. Kept him quiet. She dreaded what was to come and how it would affect George.

'Don't what?' said George. 'Let him s-speak, Pet.' George sat down in his chair and sighed.

'No...George...He's only come to tell lies. He told me...'

'I told you the truth, Martha. He sent me a letter saying that you and he had slept together...Go on...Deny it.' He glared down at George who had turned grey.

Martha waited...waited...George closed his eyes. She saw the tears start to run down his cheeks.

'See,' Albert bellowed triumphantly. 'Look at him. Too ashamed to face you.'

'George?' Martha's lips trembled. 'Why? Why would you try and shame me like that?'

He looked up at her, his eyes shining, pleading with her. 'I'm sorry...I didn't do it t-to hurt you.'

The pain was unbearable and she grabbed her coat and ran from the house. She didn't know where she was running to, her eyes blind with anger and hurt. She could hear Albert shouting after her.

'Martha. Come back. Martha.'

She carried on, running and running until she had to stop and lean against a wall to catch her breath. Albert might have come back all those years ago. They could have been together. All this time. They could have been together.

She wasn't sure how long she had been walking the streets when she heard a familiar voice. She looked up to see Sarah. She hadn't remembered coming to the market. She hadn't remembered knocking on the door.

'Lass? What's wrong?' Sarah put her arm around Martha's shoulders and took her inside. 'Is it George? What's happened? Come and sit down.'

Sarah waited as Martha tried to tell her what had happened.

'He did it...(hic)I said he would never...(hic) I didn't think he was capable...(hic) I should have listened to Albert...' She hiccoughed through every attempt to speak, trying to catch her breath between sobs.

'Whoa there. Slow down...There now. There now. Take your time.' Sarah sat and patted her hand.

'Albert said he'd...George had sent a letter...said that I had...we'd...'

'Ha'way, Lass. I think you'd better start from the beginning.' Sarah took hold of her, rocking her gently. Martha felt as if she were in her mother's arms. Safe at last. She began to tell her everything. How Albert had left her. How George had come to her aid...offered to help...even the fact that Florrie was Frank's mother and she suspected that George was his father.

Chapter 37

Sarah eased herself up from the edge of the bed and turned to leave.

'Don't go, Sarah. Please don't go.' Martha reached up and grabbed her hand.

'I'm not going far. Try and rest for a while. Sleep cures most things. You'll be able to think more clearly.'

Martha lay there, staring at the ceiling. Dear Sarah hadn't judged her. Hadn't told her it was all her own fault for letting a man do that to her outside of marriage. She'd held her and listened without saying anything and now she had made her come upstairs and lie in her bed. It was exactly what her own mother would have done. How was sleep going to make things clearer? George had said all those shameful things about her in his letter. Albert must have been so hurt by the betrayal. He thought he had left her waiting for him faithfully and it would have looked like she had let him down in the worst way possible. She could imagine what was going through his mind. He must think that, not only had she been with another man but his own brother. What about Florrie? George had left her to hand her child over to her parents because of the shame. Did he think that giving her a bit of money made everything alright?

Martha slept fitfully. Dreams charged with anger and emotion. In one dream she was walking away from George, linking her arm with Albert. George was pleading for her to come back but Albert was smiling and she couldn't look away. Couldn't look back no matter how hard she tried. She realised that Albert had his hand on her neck and was forcing her to look at him. Please, Albert. Let me look. Please.' She woke herself up, calling out, trembling. She drifted off to sleep again and she was with George and they were holding a new baby. Trying to decide her name. George wanted to call the baby Martha after her but she wanted to call her Anne after her own mother. Albert walked in saying the bairn was his and snatched it from them. She woke screaming this time and Sarah was leaning over her.

'Hush now. It's alreet. You're safe here.'

'Oh, Sarah. The dream...it was so terrible,' she cried, sitting up and wrapping her arms around the large frame. 'Albert was trying to take the baby.'

'It was only a dream. Come downstairs. I've made you a bite to eat. It's turned twelve. You've had a good couple of hours.'

Martha followed Sarah downstairs and sat at the table. Joe was already seated. Martha felt uncomfortable. What did he know? He must be wondering why she was in his mother's bed on a Tuesday morning.

'Ma sez yer not feeling so good. Had to lie down cos you felt faint. Are you alreet now, Martha?'

'Yes, thank you, Joe. Much better.' She tried to straighten her hair and pin it back into a bun. She knew she must look a fright.

'Here, get that down you,' said Sarah putting a bowl of home-made chicken soup in front of her. 'My Ma swore by chicken soup to cure all ills. Even if I had a boil on my bum she would give me chicken soup.'

Joe laughed out loud. 'Yer shouldn't talk like that in front of your grown up son. It's not right. Is it, Martha?'

She couldn't help herself and found herself grinning. 'A positive disgrace, Sarah Colby. You're a bad influence on your children.'

'Hey. Less of the children if yer dunna mind. I'm seventeen now,' Joe chided her, his voice light with laughter.

'Terribly sorry, kind sir,' she replied. 'I thought I was back with that little boy I used to look after for a moment. You know. The one who thought it was fun to catapult Mr Granger on the bottom when he was standing in the yard below us. We all had to duck down when he looked up at the window.' It felt good to reminisce. Push the hurt away for a few minutes.

Joe laughed even more. 'Aye. Do yer remember that time when Edward poured a bit of water on to your Da's head and your Da said "Looks like rain, Robert? Best be gettin' inside afore it starts proper."'

'I do. It was so funny.' Martha could picture his face clearly as he put his hand on his head and looked up at the sky.

'He knew what it was,' laughed Sarah. 'He told me and Annie when they came back inside, but your Da wouldn't let on. He didna want to spoil yer fun.'

'No. He always played along.' Martha's voice trembled as she remembered what fun her Da had been.

'They were good men, both Robert and Cyril.' Sarah wiped her eyes roughly. 'Come on, yoos two. I didna make this soup so that yer could let it go cold afore you ate it.'

The three of them tucked in. Martha savouring happy memories from before the war. The other two seemed lost in their own thoughts. The war had robbed them of the most precious thing they had. Family.

Sarah saw Martha to the door when they had finished eating. 'Go and see Florrie. Ask her straight out. It's for the best and then you'll know for sure.'

'You've been gone a long w-while,' George said, his face twisted with worry.

'Dunna go on at her, George.' Edith was changing Percy's nappy. ' Yer canna blame her for wanting a bit of peace. She's not used to having a bairn around all the time.'

'She is,' said William, taking his coat off. 'I've been here a long time.'

'I meant a tiny bairn, like Percy, not a big lad like you. Did yer have a good day at school, William?'

It crossed Martha's mind that Edith had completely lost the Scottish accent now. It must be with being back on home soil.

'It was alreet, but I wanted to come home and see Cousin Percy...even if he is a bit noisy when I'm trying to sleep.'

'William.' Martha's tone was firm. She had specifically told him not to mention it when they were walking back from school.

'He's fine. We know the wee one is a nightmare.' John stood up as he spoke. 'You look aboot done in, Martha. Sit doon, Lassie.'

'No...It's fine. Let me wash that for you Edith,' she replied holding her hand out for the soiled nappy.

'Ha'way, I canna have yer doing my washing for me. Yoos've made us welcome enough.'

'Please...I'm happy to do it for you.' Martha took it from her hand and went outside into the backyard. After emptying much of the contents down the netty, she put it in the bucket along with the dozen others that Edith hadn't managed to wash yet. It's a good job it's not summertime, she thought. The smell was bad enough as it was. It would have been unbearable on a summer's day.

Martha put several pans of water on to boil and poured them into the large, metal dolly-tub she used for washing. It was dark and cold outside when she started to scrub the muslin squares with carbolic soap and a stiff brush. She didn't want to look at George anymore than she had to, so she made the work last as long as possible. Edith and John must be aware of the tension between them, she thought. Had he said anything, she wondered? Told them what he had done? When she went back inside she hung the squares on the drying rack above the fire. The room filled with steam and the unmistakeable aroma of what babies do best along with the more acceptable hint of warm breast milk. Edith was wiping Percy's mouth as his little head lolled back in a contented sleep. There wasn't even the tiniest murmur from him as she tucked him into his make-do bed.

Ten minutes later, they sat down to a simple meal of bread and cheese. Martha hadn't cooked and Edith hadn't volunteered. No-one complained.

'We'll be leaving tomorrow. If I can manage to have a word with Albert. Is he likely to come around again? I missed him this morning,' Edith asked. 'I canna leave without talking to him.'

Martha wondered what Albert had said to George after she had run out this morning. George looked over at her as if he had read her thoughts.

'Aye. H-He said he'd come back in the m-morning. He didn't stay after Martha left.'

'I think it's time John and I went up... Get some sleep afore he starts.' Edith tapped John's elbow and he picked the tin bath up, ready to carry it upstairs.

'Yes, William and I are tired too. Off we go,' she said standing up and holding her hand out.

'Do we have to, Ma? I'm not tired yet.'

'Of course you are. You didn't sleep very well last night.'

'I'll p-probably stay down here...be company for Edith when the b-bairn wakes up.' mumbled George. She didn't answer.

William groaned but took Martha's hand and went upstairs with her.

As they lay in bed, Martha was glad that William was sleeping with her. She wouldn't have to make excuses as to why George was staying downstairs. They would think it was because the floor in the bedroom was too uncomfortable.

'Are you coming to school again, Da?' asked William. Martha threw George a look that said definitely not.

'Not this morning, lad. Yer Da's a bit t-tired. I'll come with you tomorrow. I promise.'

William's chin fell, but he gave his father a hug. 'You'll be better soon, Da,' he added before following Martha out onto the street.

Martha dropped William at school. She looked for Florrie. She had sent a message with Frank yesterday, asking if she could go into work a little late and meet her at the school gate. She was about to give up and go when she saw Florrie running up the street towards her. She stopped, flushed and trying to catch her breath.

'I...I've had to sneak out.' She took a deep breath, trying to get the words out. 'I asked one of the girls to cover.'

'Thank you, Florrie. I'm sorry to pull you out of work. I...There's something I need to talk to you about.'

'It'll have to be quick. I need to get back afore anyone notices I'm missing.'

'We can talk as we walk back to Gray's. I wouldn't do this if it wasn't important.'

They walked back along the street. Florrie threaded her arm through Martha's. 'What's all this about?' she asked.

Martha felt uncomfortable. How could Florrie be so intimate when she had held this secret from her? 'It's...It's a bit delicate...I don't want you to think I blame you in any way.' Martha was finding it difficult to find the right words.

Florrie stopped to face her. 'Dunna blame me for what?'

A woman was kneeling on her front doorstep, wiping it down ready to apply the donkey stone set down beside her. Martha took Florrie's arm, taking her further up the street. Keeping her moving along the pavement. She looked straight ahead. 'Frank...Is he?...' She paused. This was so difficult.

Florrie snatched her arm away, stopping in her tracks. 'Who told you? Was it one of the girls from work?'

Martha swallowed hard and looked at her friend. ' No... I...It was...

Florrie threw her hands up in air. 'Why can't people mind their own business. It was a long time ago. I was only sixteen.'

'I'm ...I'm sorry. I didn't mean to upset you. I...I needed to know.'

She turned on Martha, eyes flashing, cheeks burning. 'Why did you need to know? What the hell's it got to do with you?' I suppose you'll do like all the rest and tell me I'm not good enough to be seen with you. That I ought to keep Frank away from your son? Is that it? Well you dunna need to tell me twice, Martha Hubbard. I thought you were better than that.'

Florrie marched away, pushing passed an elderly couple. The husband shouted out to her, 'Watch where yer going,' but Florrie didn't stop.

Martha apologised to them and chased after Florrie, regretting having asked her. 'No..No...that's not what I'm saying. Wait. Please wait.'

Florrie slowed down, finally stopping close to the factory gates.

Martha caught up and took hold of Florrie's arm again, turning her so that they faced each other. 'I'm so sorry George walked away from you. I wanted to be sure before I confronted him. Please forgive me for embarrassing you, Florrie. No-one will hear it from me. I promise.'

'What?' Florrie's mouth dropped open. 'What are you talking about. George didn't walk away from me. He helped me. Why would you think...?'

Martha looked down at the pavement. 'I was there...at the house. You told George he didn't need to support Frank anymore now that you had Sam. Oh, Florrie. I'm so sorry he put you through this. I don't think I can ever forgive him.'

Tears rolled down her cheeks as she forced herself to look up. Why was she grinning? How could she think any of this was amusing?

Florrie tried to stop herself from laughing out loud, clasping her hand over her mouth.

'I don't understand...why are you laughing?'

'Oh my dear, Martha. You think Frank is George's child. Come here you silly woman.' She took Martha and pulled her close. 'George is not Frank's father, Rupert is...was.'

'Rupert? '

'Yes. We were going to get married when we found out I was expecting but he was killed. He fell off the scaffolding...George loved him so. He wanted to help look after Rupert's son.'

Martha couldn't believe what she was hearing. 'Why didn't he tell me? I don't understand.'

'He promised to keep it secret. For me. To stop people gossiping about me. Saying I behaved like a slut. Me and Ma had to keep it hidden until he was born. It was funny really. Me wearing clothes that were too big and her stuffing things up her frock so that she looked as if she were having a baby.' Florrie held Martha at arms length, looking straight into her eyes. 'Your George was an angel. He gave what he could afford every week to make things a bit easier for me and my family. We had to be sure no-one ever saw us together so that he wouldn't be blamed. I told him to stop when he said that you and him were getting married, but he insisted on helping until Frank was old enough to work. Your George is the kindest person I've ever known. I'll always be grateful to him.'

Martha felt foolish and ashamed of herself. How could she have thought such things about the man who had loved her so devotedly since the day they married. It made her feel physically sick to think she had misjudged him so easily. Had betrayed him so easily. Her heart was beating wildly. She knew at that moment how much she really loved him. How she couldn't bear to lose him. That whatever the reason was for George to send that letter to Albert, it was done purely for love and protection of her. She decided to confide in Florrie about Albert wanting her to leave George and about the letter that George had admitted sending to Albert. She asked her what she thought his reasons might be.

'I canna answer that, but I can tell you that George loves you more than life. He must have had a good reason for doing it. You need to ask him, Martha. Dunna let it come between you. It'd kill him if he lost you and William.

'He won't lose me or William if I can help it. I only hope he can forgive me for almost ruining everything we have.'

Florrie hugged Martha. ' If I know George, he will. I have to get back in. I'll come and see you soon. I promise.' Florrie kissed Martha's cheek and slipped in through the wrought iron gates.

'Wait for me.' Albert's voice coming from behind made her jump. She didn't stop walking as he matched his stride with hers. 'I saw you outside with Florrie.' He didn't enquire why she was out of work. 'What did he have to say for himself then?' he asked.

'We haven't spoken about it.'

'What?' Albert stopped her from walking on. She tried to pull away. 'Look at me...Look at me, Martha.' His hand grabbed her chin and pulled her face around so that he looked straight into her eyes. 'Why? You need to have it out with him. You need to hear it from his own mouth so that there's no doubt in your mind. You'll know for sure what a devious man he is.'

It took Albert less than a minute to confuse her thoughts.

'I can't. I don't understand why he would do it. He was trying to get you to come home so that I could speak to you...tell you...'

'Tell me what? What did you need to tell me that was so urgent if it wasn't to say you'd slept with him? Don't tell me you're finally going to tell me the truth? You think I haven't worked it out? That I haven't wondered all these years?. Whose he was? How you told everyone he was born early. I knew it when I came down for Granda's funeral. I haven't stopped thinking about him. That's why I came back. William's my son and I'm taking him.'

Chapter 38

1910

'I canna believe how lucky I am,' George kissed Martha again. 'You're the most beautiful bride there ever was.'

Martha tried to look happy. George was so kind, so thoughtful, but she didn't love him. He hadn't heard what his so-called friends had said about him, calling him a fool for taking Albert's *leftovers*. He didn't know she had overheard them whispering at the reception. She had begun to feel unwell earlier and was glad to be back at George's house. Glad it was finally over and she could stop acting like the blushing bride.

'Are you alreet, Pet?' he said as she placed her hands on her tummy and doubled over in pain.

'I...I don't know,' she gasped as another pain ripped through her. She sat down on the bed. 'I'm sorry, George. Can you ask Ma to come upstairs please?'

George left Martha in his bedroom...their bedroom now she thought, looking around as he raced downstairs. It struck her that she wouldn't sleep in the house on Tankerville Street ever again. She wouldn't see Da every morning. Ma wouldn't have her breakfast waiting. She wouldn't be able to kiss her goodbye and go off to work at Turnbull and Tilley solicitor's anymore. Wouldn't go home and sit down for supper with her and talk about what had happened at work. Ma was always interested to hear about the goings on where she herself had worked before marrying Da. Martha's old life had gone forever. She wanted to lie down and curl her knees up. Perhaps that would ease the pain. She stood and took her skirt off.

That's when she saw the dark red stain. She looked at the bed. There was blood on the blanket too.

'Martha?' She turned to see her mother staring at her, staring at the skirt. 'Oh. Martha.'

Martha lay down on the bed, turning her back on Annie. She made no sound. Annie sat down on the bed and stroked her daughter's hair.

'I'm so sorry, pet. It often happens with your first. At least you won't have the dreadful sickness anymore. I used to get it from the very start too. I suspected that was what was wrong with you. Your Da and I went through this three times before you came along and even then you were born early. Fighting for all you were worth. Try not to dwell on it too much. There will be others.'

Martha turned over and looked up at her mother. She looked so smart in her navy blue dress and jacket. Her hat with its broad brim cast a shadow over her eyes. Martha couldn't see whether she was upset or relieved with this outcome. She hadn't shown surprise or anger when she and George announced their intention to marry, but her eyes had shown the deep hurt she was feeling. Martha knew her mother had wanted her to continue the dream she herself had had as a young woman starting out on a career.

'Why didn't it happen sooner?' Martha asked. 'Why today?' Martha saw her mother's back straighten in an effort to look more positive and in control. She had always done that whenever there was a problem to be solved.

'Come on now. Don't talk like that. George is a good man. He'll make a good husband. What's done is done. No point chasing something that's gone. You'll have to make the most of things. Lie there and I'll be back in a couple of minutes.' Annie left the room. Martha heard her go downstairs and sighed. Why hadn't she waited a little longer? Why had she gone along with George and got married so quickly. He'd only suggested it less than two weeks ago. Ma was right. There was nothing she could do about it now. The deed was done.

Annie returned with a bowl of warm water, some hand cloths and a towel.

'Let's get you cleaned up,' she said. 'Then you can rest.'

'I can't be pregnant again. Not so soon. It's only two weeks since I last...We've hardly...,' she said, taking the glass of water from George. She wasn't used to speaking so openly about such intimacies with anyone, particularly when it was a man. The taste of bile burned her throat. She rinsed her mouth and spit into the bowl he'd brought when she had started retching.

'You must be. You were like this when ...' George stopped himself from saying it. 'It'll be grand, Pet. A new baby's the perfect thing to brighten you up. Help you get ower...the loss.' He turned from her. 'I...I'm sorry. I allus say the wrong thing. I dunna want to upset you.'

Martha reached out to him. 'You haven't, George. None of what's happened is your fault, but I don't know if I'm ready to go through it all again so soon. What if I lose this one as well?'

She could see how he always acted as if he was treading on eggshells around her. Trying to say the right thing. Trying to make her love him. She wished she could, she wished more for the love she'd lost. Whenever she was alone she only thought of Albert and what could have been.

'I'll make you and our bairn so happy. I promise,' he said taking hold of her hands. 'I'll even make you love me one day.'

Martha smiled affectionately at her good friend and new

husband. 'I know you will.'

Chapter 39

'I knew what he said couldn't be true. I'm going to get my son, Martha. You can come with me if you want to see him, but I'm taking what's mine. I'm not having him bring up my lad.' Albert left her standing. He marched off towards her home and George. His stick seemed to strike the pavement so hard, she was sure it would snap.

'No...Wait...Albert wait.' Martha raced after him, but he was too fast for her. By the time she turned into Tankerville Street he was banging hard on the door. Someone opened it and he disappeared inside.

She had to stop and catch her breath as she went inside. Albert's voice sounded so bitter as he leaned over George, holding his stick as if ready to hit him with it.

'I should knock every last breath out of yer. You lying bastard. Did you think I didn't know he was mine? You aren't fit to wipe his nose, let alone bring him up.'

'Stop it!' screamed Edith trying to pull him away. John grabbed Albert around his waist and yanked him away.

'Am no having this in front of my bairn,' John said calmly. 'Sit down, laddie, or I'll have to cowp thee.

He pushed Albert down on to a chair.

'Stop it right now,' said Martha dashing in to the kitchen. 'No more. No more.'

'Tell him your coming with me and bringing my son with you.' Albert fought to free himself from John's grip, but to no avail. John might have been small, but he had the strength of two men.

'I'm not coming anywhere with you, Albert. This is my home.'

'Suit yersel, Martha. Yer a fool, but I'm taking my son with me. You canna stop me doing that.'

'William's not your son, Albert. George is his father.'

'Stop yer lying. I knew George was lying when he said he was the father. Why would you want him when you could have me? That's why you wanted me to come back. '

'If you'd worked it out, why didn't you come back for me? Why did you leave George to make things right? Why wait all these years?'

'Miss the chance of a good job and spend the rest of my life here wishing I'd gone? I'd have come back when I was ready. You couldn't wait could you? Well now it's my turn to have a say in what happens to him.' Martha smarted at his cruel words.

'He's not yours, Albert. Listen to me. I was having your child but I lost it.' Her eyes dulled at the memory. 'The day George and I got married. Believe me. William is George's son. Not yours. 'Martha remembered how William's fight for survival had brought her and George to their knees when he was born nearly two months early.

Albert glowered at her, searching her face. She held her gaze so that he would know she wasn't lying. He turned on George again. 'He dunna deserve a child. He's not fit. Look at him sitting there and taking it. Come with me, Martha. You love me, not him.'

'No, Albert. I'm not going anywhere. Whatever else happens today, I won't be going anywhere with you.

Whatever George has done, I still love him. I could never take his son away from him.'

'And what about the bairn that Morag McKay is carrying? Has she got to find someone else to marry as well?'

It took a second or two for it to register. Martha spun round to look at Edith. 'What? Who's Morag Mckay?'

'The woman he left to come crying to me, a belly as big as a house. She said she had written to you, begging you to come back, but you never answered her letters. I came to ask you to come home, Albert.'

'I...I didn't know. Stupid woman. It's not my fault she threw hersel at me, is it?'

Martha could hardly believe what she was hearing. 'Get out! Get out of my house, right now,' she screamed at Albert.

'It wasn't my fault, Martha. She should have done away with it. I told her I didna want anything to do with it when I left.'

'How could you do that, Albert,' Edith shouted. 'It's you who's not fit to be a father. Don't you care what happens to them? Her ma and da have thrown her out. She's staying at ours but there's barely room for John and me. You had the cheek to turn your nose up at me when I fell for John's child. Acting all disgusted as if you were the innocent brother whose sister had shamed him. You disgust me.'

'Yer all the bloody same you women. Expect men to be made of stone when you tease 'em. Yer should keep yersels to yersels.'

George stood up and punched Albert in the face. The sound of his nose cracking was sickening. He dropped like a stone and lay dazed on the floor. The blood trickling down his cheek. John dragged him to the door and pushed him outside to lie on the pavement in a heap.

A minute or two later and they all heard Albert banging on the door, shouting loudly.

'I only came back for my son. I only wanted Martha so's I could teach George a lesson. Show him no-one takes what's mine and gets away with it. She loves me George. She'll never really be yours.'

George started for the door, but Martha stood in front of him.

'Don't. It's finished. No more.'

She left them standing and went upstairs to her bedroom. Throwing herself on the bed, she cried herself to sleep.

'I've brought you a drink, Pet?' George was sitting on the edge of the bed stroking her hand.

Martha tried to wake up. What time? Where? She remembered what had happened.

'I need to go and collect William. What time is it?' She tried to sit up, but George pushed her down gently.

'Plenty of time for that. It's b-barely lunchtime... We need to talk.'

Martha saw the sadness in his face. He looked so tired and grey. 'Tell me why, George. I need to know.'

'I'd n-n-no right to do it, I know. It was b-because...because of Albert's reply.'

'Reply? I'm surprised he replied at all.' Martha didn't understand. He must have sent the letter before Albert replied?

'No, not to that l-letter. The first letter. The one you asked me t-to write to him.'

'You wrote twice?'

'Yes. I wrote to ask him to c-c-come home. That you had s-something important to tell him. That it was urgent. It was his reply to that l-l-letter...I would n-never have told you. I knew how m-much it would hurt you and so I wrote the letter to m-m-make sure he didn't have a need to come back. I'm s-so sorry, Martha.'

Martha reached out to him and stroked his face. 'Tell me, George. Tell me what he said in his reply. He can't hurt me anymore than he already has.'

'He said that he hadn't time to come running back to you every time you had something to tell him. He said you'd become a bit c-c-clingy and now he'd seen the amount of available l-lasses up there, he'd no need to travel half the c-country to get what was there on his doorstep. I'm sorry, M-Martha. I would never have t-told you. I sent the letter and I'm sorry for l-l-lying, but I couldn't bear to see you hurting so m-much.' George pulled her into his arms, kissing her head.

'Oh, George. I don't deserve you,' she mumbled into his chest. 'How could I not see what he was really like?' She pulled herself free, looking earnestly into his face. 'I won't lie to you, George. When you were away...fighting...' She felt ashamed now. 'I nearly... He said he loved me...You'd been gone so long...We didn't...I wanted to but we never actually—'

He put his fingers to her lips. 'Sssh. It's alreet, P-Pet. I know how much you loved him. I allus w-wished that you might love me that way one day. I'd s-s-settle for half as much if it meant we stayed together.'

'Oh, George...We will...I will...I do.'

He kissed her hard on the mouth and climbed into bed beside her.

Martha sat up, panic striking her. 'Where's Edith and John? We can't—'

George pulled her back down again. 'Gone to find Albert and g-give him one last chance before they go for the train. They won't be back. They said to t-t-tell you how s-s-sorry they were. Now w-where were we?

He's due to go back tomorrow. There's not much hope of hearing from Dr Rose before then. Edward would have barely got back there. There might not have been time for him to speak to her. How was she going to keep him here for treatment? He was definitely a lot better, but he still wasn't in any fit state to be back out there fighting on the front. Martha lay basking in the warmth of the sheets that George had occupied with her for the last couple of hours. She could still taste him in her mouth. Smell him on her skin. Her happiness was being snatched away again as she thought about him going back to the front. She couldn't lose him again...so soon after they'd finally, finally found each other. She got out of bed reluctantly, dressing slowly, trying to think of something that might let him stay at home. She glanced in the mirror on her dressing table as she pinned her hair up. Her skin was flushed. It almost looked as though she had caught the sun against the shine of her hair. She felt like a young girl again. How much time had she wasted on something that was worthless?

'We're back, Ma. Da says we're going out for tea. Can we, Ma? To a real restaurant?'

Martha came downstairs.

'I thought we might do s-summat special. Being my last day an all. What d-d-do you say?' He was staring at her like he'd only seen her properly in that moment, truly seeing all her love coming straight at him. She could read the love in his eyes and she felt a warm flutter inside.

'That would be lovely,' she answered, trying to hide the fear of losing him. 'Where were you thinking of?'

'I thought we could mebbe go the R-R-Royal seeing as that was the first p-place I took you. That was where we started wasn't it?'

'It was.'

'This was on the hall floor when I left to pick William up from school.' He passed her a piece of paper.

'Martha opened it and read Edith's note...

Dear George and Martha,

We are catching the four-o-clock train to Darlington. I have managed to convince Albert to come back with us. I think he will come around to facing up to his responsibilities when he sees Morag. He'd be a fool to turn his back on the chance of a family for a second time. He has told Mr Castleton he's leaving and he isn't best pleased. Says he will have all on to find a replacement foreman.

Albert is keeping his fingers crossed that he won't make it difficult for him to get his old job back up in Govan. I know you and George will work things out and I wish you both well. Don't worry too much about George, Martha. He's stronger than you think.

Thank you for all your kindness while we stayed with you. I hope you get the chance to visit us someday soon.

Love

Edith, John and baby Percy.

'I wonder if Mr Castleton would consider a woman foreman.'

'Sorry?'

'I should have as much right as a man to apply for the position. Don't you think so?'

George grinned. 'That's my girl.'

Martha kept William off school the next morning. They would go with George to the station to say goodbye properly. Martha could barely keep herself from crying. Why hadn't she heard from Dr Rose? She could have sent a telegram. Edward would have told her that George's leave ended today. They were eating breakfast when someone knocked on the door startling Martha.

'I'll go,' said George. 'It's probably him.'

'Who's him?' asked William.

'Sam. He wanted to see your Da before he left.'

Martha heard voices, female voices.

'It's Mrs C-C-Clarke and Mrs Wicklow. I've shown them through to the front p-parlour,' said George. 'Said they want to talk to us about s-something important.'

Martha brushed her skirt off and primped her hair before going through.

'Celia, Mrs...Gladys. How lovely to see you both. Can I get some tea?'

'No, that's not necessary. We wanted to talk to you and George about something. It won't take long.' Celia looked her usual smart self in a black wool coat and matching hat. The colour turned her eyes from their natural grey to dark charcoal. She was as thin and frail as she had been the last time Martha had seen her. It was sad to see both women wearing such dark clothes. She hoped she would not have cause to wear them for a very long time. Mrs Wicklow had her arm in a sling, but it was black to match her suit instead of the customary white. It made Martha smile. That woman would never let anyone see any weakness in her.

'I'm afraid William is here today. I kept him off school so that we can both go to the railway station to see George off. He goes back to the front today.'

'We know,' said Celia. 'That's why we are here. Ask George to come in will you? He can bring William with him.'

Martha invited them both to sit down and went back to the kitchen to ask George and William to come through.

'Hello, Mrs Clarke,' said William, beaming up at her. 'Did Mrs Finch make some cake?'

'William. That's not the way to speak to guests,' said Martha looking down at her son and frowning.

'What's a guest?' he asked.

'We are,' said Celia, laughing. 'Mrs Finch hasn't baked today I'm afraid, William. Maybe tomorrow.'

'How can we help?' asked Martha, expecting it be something to do with the cause.

'Well actually, we might be able to help you, or should I say Mr Hubbard,' said Gladys.

'Yes,' interrupted Celia. 'Daisy told us about your condition, George. I hope you don't mind. We had a word with the senior doctor at Normanhurst. Gladys and I have had plenty of dealings with soldiers suffering with neurasthenia. Mainly officers, but he agrees and can see that the ordinary soldier is just as likely to get the condition. He says that there are specialist hospitals around the country. In particular there is one in Edinburgh that is supposed to be very good and — '

'For goodness sake, Celia. Get to the point...What she is trying to say Mr Hubbard is that he is happy to have a look at you. Check your symptoms, and if neurasthenia is the case he will refer you to Edinburgh for treatment.'

'Oh Celia...Gladys. How wonderful. I can't thank you enough. We can't thank you enough, can we, George? '

'It's kind of you and I am g-g-grateful to you, but I have to report b-back tonight and my train will be leaving soon. Dunna think I don't appreciate it...I d-do, it's just that...'

'George, what are you talking about? Of course you'll go and see the doctor. The train doesn't leave until this afternoon. You can be up to the hospital and back again if he says you're fit.' Martha voice began to rise as panic took over.

'It'll be alreet, Martha. D-Dunna get all worked up.' He put his arm around her shoulders. 'I'll see you both out and th-thanks again for thinking about me.'

Celia and Gladys were puzzled.

'Why don't you want to go...if you don't mind me asking?' said Gladys.

'I dunna mind going back. It doesn't feel r-right to be here when all the other lads in the b-battalion are still out there.'

'But it's not your fault you're ill,' Martha pleaded. William clung on to her skirts.

'Why are you crying, Ma. Da's a hero. He'll be alreet.'

'You're a credit to your country, young man,' said Gladys. 'It can't be easy to go back when you know the risks and someone offers you the opportunity to stay.' She held her hand out to him. 'I'm very proud to have met you. If you change your mind before the train goes, please come up to the hospital and Celia and I will make sure you see the doctor.'

'Of course,' added Celia. 'You've still got time to think about it.'

George saw them out.

'William. Can you go and play in the b-bedroom for a while. I need to talk to your Ma.'

'Ah, but...'

'There's a good lad. I'll only be a few minutes.'

William raced upstairs.

'Come and sit down, Pet.' He guided her to the chair and eased her down. 'I have to g-go, Martha. You know it's the right thing to do.'

'Nothing's right about it. I'll lose you. I know I will. Please, George. Please go to the hospital.'

'Martha, listen to me. Out there the men live in f-f-fear every second of the day. They don't know whether they'll get home or not. Sam made me realise how much they d-depend on each other...me. D-D-Depend on the Shepherd. If word gets out that he's no longer there they may lose hope. I haven't been out looking for wounded men since B-B-Bess died, but they dunna know that. There are other men who do it now. With their own dogs. As long as they think that someone will be in no-man's land looking for them if they get hit that makes it easier for them to go over the top and fight. I've been on wire c-cutting duties for w-weeks. And that's a very important j-j-job too. Making sure the men d-dunna get caught up in it. I c-canna let them down.'

Martha knew there was no use arguing. He had made his mind up. 'Promise me you'll come home to me,' she whispered as he pulled her up out of her seat, squeezing her tight.

'You make sure you and William are waiting for me and I'll do everything in my p-power to come back, Martha.'

He rocked her gently in his arms, singing softly into her ear. Not once did he stutter...

'Sweet and low, sweet and low
Wind of western sea,
Low, low, breathe and blow,
Wind of the western sea!
Over the rolling water go,
Come from the dying moon, and blow,
Blow him again to me,
While my little one, while my pretty one, sleeps.'

C J Richardson

I live in a small village in North Yorkshire with my husband. This is the second time around for both of us and we have six grown-up children and fifteen grandchildren between us.

I started writing when I retired about eight years ago. Firstly joining a beginner's class and then forming a writing group with some fellow students. We meet regularly to share our work and also to critique and help each other.

I have studied A215 and A363 with the Open University and gained a distinction for my year three A363 course in Creative Writing. I am currently studying with Open College of Arts and hope to gain a BA(Hons) in creative writing over the next couple of years.

The idea for North Sea Shells came from my final piece for the Open University where I had to write the opening four thousand words of a novel. This was in 2014 and the whole country was getting prepared to commemorate the one hundredth anniversary of the start of World War 1.

I was fascinated to hear that German warships actually attacked the north east coast of England in December 1914 and began to research the events of that terrible day. Once I had completed those first four thousand words, I knew I had to finish the story. Although fiction, it is loosely based around the events of that December morning and the consequences that followed for my fictional family.

This is my first novel and I hoped you enjoyed it. If you wish to find out more about my work and my plans for the future, please visit my Website or Facebook page below. I expect it to be a long journey and would love your company whilst *climbing the writing hill...*

http://www.cjrichardsonwriter.com/
https://www.facebook.com/cjrichardsonwriter